THE
CYPRUS
PAPERS

C.W. Bordener

To my wife and daughters. You get one life to live.

Live it like it's your last, because it is.

We take this ride together!

ACKNOWLEDGEMENTS

There are so many people to thank for making this novel a reality. First of all, thank you to my awesome wife and two beautiful daughters. Without their inspiration and support, this novel would have never happened.

I'd also like to thank my editors and beta readers. In addition to their thoughtful work and dedication, the personal advice and kind words of encouragement I received throughout this process are very much appreciated.

An additional thank you to all of my mentors. I've had many throughout my career and each has taught me valuable lessons, both professionally and personally.

Lastly, but certainly not least, I'd like to thank all of my friends and colleagues. I've had an amazing experience in this world so far. One that has inspired my characters and guided their adventures. I sincerely hope you all enjoy reading this novel.

THE
CYPRUS
PAPERS

Foreword

TWO YEARS AGO.

The capital city of Tashkent, Uzbekistan, was quiet in the pre-dawn hour. Two men dressed in black with ski masks and army-issued AK-47s exited a nondescript white van that stopped in front of a house on a tree-lined residential street near the city center. A third man turned off the engine and adjusted the mirrors to get a better vantage of the street.

The "Stone City" had always enjoyed a large Islamic population, but the contemporary spelling of its name stemmed from its Soviet influence. An earthquake leveled much of the ancient city in the 1960s. Its rebirth during the Soviet-era occupation contributed greatly to the city's grim architecture. Most buildings were little more than concrete blocks dotted with undersized windows.

The two men quickly and quietly approached a waist-high old stone wall that separated the homes from the street. The wall now served to house the landscaping beds and to accentuate the architectural entrances of the aging homes.

They closed in on the home with a BMW 5 Series parked in front with a rental barcode attached to the upper-left corner of its windshield. The luxury car was a stark contrast to the Russian and Uzbekistan cars that lined the street.

From one of the neighboring homes, a dog barked. Both men stopped and crouched behind the stone wall. They waited until the dog was quiet, then indicated to the man in the van they were ready to proceed. They advanced cautiously toward the house.

In a bedroom on the second floor, Stan Murphy slept next to his beautiful and much younger companion. Stan was a hedge fund manager. After his education at Wharton, he began his career at a boutique hedge fund firm in New York. A diminutive man with average looks and a receding hair line, he relied upon his bullish personality and financial acumen to quickly progress through the ranks.

Stan's core competence was his ability to uncover international investment opportunities with unique tax benefits. His willingness to oversee their funds in off-shore tax havens was also attractive to his clients. The massive recession, however, had shrunk his clients' bankrolls. Investors developed an appetite for "less risky" investments like gold, and began closing their accounts.

On the verge of losing millions of dollars in management fees, Stan developed an international investment to capitalize on his clients' risk tolerance. He uncovered an opportunity with a defunct gold mine in Africa. Mine investments were capital intensive and required corporations to absorb significant financial risk. These corporations typically had a large portfolio of investments. Pressure from shareholders to manage earnings created a willingness to exit underperforming investments at a significant discount.

His strategy worked and yielded a significant return to his clients. Unfortunately for Stan, his subsequent investments in defunct mines were unable to match his initial success. His partners became frustrated after a few key clients closed their accounts.

Stan needed to prove that a defunct gold mine in Uzbekistan was worth the risk. He had previously secured two rounds of financing to exploit the remaining gold, but its potential had yet to materialize. This was his third trip to the Uzbekistan capital in the past six weeks. The mine was located in the Kyzylkum Desert, a four-hour drive west of the city. He was scheduled to meet a gold mine expert in the morning to validate the investment's potential. He wasn't looking forward to the meeting that had been arranged by his firm.

He knew his partners and investors were unhappy. In addition to lackluster returns, a financial crisis in Cyprus—where most of his investors' accounts were housed—was severely impairing his tax haven strategy. The Cypriot government had recently approved a fifty-percent levy on foreign accounts to cover the country's financial collapse. The levy would result in massive losses to his wealthy clients and destroy his reputation.

Stan assured his firm that the funds under his management could be transferred out of the country before the levy. After multiple attempts to get the funds out through official channels, he now wasn't so sure. The government actively monitored all banking activity and denied any withdrawal requests.

He had met with a client in Cyprus just a day before in another failed attempt to get the money out of the country. Desperate and unbeknownst to anyone, Stan initiated a withdrawal of the more accessible funds to a personal account he held in Switzerland. He paid handsome bribes to his banking contacts to use these channels that were outside the eyes of the watchful government. With great uncertainty, the funds were scheduled to be deposited tomorrow morning. His fate hinged on the success of the money transfer. If it failed, he only had a day or two before his house of cards fell apart.

Stan woke to a large bang. Disoriented, he pushed his young companion off the bed before falling to the floor. He stumbled to his feet as he regained his faculties. His thin frame, clad only in plain white boxer shorts, shuffled across the room. He locked the door. His chest, covered in gray and brown hair, heaved as he contemplated his next action.

He heard two sets of feet race up the stairs to the second floor. *Investors must have learned about the account withdrawals,* he thought. His investment strategy garnished interest from a global pool of investors. As he had learned from the African mine, gold also attracted a class of investors he'd never dealt with in the past. He fumbled through his crumpled pants on the floor to grab his cell phone.

"Stan, what is happening?" asked his companion in broken English. Trembling, she haphazardly covered her naked body with the bed sheets before cowering against the side of the bed.

"Be quiet!" he demanded. He dialed the first number listed in his cell phone.

Stan ran into the closet and held the door closed as he pinched the phone between his shoulder and ear. It rang a second time. "Shit, answer the phone," he whispered as he stared at the closed door. He could do nothing but wait. The feeling was as helpless as it was desperate.

After three loud thuds from the bedroom, he could hear the door being torn off its hinges. Stan cringed when his companion screamed. Her scream was brief, as an eerie silence took hold. Then a male voice spoke with an unnerving calm demeanor.

"Where is he?"

Engulfed in darkness, Stan strained to hear a reply, but none came. The first strike against the closet door startled him. His face recoiled, but his firm grip on the door handle with both hands remained. He knew his efforts were futile, but he needed time. Finally, the ringing in his ear stopped, but it was too late. The flimsy door splintered with the second strike. He let go of the doorknob, which dropped to the floor without the integrity of the wood structure.

Stan's eyes repeatedly blinked from the bright light shining in his face. The small, powerful light was fixed to the end of a rifle barrel that was just a few inches from the bridge of his nose. He could only see a faint outline of the man standing in front of him as he raised his arms above his head.

Without words, the man motioned him to exit the closet using the rifle barrel. Paralyzed with fear, Stan didn't move. With a swift action, the man lowered the weapon to his side, as it remained held in place by a rifle strap. He grabbed Stan and pulled him from the closet.

The half-naked man fell to the ground and began kicking wildly. The assailant punched him into submission. He dragged the hedge fund manager out of the closet and across the floor, leaving a trail of urine.

"Don't kill me!" pleaded the frightened man.

The phone he had clutched remained on the closet floor. A voice on the other side began to speak. "Hello? Stan, is that you? What's going on? It sounds like World

War Three over there. Don't worry, I'll get you out. *Trust me*. I'm your lawyer and I know what to do. I'll find whatever prison they send you to."

Stan tried to regain his composure as he viewed the two armed men from his position on the floor. "I'll pay you double whatever your employer promised. Just let me go."

"I'm afraid we can't do that," replied the second assailant in a heavy Russian accent.

"What do you want?" asked Stan. Perspiration beaded on his forehead.

"We're here for you, Mr. Murphy. You have some valuable information related to a Cyprus bank account you liquidated." The last thing Stan saw was the butt of the man's rifle rapidly approaching his face as he attempted to lift his arms in protest.

From a rooftop across the street, a dark-skinned man with emerald green eyes had witnessed the commotion in the bedroom. In the dark, he studied the movements of the two military-trained men. He too had come for the man in the house, but had arrived just after the men exited the white van. He tapped his earpiece and it began to ring. It would be early evening to the recipient.

"Yes?" came a voice on the other end.

"Our information came too late. The Russians have entered the picture. They have him." He didn't need any instructions to determine the next move. "I am in place," he added.

"You know what to do."

"Yes, I do." The man ended the call with another tap of the earpiece. His assembled rifle included a silencer to suppress both the sound and flash. With the night-vision telescope raised to his left eye, he focused his attention on the front door.

Moments later, the hedge fund manager exited the house with assistance from the two men. With the unconscious body wedged between them, they bore the weight by holding the man's lifeless arms over their shoulders.

The man on the roof concentrated the crosshairs on the target. He blinked twice to wet his eyes. He wouldn't blink again until his work was finished.

When the three men reached the concrete stairs that led down to the sidewalk, he placed his finger on the trigger. He learned their body movements after the first step and calibrated his aim during the second step. When they reached the third step, he pulled the trigger. The small-caliber bullet penetrated the target's heart with precision as the three bodies moved in tandem.

"Be careful," barked the alpha male to the other man as he responded to the slight movement in the body.

"I've got him," replied the man in his native tongue.

The man from the rooftop knew the two men would not discover the dead body until they reached the van. He quickly separated the rifle into three parts and packed it in a black backpack.

He quietly retreated down the side of the house, through the backyard, and down the alley. The rental car was located a few blocks away. He checked his watch. He had four hours to kill before his plane was scheduled to depart.

Part I

Chapter 1

The room felt surreal to Emily. The elegant cranberry-colored drapes framed the magnificent view of the Capitol Building and flowed from the ceiling into delicate pools on the swirled white marble floor. Three oversize white crystal chandeliers cast a warm glow on the crowd and provided an intended degree of anonymity.

Meticulously dressed waiters in tuxedos wore emotionless smiles as they served tiny appetizers and champagne to the guests. At five hundred dollars a ticket, food was not the main attraction at the political fundraiser. Garbed in tailored gowns and tuxedos, and adorned with expensive watches and jewelry, the guests glided around the room in search of conversation.

"I hate these events," Emily said to herself. She could think of much better ways to spend a Saturday night. *Why does my boyfriend drag me to these things?* She hated everything about them, from the boring political conversations to the brush-offs from people after learning she was not actively involved in politics. She had never even voted before. A point she planned to intentionally omit tonight.

These events were just about political affiliations and false idealism. *I'd like to see these people live off the wages of the ninety-nine percent,* she thought.

Emily scoured the room, but she could not see him. *He's probably just running late.* Across the room and toward the far corner, was an elegantly polished wooden bar with only a few people. "Perfect," she said as she started to squeeze her slender build through the sea of people.

"Hello there," said a familiar voice. Emily turned around to see one of the partners from the consulting firm where she worked. The woman wore a dark blue gown with a miniature US flag pinned to her chest.

"Hello, Claudia," replied Emily, not surprised to see her at the event. Claudia Briggs was one of the founding members of her firm, and the only one who held a law degree. She had worked at the US Attorney's Office in New York and also served as an associate counsel for the president before launching a career in consulting. Claudia was well-connected in both the legal and political arenas, which had a significant impact on the firm's success. Standing just over five feet tall, her short stature was more than compensated for by her naturally loud and often opinionated voice.

"What brings you here?" Claudia asked with a broad smile.

"I'm Scott's plus one."

"Of course," she responded. "He's such a nice boy. And handsome too." She winked, then shifted her gaze toward the room. "I hear such positive reviews regarding your work. You know, this scene is a hotbed of connections. If you build a book of business, the sky is the limit for you, my dear." She raised her short arms for emphasis as she gestured toward everyone in the room.

Although she knew she could learn a lot from working with Claudia, Emily's time was monopolized by one of the other founding partners of her firm.

"I'll certainly take that advice." Emily smiled.

"I see that you don't have a pin," stated Claudia as she glanced at Emily's plain, black cocktail dress.

"No, I don't."

"Don't you worry, my dear. I always carry a spare." The woman opened her small black clutch and dipped her stubby fingers inside. She pulled out an ornate pin in the shape of the US flag. She reached up to gently pin it on Emily's dress strap.

"That's much better," said Claudia when she reviewed her work. "You must always demonstrate your allegiance to this beautiful country. Besides, you don't want to be one of the few people without one."

To Emily, generating business was always secondary to executing the work brought in by people like Claudia. She was hesitant to step outside of her comfort zone to begin developing contacts. That needed to change if she wanted to make partner.

"Speaking of that, I see my next target is free." Claudia reached out and gently touched Emily on the elbow. "I'll see you in the office, my dear. We can continue our conversation there, if you would like," she added with a pleasant smile.

"I'd really like that," responded Emily. Before she could say any more, Claudia began to shimmy her pear-shaped body through the crowd.

After avoiding eye contact on three separate occasions to thwart unwanted conversations, Emily finally made it to the bar. Top-shelf liquor lined the antique mirrored walls. The friendly-faced bartender provided a sharp contrast with the dour expressions of the other event staff. Emily studied the vast bottle selection while he attended to a man standing next to her.

"Hendrick's," said the man.

Caught off-guard, she answered, "Yes?" as she looked toward the man who had spoken.

He offered her a queer expression, then smiled. "Hello."

"Do I know you?" she asked.

"I don't think so. I think I'd remember you."

She blushed before responding. "You called my name."

The bartender set a drink in front of the man. "Unless your name is Hendrick's,"—he picked up his gin cocktail for emphasis and tilted it toward her—"you must have misheard."

She blushed before responding. "Sorry," she said. "My mistake."

"What can I get you?" the bartender asked politely.

"Sapphire and tonic, please."

"You can do better than that," said the man as he continued the conversation. Emily turned to address the man, but his attention was with the bartender. "Get her a Hendrick's and tonic, please."

Before she could protest, the bartender turned around to make the cocktail. "That's a little presumptuous."

"It's a better gin."

"That's not the point—"

"I think we got off on the wrong foot. Hi, my name is Owen. Owen Templeton. Nice to meet you, Miss..."

"Hendricks. Nice to meet you as well," she stated as she moved her left hand through her shoulder-length medium brown hair.

"Ha, so you're a *Hendricks*. I should have figured that out." He laughed.

Conscious of her involuntary movement, she turned slightly away from him and toward the bar to discourage any unwanted advances. There was never any shortage of predatory men at these events, and their perceived power typically invited poor judgment and inappropriate behavior when it came to women.

"If I may say, you don't look like you're having a good time." He casually scanned the room before continuing. "This isn't your scene, is it?"

"Not so much," said Emily as she turned slightly to face him, but not enough to indicate she was interested. "I'm much more comfortable in a pub or some dive bar in Adams Morgan."

"DC is such a great city. I've lived here a few years, but I split my time with upstate New York. Work consumes much of my time, and I really don't get out much. Tell me what I'm missing. Where are the *in* bars?"

"I'm probably not the best tour guide," she stated. "Besides, I spend too much time at work myself."

"Ah, so you're an attorney. I knew there was something familiar about you. I'm an attorney, as well. Harvard Law. Where did you attend law school?"

Emily tried not to dislike people she met from ivy league schools, but they were always so quick to state their school affiliation as a badge of honor. Emily was proud of her school—a well-respected public institution—but she didn't flaunt her alma mater like it was her only identity.

The bartender carefully laid a napkin on the counter and placed her drink on it before turning his attention to other guests.

Emily gently squeezed the lime into her glass, stirred, and took a sip before she replied. "An impressive pedigree," she said. "But, I didn't attend law school and I'm not a lawyer. I'm in litigation consulting."

While Emily spoke, Owen squeezed a lime and placed it in his glass. He picked the straw out of the glass and gently poked the lime before discarding the straw on the napkin in front of him. He casually lifted the glass to his mouth and took a long drink.

"I'm not sure I follow," he said, his voice trailing off. "You're in litigation, but do not practice law?"

"Exactly," she said. "I work with law firms. I provide consulting and analytical services. I essentially piece together financial stories to provide expert reports and testimony for complex commercial disputes. But I am certainly not a lawyer. I have too much integrity."

"Ouch," he said with a pained expression.

"Sorry. I didn't mean it like that," she lied. "I meant that, yes, I work with lawyers, but am not one myself."

She decided to keep it simple. Lawyers were by nature argumentative. She had found herself in a few unpleasant conversations in the past over trivial topics. After perusing the room for an excuse to leave, she politely turned to Owen when he began to speak.

"I get it. Law is an unusual profession, in which there are many unscrupulous people. I can't really think of another profession that is even remotely similar... unless you consider prostitution."

Emily snorted. She immediately covered her mouth with her hand as she smiled and tried to conceal her embarrassment. "That's what I was looking for," he stated with a smile of his own. "Was that so hard?"

"Thank you, I needed that," she said. "These events really are not for me."

"I agree, but, unfortunately, I find myself at such things far too often."

"You're a politician?"

"Guilty," he admitted and laughed.

For the first time, Emily got a good look at Owen. From the crow's feet around his eyes and gray peppered hair, she reasoned he was in his late forties. His tall, slender physique combined with a youthful spirit made him appear younger. *It's probably served him well*, she thought. She had to remind herself to keep her guard up. Politicians' words could rarely be trusted.

Emily had two classifications for politicians: old school and new wave. The old school typically were overweight, over indulged, and adhered to the good ole boy network to achieve their agendas. The new wave utilized a more modern and slick approach. They tended to be more approachable and used a Kennedy-like charm and, often, good looks to influence people.

Owen clearly fell into the new wave category. In the end, it didn't really matter. She always kept her viewpoints guarded at these events.

"I understand why you don't like these events," stated Owen. "I look around this room and see very unhappy people. They go through the motions of life, but have very little concern for others. It's really quite sad. Let me tell you a story—"

"Oh, here we go," Emily jested. "This is usually where I exit the conversation." She pretended she was about to walk away.

"No, seriously. I grew up in a middle-class neighborhood, but my parents always reinforced the idea of family and helping out the less fortunate. I've made it my mission to help out others, no matter how dire their situation. Everyone deserves a chance in life."

"Well, that's quite admirable," Emily said in a surprised tone. She could usually tell when someone was not sincere, but had difficulty reading Owen.

Scott appeared about ten feet away. With a broad smile on his face, he approached her.

"What?" asked Emily to Scott when he got closer.

"You know this guy?" Owen asked.

"Of course she does," interrupted Scott as he leaned over and gave her a quick kiss on the lips. "I was going to introduce you two today. I guess I don't need to now," he said with a contented smile.

"So, you're *Congressman* Owen. I thought you were just *an* Owen. I should be mad at you. You're the reason I've been seeing a lot less of him," she said, pointing to Scott.

Owen laughed. "There's always a lot to get done. You need dependable people. Do you know of any?"

"Hey!" Scott protested.

An individual appeared and leaned toward Owen. The man whispered briefly into his ear. Immediately, Owen's demeanor changed and his eyebrows furrowed.

"Scott, let's connect later. We have a lot to discuss before our next trip." His charm returned when he addressed Emily. "Emily, it's been lovely chatting, but unfortunately, duty calls. I need to shake some money trees," he added with a smile.

He reached out to gently hold her hand. "I genuinely hope that we'll meet again." His hand lingered momentarily. "Enjoy your Hendrick's." Before she could withdraw her hand, he presented a slight smile, and then he was whisked away by his assistant.

"So, he's the one, huh?" Emily said to Scott. "He certainly is a schmoozer."

"What was that all about? *Enjoy your Hendrick's?*" Scott asked with a forced casual tone.

"Jealous, are we?" she replied with a grin.

"Always. I need to keep my eye on you before you realize you can do better than me." He reached around her waist, resting his hand on her left hip.

He held her like he used to when they first dated. She requited his touch by reaching a hand gently around the back of his neck. Emily shifted her weight so that Scott had to put his arms around her.

Their heads remained only inches apart as they ignored the rest of the room. He gazed at her and said, "You have the most beautiful brown eyes." After a gentle kiss on the lips, their tongues briefly met.

"Stop... not here," she said as their eyes met again.

"Okay, but later, you're mine..."

Chapter 2

TUESDAY. 9:12 AM.

Emily worked at Sufferton & Waine, LLP, a boutique consulting firm on K Street, just east of the White House. Like so many buildings in downtown DC, Ionic columns and limestone facades wrapped street-facing sides of the neoclassical low-rise.

The firm's main service line focused on litigation consulting. Its partners were well-connected in DC and had a surprising amount of high-profile engagements and clients for such a small office. The team consisted of four partners and twenty-seven consultants.

Emily sat at her desk with the door closed while she diligently worked to put the finishing touches on a report involving a class-action lawsuit. The Ferris Report, as it was known internally, was the culmination of nearly six months of reviewing countless documents, attending endless meetings, analyzing too much data—and losing too many nights and weekends. But she enjoyed every bit of it.

Emily's work strained her relationships with friends and family, but the satisfaction of putting her best effort against an opposing expert's and coming out ahead could not be matched.

She paused her typing to take a casual look around her office. It was beginning to lose the "new carpet" smell. She enjoyed the smell, even though she knew it was just the toxins being released into the air.

The firm had been experiencing a growth spurt. Three months earlier, they added seven staff members and moved into a new office building. Emily exhaled slowly as her eyes moved away from the bookcase of rarely referenced textbooks and toward the endless piles of research papers and client documents splayed across her desk.

Finally, her eyes focused on the computer screen in front of her. She finished gathering her thoughts and began tapping the keyboard. With a renewed focus, the day quickly slipped away.

A knock at the door startled Emily. "Come in," she announced. After a moment, she exited her trance to greet her visitor.

Terrance Sufferton, the founding partner who monopolized Emily's time, stood in the doorway. His Ivy League education contrasted his unique blend of humility and eccentricity.

She took a long look at him. He wore suspenders to hold up his pants. His striped shirt contrasted horribly with his paisley tie. His dislike for shaving was evident from the Santa Clause white beard that clung clumsily to his round face.

What he lacked in polish, he more than made up for as an expert testifier on the stand. He was a fierce competitor in the courtroom. Unflappable and credible, he was an opposing counsel's worst nightmare. Even his lack of polish was an asset. It gave him instant *street cred* to juries, who typically couldn't relate to smooth-talking expert witnesses. Most of all, Terrance was a good friend and mentor to Emily.

Her father died a while back. Terrance's friendship and guidance had served to fill that void. At least in part. He also proved instrumental to her career and presented opportunities that she likely wouldn't have received elsewhere.

"How's the Ferris Report coming along?"

"Fine," replied Emily as she collected her thoughts. "I should be done by the end of the week."

"That's cutting it close. We need to provide the draft report to the attorneys mid next week, and I still need to review it."

Emily just gave him a knowing look. His reviews mostly consisted of recommending a few personal word preferences, and little else. She did outstanding work that didn't require much revision.

Immediately, he softened his tone. "Well, someone has to read it," he stated with a grin. "I hear you attended the reception on Saturday. Make any good contacts?"

"You've been talking to Claudia. Yes, she drilled me on my need to get out of my comfort zone to develop new business. I got the message loud and clear." She smiled.

"Good."

"I didn't see you there."

"Those events aren't my thing. I'm a behind-the-scenes person when it comes to politics." He patted his guilty belly for emphasis.

"Where's Claudia? She's not in the office today."

"She was called to a client site. She'll be back tomorrow."

"Gotcha. I just wanted to touch base with her. But I'm sure you already know that."

"I do."

Terrance smiled and started to exit. He stopped and turned back toward Emily. "I have a new case for you."

"Not another," she protested in jest. "Please tell me we have at least two months to finish it. I'm getting behind on my other engagements."

"I really don't think it's going to be too bad. They don't even want an expert report. Just a simple fact-finding exercise and a summary analysis. Lisa was slated to work on this, but she's not available."

Something in his voice alarmed Emily. "What happened?"

"I'm not sure. She had some family emergency she needed to attend."

"Oh my. I hope everything's okay."

"Claudia briefly spoke to her on the phone. It looks like she'll be out for a couple of weeks."

"Lisa already left?"

"She flew to Seattle last night. I really don't know anymore. I'll let you know when I hear something."

"Okay. Thanks. I'll send her a quick note later," said Emily.

"I'm sure she'd like that," he replied.

"Since you're taking the lead on this one, I wanted to let you know the timing is a bit tight. We're going to need the summary analysis done in two weeks. Sorry."

"Two weeks? You really don't like me, do you?"

"I've set up a meeting tomorrow with one of the client's representatives. I'll send you a meeting invite."

"Great. I look forward to it," Emily stated sarcastically. "Can you tell me anything else about the engagement?"

"I really don't have much visibility in the matter. Just meet with the client and figure it out. I trust your judgment."

"Will do," said Emily as she turned her attention to her computer and started typing.

"Don't you have dinner plans or something tonight?" asked Terrance. "It's Tuesday."

Emily always met Scott for dinner in Georgetown on Tuesday. They coined it their Tuesday Night Club and had enjoyed the ritual for as long as they had dated. As their careers progressed, it required more effort to carve the time out of their schedules. Lately, Scott's job required lots of days out of town. Emily still made an effort to attend, even if it was just to catch up on some work or enjoy some quiet time with a book.

Emily looked at Terrance. "Yes, but it's not until seven thirty."

"It's seven thirty now."

"Shit! Where do my days go!"

Emily quickly packed up her computer and threw it into her work tote. She added a few key files so she could work later in the evening. After putting on her coat, she walked down the empty hall and past the other offices to the bathroom. When she exited, she thought of something she meant to tell Terrance. She jogged to his office.

Emily slowed down as she approached his door. She lifted her hand to knock, but paused when she heard Terrance yelling.

"No. I had to change the lead consultant on the engagement. As you are well aware, the first one I tagged is having a fucking family emergency!" *I've never heard him this angry,* she thought. He continued his rant. "We may need more time, or have to come up with an alternative." His voice trailed off.

After a few moments, his demeanor changed. "Fine. I'll handle it," he said with resignation. "I understand." There was a loud bang as he appeared to slam the phone onto the receiver.

Emily lifted her hand once again to knock. This time, she didn't have a chance. The door abruptly opened.

"Oh," Terrance exclaimed softly as he stood in the doorway. He looked surprised to see Emily standing outside his door. "You're still here."

With some embarrassment, Emily spoke. "Sorry, Terrance. I didn't mean to interrupt."

"You didn't interrupt," he said. He flashed her a friendly smile.

"I just wanted to remind you of an upcoming conference call with the attorneys of the Ferris Report."

"It's on my calendar," replied Terrance. "Are you okay?"

"Yes, it's just..."

"Don't worry about it," he said in a reassuring tone. "It's just... *consulting*," he added, pointing to the phone on his desk. "Clients can be a huge pain in the butt. It's my job to shield some of the ugly side of business from the people who work with me."

After a brief pause, he continued. "You'll understand when you have clients call you at God-awful times. I once got a call on Christmas Eve. He chewed me out for over half an hour without giving me a chance to speak. In the end, we didn't even do anything wrong. In fact, he was at fault, but I didn't tell him that. I did charge him my standard hourly rate, though," he added with a grin.

"I wasn't trying to eavesdrop."

"Why would you want to? Go enjoy your evening," he said with a laugh as he patted her shoulder. "I'll be out of here soon myself."

Before she could respond, he walked past her and down the hall.

Chapter 3

TUESDAY. 7:48 PM.

Emily exited the building, noting a slight chill in the October air. The hot summer that lasted through September was now giving away to fall. The trees that lined K Street were showing off their best fall colors.

Even though Emily often complained about the summers, there was no place like DC in the fall. She had done a fair amount of traveling abroad and decided it was the most European US city. She welcomed the multitude of languages she heard when she walked the streets. If she closed her eyes, it was as if she were three thousand miles away.

She hailed a cab with a quick raise of her hand. "Clyde's, in Georgetown," she said as she climbed into the back seat. She reflected on the day's events and sank farther into the seat. The cab quickly crossed town while the city lights danced throughout the cabin.

The cab ride was exactly what she needed to unwind and clear her head before dinner. Emily checked her phone and noted a meeting reminder for dinner and a missed call from her mother. She didn't want to talk to her anyway.

There were only so many conversations a person could have with someone who didn't understand their life choices or the fact that the world had changed in the past three decades. Having a career and not being married with two kids when you're in your thirties was not a bad thing anymore. *God, I can hear the conversation without even talking to her*, Emily thought with an annoyed smile.

Her mind drifted to when she first met Scott at Clyde's, three springs prior. She had been sitting in a booth studying for a final. Scott was there for a fundraiser, and the clean-shaven, political strategist with slicked-back hair had approached her booth with a certain unassuming confidence.

He sat down and just started talking like they had known each other for years. Her first instinct was to wave him off as she had many courters before, but his engaging blue eyes and awkward smile kept her attention. They talked all night and joked later that the reason his candidate failed that election was because they spent the entire summer enjoying the spoils of the city.

Recently, however, there had been a divide in the relationship. Emily was spending too much of her time and attention on work. Scott was equally guilty, spending most of his time with Owen.

Scott spoke glowingly of the man's work ethic and vision, but the amount of time he spent with Owen made her jealous. She couldn't compete with his demanding schedule.

Scott had met the congressman the past summer while campaigning for someone else. They made an instant connection, and Owen offered him a position on his campaign team two months ago.

The taxi dropped her off across the street from the restaurant, a three-story structure with a colonial brick facade. The first floor was clad in wood paneling to replicate what an "old colonial building" might have looked like two hundred years ago.

Emily stepped into the bustling restaurant and quickly made her way to the booths across from the main bar. Scott faced the entrance, but his attention was focused on the flat-screen TV. He nursed an almost-empty pint while watching a hockey game.

"Sorry I'm late," she said as she kissed him on the cheek and sat down across from him. "I totally lost track of time."

"That's okay. I got here a few minutes early and was able to catch up on some work."

"How's the campaign? Have you guys picked out the drapes yet?"

"Very funny."

"Seriously, how's it going? I really haven't had a chance to ask."

Scott made eye contact with the bartender, held up two fingers, and pointed to his beer. "Honestly, it's going very well," he stated. "We're starting to get some major funding. It's really taking off faster than I can handle. I may be in over my head."

"I'm sure you'll be fine," Emily reassured him. "You've always been ahead of your time. What you see in politicians, I'll never know. You are the polar opposite. Integrity, intelligence, humility. Maybe not the charm, though," she added with a smile.

"Hey!" protested Scott. "What I lack in charm, I more than make up for in physique. You like it," he said as he made a presenting gesture with his hands to his body.

"I don't know about that." Emily laughed. "That certainly wasn't the selling point when we met. I honestly don't know what I saw in you that night."

"You saw a handsome man with a budding career and a wickedly good sense of humor," he said with a huge smile.

"Ha. I guess I chose poorly, huh?"

"Very funny," he said as he took a gulp of his beer. "So, what did you think of him?"

"Who? Owen?"

"Yes."

"Are we going to talk about him all night?"

"I'm just curious. I can't believe it took so long for you two to meet. So...?"

"Well, he's handsome and likes to drink. He'll certainly assimilate well into the DC culture."

"He could be our future leader," said Scott.

"You think he has that much potential? But he's just a congressman."

"Without a doubt, I do," Scott quickly replied. "Besides, many congressmen have become president. Nineteen, to be exact."

"You looked that up." She laughed. "You're such a nerd."

"I wanted to know. I'm telling you, he has a legitimate chance, and I'm not the only one who believes it."

"I've always wondered what the White House looks like on the inside. In person, I mean. The White House tours stopped before I moved to DC."

"I could be your personal tour guide."

"I'd rather have Owen be my guide," she said in a seductive tone.

"You do find him handsome. I knew it."

"He's too old for me. I think you'd be a better fit. You certainly spend enough time with him. You know, some lifts might help your overall situation," she jested in reference to his shorter-than-average height.

He replied with an annoyed smirk. Before he could respond, his phone rang. "Damn it. I need to take this. Give me a minute. Sorry, babe."

"Speak of the devil," she said with a smirk. "Make sure your hair is in place in case he wants to chat over video," she added as Scott appeared to ignore her.

He got up from the table and quickly made his way out of the restaurant. He paced the sidewalk as he talked, while motioning with his free hand.

The bartender approached the table with two draft beers. "Hi, Emily."

"Hey, Tom. Long time no see," Emily said with a smile as she lifted the glass to her lips. She wiped the foam mustache from her face and set the beer neatly onto a coaster.

"If he ditches you again, just give me a holler and I'll fuck him up for you," Tom said with a half-smile.

"Thanks, Tom. I may take you up on that," said Emily before he strolled back to the bar.

Two minutes later, Scott hurried to the table with a surly look on his face. She knew what it meant. "Emily, I'm sorry, but I really need to head back to the office. Everything is moving so quickly, and if I want to keep my job, I'll need to stay three steps ahead of everyone else. Is there any way I can make it up to you?"

"Dinner! Saturday night. Bombay Club. Nice clothes, no jeans. And please don't be late," she said as she looked deep into his blue eyes.

"You're the best," he said. He packed his things back into his work bag and grabbed his jacket. He started to leave, but quickly turned around. "Are we good?" he asked.

"We're fine," she lied.

"Good," he said. "See you Saturday." He gave her a kiss on the cheek, then walked out the door.

Emily looked at the two full beers on the table and sighed. She opened her bag and placed her laptop on the table. *I might as well be productive.* She glanced at the television and noticed Tom was looking at her with a smile. He made a fist with his right hand and playfully punched his left. He lifted up his sleeve to show off his Special Forces tattoo. He was proud of his military service and generously offered free rounds to servicemen visiting the bar.

Tom mouthed that the next round was on him. Emily gave him a thumbs-up and began working on the report for Terrance.

Chapter 4

Emily stepped into the restaurant and gave her party's name to the hostess. "I'm here to see Ben Nelson."

Standing behind an imposing mass of wood and high-gloss polish, the young, bleached-blonde hostess checked the computer. After a minute, she finished her task, looked Emily up and down, and said, "Right this way, please." She appeared from behind the computer wearing five-inch heals to lead Emily toward her table.

The Old Ebbitt Grill was a DC institution that was almost as old as its politics. It had been a while since Emily had last been there. She admired the detailed wood finishes and antique paintings throughout the establishment. It was equally occupied by members of the legal community and casual diners visiting the city.

After a long, winding walk through crowds of people, the hostess stopped. She stood before a corner table at the farthest point of the restaurant.

Ben Nelson waited patiently at the table. His form-fitted suit gave a hint to his muscular frame. She guessed he must be well over six feet tall. In contrast to his formidable appearance, he wore a warm smile.

"You must be Emily Hendricks," he said as he stood up. "Ben Nelson." His suit didn't show a single wrinkle when he offered his left hand. Emily quickly dropped her right hand, which she had naturally raised. She awkwardly accepted his hand with her own left. Her arm shook like a rubber hose from the sternness of his greeting.

"Hi. Nice to meet you," Emily said with a polite smile.

"And you, as well, Miss Hendricks," he said. His confidence and mannerisms indicated he was the kind of man who knew how to handle himself in a crisis.

"Please, call me Emily."

"Certainly, Emily. I hope you don't mind, but I'm not much for chitchat. Let's get down to business."

"I'm sorry, but I'm still getting up to speed on this assignment. I really don't know much about it."

"Of course," he said. "And my sincerest apologies. We certainly did not intend to keep you in the dark. We just wanted a certain degree of discretion."

"Terrance stated that you needed a quick turnaround with our services. Could you elaborate?"

"Mr. Sufferton has been most accommodating," he said with a dry tone. "Essentially, we are asking for an assessment of our campaign finances. Our goal is to reassure our funders and constituents as to the soundness of our campaign quality."

"Have you had any issues historically regarding the campaign's soundness?" asked Emily.

"We simply want an affirmation from your firm regarding our current finances. A stamp of approval, really. Nothing more. We've never had any issues. We run everything by the book."

"I understand."

Ben continued, "You will have banker boxes with our complete financial history, donor information, and expenditures with supporting receipts first thing in the morning. We are completely transparent and want to facilitate your due diligence."

Emily had a flashback to her early consulting days before the prevalence of electronic information. Budgets were often consumed with the discovery process. Developing an understanding of the provided documents was necessary before even a basic analysis could be completed. It was a time-consuming and inefficient process.

"We really need the information electronically," Emily said. "If we are to meet the deadline," she added.

"I'm afraid that is just not possible. We are fairly primitive and do not possess any sophisticated financial tracking systems," replied Ben.

"Terrance mentioned a two-week turnaround. Is that still the case?"

"Yes, and unfortunately, Emily, we really don't have much flexibility."

"I see," said Emily. "In terms of budget, what are we talking here?"

"Budget discussions have already been addressed with Mr. Sufferton."

"But I need to know how this is going to be staffed. In order to meet the deadline, I'll need to bring in supporting staff."

"Absolute discretion is necessary here. It was our understanding that this engagement would be seen through its entirety by only one individual. This was previously discussed with Mr. Sufferton," Ben stated with a slight irritation.

After the meeting concluded, Emily left the table when Ben picked up a menu. She had politely declined a lunch offer based on a false pretense of a prior commitment.

She walked back through the restaurant. She fought to hide the annoyed look on her face. She couldn't believe the deadline, or Ben's arrogance. This assignment was going to be an absolute nightmare.

The bar was bustling with activity. As she passed through it, she came to an abrupt stop. *It can't be*, she thought. She saw Terrance seated at a high cocktail table near the bar. A white-shirted waiter carefully placed a sandwich in front of him. His seat directly faced the table she had just left. He greeted her with a smile.

"Fancy meeting you here, Terrance," said Emily. She found it impossible to conceal the annoyed look on her face.

"How's my favorite consultant?" he quipped. "Aren't you supposed to be completing some work for me?"

"I'm always working. Don't worry, I'll have lots of billable hours this month."

"Take it easy, Emily," Terrance stated with a look of genuine concern as he raised his hands to complete a downward motion gesture. "I'm really not worried about your hours. You know I never am. Sit down and have lunch with me."

"I probably shouldn't. I have a lot of work to complete for *you*," she replied as she shot him a stern look.

"In that case, you have no excuse. You can give me a summary of where we stand on all of our engagements. Wait a minute," he said as he got out his phone. After quickly typing on the keypad, he returned his attention to Emily. He didn't say anything, but she knew he was up to something.

"What?" Emily finally asked. His silence continued. Her phone buzzed. She checked it to find a meeting request from Terrance to "review engagement status." The meeting was slated to start in five minutes. Emily laughed as she shook her head and accepted the invite. "Fine."

Terrance sat silently as Emily removed her suit jacket and elegantly folded it over the back of her chair. She noted Terrance's smirk as she sat.

She didn't know if it was meant for her compulsive mannerisms or the fact that he quickly persuaded her to sit down and have lunch with him. She didn't care either way. She always enjoyed his company. The fact that she was getting some much-needed time away from the office also helped.

After she ordered a drink, she waited for Terrance to speak. As the silence continued, she laughed.

"What...?" he asked.

"Nothing," said Emily as the waiter placed a drink in front of her.

"Seriously, what's so funny?"

"Are you really not going to tell me what you're doing *here*? Charades are not your strong suit."

"I really don't know what you're talking about," Terrance stated in his mostly forgotten Northeastern accent.

"Come on, Terrance," Emily added quietly. In a more deliberate tone, she added, "What are you doing here, at this specific restaurant. The same restaurant as my meeting with Ben, which you set up."

"Having a drink," he replied, taking a sip of his cocktail.

"Are you checking up on me?"

"Of course not. You know I never interfere. I'm the face and you're the brains. Clients love seeing me and don't realize that I don't do any of the actual work. My job is to let you do your job and then take the credit."

"Thanks. I'm glad we settled that mystery."

"You know the game. And everything is a game, whether you like it or not. I'm not telling you anything that you don't already know," Terrance stated with a fatherly tone. "Maybe I *was* checking up on you, for once."

"What the fuck, Terrance? Really? First you lie and now you say you don't trust me?"

"I didn't say that, and you know that's not the case. I just like your company. And keep your voice down, young lady. That language is quite unbecoming." Emily looked around the room, noting a few heads turned her way.

She also noted a gentleman draped in a dark blue suit. He was angled toward her and Terrance. He had jet-black hair streaked with silver. A black fedora rested on the table. The magazine in front of him obstructed any view she might have had of his face.

"What aren't you telling me about this case? I don't even know who the client is. There's a lot I don't know, in fact. I'm completely in the dark. This isn't how we do things."

"Okay. One step at a time. Yes, this is going to be a high-profile case. Sorry for not telling you sooner." Terrance's eyes momentarily drifted to the floor, and he caressed his drink.

"Just how high-profile?" asked Emily.

"Our client is a smooth-talking politician that has quickly risen through the ranks. He has potential to go much higher. Like any politician, he needs funds to feed the machine and keep the momentum moving. Stalling any momentum could be catastrophic," explained Terrance. "His ascension within the Republican party has garnered the attention of its leaders. Before any funds are funneled into his campaign chest, they want us to shed light on any unknowns."

"Go on."

"That's essentially it. You're caught up. We investigate his personal and campaign finances. If everything looks good, he continues to get funding. End of story."

"Who's the politician?" asked Emily.

After a brief pause, Terrance replied. "Owen Templeton."

"Our client is the Congressman Owen Templeton."

"Yes."

"You know that Scott works for him. He's a part of his campaign team."

"Is that going to be a problem for you?" asked Terrance. "I'm assuming you won't divulge any of our work."

"Of course it's not going to be a problem," said Emily after a brief pause.

"You don't sound so sure."

"It's just a crazy coincidence. I just met him over the weekend. Did you know Scott worked for Owen?"

"I didn't when we accepted this engagement. Claudia informed me this morning. I didn't think you would have a problem with it. Separation of church and state," he said, smiling.

"It's definitely not a problem. What about the timing? Ben stated they needed everything done in two weeks? That's tight, especially if I can't get any supporting team members to help."

"Honestly, Emily, we can't have many people involved; they really are sensitive with their information, but you can involve an associate, if it'll speed things up."

"But Ben said—"

"I don't care what Ben said. We'll get this done in time and they'll be happy." Terrance casually glanced over her shoulder.

"Who is that guy? I noticed him earlier too."

"I don't know," said Terrance. "We need to be careful on this one."

"Terrance, why would we need to be careful? What aren't you telling me?"

"Nothing. I just mean that we need to do a good job, like we always do. Nothing more. Please don't read into this too much. Let's get back to the subject at hand. When will the documents be available?"

"Tomorrow," replied Emily.

"Perfect. I want your initial assessment on Friday."

"Monday," she insisted.

"Fine, but get it done quickly."

"I'll get it done, but it'll take time to review everything. As you know, we're not getting anything electronic. Banker boxes? I can't believe they're not more sophisticated. What exactly are we looking for?" asked Emily.

"Any irregularities in payments, companies, donors. There shouldn't be any red flags. That includes his personal finances too. I'm expecting this guy to be squeaky-clean. At least he better be if he wants his large donors to come through for him."

Chapter 5

THURSDAY. 8:15 AM.
CHEVY CHASE, MARYLAND.

At exactly a quarter past the hour, a black town car stopped in front of the long, black gate. It blocked the entire driveway of the large house in Chevy Chase, an affluent suburb located just outside of Washington, DC.

A hidden camera focused its lens on the street side of the gate. After the remotely operated camera confirmed the identity of the vehicle, the gate slowly opened to reveal a driveway of hexagon-shaped pavers laid with precision. The car stopped when the rear driver's side door aligned with the walkway to the front door.

Like many neighborhoods in the metropolitan area, real estate was expensive and the homes consumed much of the lot. The two-story English Tudor was no exception. Only some thoughtfully selected and purposefully placed privacy shrubs shared the space.

The center of the house was constructed of large multi-colored slate stone squares. Small, ornate slate stones outlined the elegant antique red door with aged brass hardware. Flanking the center of the home were the east and west wings. Built using a traditional interlay of red brick and brown wood beams, they punctuated the home's timeless elegance.

The driver exited the vehicle and closed the door. After tugging on the sleeve to adjust the fit of his uniform, he stood next to the car with his hands clasped in front of him. He remained motionless as he waited.

His dark blue uniform was the same as every other officer of the Judicial Security Division. The elite division provided security detail to the US Supreme Court Justices and was under the jurisdiction of the US Marshall Service. The prominence of justices and the importance of the court cases they presided invited increasingly more actionable threats against them.

The red door opened to reveal a tall, slender woman in her late fifties. Her silver-gray hair deliberately curled toward the neck just before reaching her shoulder. It was a style that she had enjoyed for nearly two decades.

The woman walked with a sense of purpose that was unmatched by a much younger and fuller-framed assistant that trailed with a pen and notepad. The younger woman diligently wrote down every barked order as she struggled to keep an oversize purse on her shoulder.

The older woman was Lara Belinski, a second-generation US national of Polish descent. She had been appointed to the US Supreme Court after being nominated by a Republican president.

Her qualifications were overshadowed by a high-profile account of infidelity. Her involvement with a student aide during her tenure as a Georgetown law professor had surfaced just before her appointment, and nearly cost her the position.

When she approached the town car, the driver opened the door. The younger woman hurried to climb in first and moved to the passenger side of the car to clear the seat usually occupied by the Justice. After adjusting her skirt, she waited in earnest with a pen and paper.

Lara typically didn't pay attention to her driver, but she shot him a disconcerting glance when she noted his uniform jacket was an inch too short for his arms.

"It was one of those mornings, ma'am," he stated with a formal tone.

"Where's my regular driver?" she asked, stopping at the opened door. She looked directly into the man's emerald eyes.

"Vincent's out today. My name is Sean."

"Next time, please dress appropriately," she said as she entered the vehicle. "We are representatives of the US court system and should reflect such."

"Certainly, ma'am. It won't happen again," said the driver before he closed the car door behind her. After buckling his seat belt, he checked the rearview mirror to ensure his passengers were ready.

Though his given name was Sean, people who really knew him called him the *Irishman*. In his rural hometown, he stood out due to the combination of his skin and eye color. It had been the root of much teasing when he was younger.

His father must have been one of the few black people in his hometown. He had never met the man, but knew he was black because his mother was white. People he met often commented on his skin color given his Irish descent. It annoyed him. He couldn't remember if his nickname stemmed from his eye color, heritage, or because he was a black man from Ireland. In the end, it didn't matter. It had stuck.

With a quick twist of the key, the engine hummed. He placed the transmission in drive, and began the Justice's typical commute to the courthouse.

In the back, Lara spoke to her assistant regarding a brief she had been working on. She knew her viewpoint wouldn't be shared by the left-wing justices. The brief needed to be carefully crafted so that her viewpoint wouldn't be overshadowed.

"I need to have your research completed by the weekend," Lara said in an emphatic tone.

Her aide reacted to a stutter in the woman's speech and paused her writing to make eye contact. Lara had two summers of therapy to eliminate the stutter as a child, but it occasionally came back when she was overwhelmed.

After Lara gave her a dismissive look, the aide continued to write on her notepad. "I will have it to you by then," she responded submissively.

"Good."

Lara wasn't really concerned at all about the brief. That matter was relatively minor. She had an important meeting scheduled later in the day that she hadn't shared with anyone. She was to meet an acquaintance from the FBI. She planned to get ahead of a major political storm that she thought was about to brew out of control. If she didn't act now, her legacy as a Supreme Court Justice would be ruined.

Lara continued the one-sided conversation as the driver turned onto Rock Creek Parkway. The parkway ran through Rock Creek Park, a US National park that spanned two and a half square miles. It was a popular thoroughfare to the Capitol.

After the town car passed through the winding roads, it resurfaced onto Constitution Avenue. Lara looked over at the sun-drenched Lincoln Memorial. They passed many other famous monuments located around the National Mall before turning onto one of the most well-known streets in the country, Pennsylvania Avenue.

Their destination, the US Supreme Court building, was located on the other side of the Capitol Building. The sedan deliberately slowed to catch a red light that sat equidistant between the White House and the Capitol.

"This is where I get out," said the Irishman in a monotone voice. He placed an old European-styled herringbone cap on his head, then opened the door and casually exited the vehicle.

Lara and her assistant, Molly, gave each other curious glances when the vehicle locks were engaged. Their driver was quickly lost from view as he blended into the pedestrian traffic. No words were exchanged as the two women began to look around the car for any indication why their driver would abruptly exit the vehicle.

"What the hell is going on?" Lara asked. "Where could he possibly be going?"

Annoyed, Lara grabbed the door handle and pulled. The door didn't budge. She repeated the action three times with the same result. Molly tried opening the other door. The women looked at each other. Their confusion quickly turned into fear, and then panic.

Molly moved to the front seat to try the doors and windows. "What about the trunk?" she asked. "Aren't they supposed to have a quick release so people don't get stuck in there?"

"I think you're right," replied Lara. She turned around and knelt on the rear seat. She opened the latch and moved back to allow the back of the seat to move forward.

"Oh my God," said Molly as she peered into the trunk from her front seat vantage.

Six five-gallon canisters lined the trunk. The smell of gasoline quickly permeated the cabin. Lara and Molly gasped.

Awkwardly positioned against the side of the trunk and the canisters lay a contorted body. Their regular driver, Vincent, stared blankly at them, dressed in only his socks and underwear. His deep purple face showed obvious signs of strangulation.

Molly's panic turned into resignation as she began praying and made a cross gesture on her chest. Lara, a proud atheist, chanted a silent prayer while she pounded on the window.

The explosion came in two bursts. The first engulfed the interior of the vehicle in flames as the Supreme Court Justice and her aide banged furiously on the window. A look of horror lined their shocked faces. Bystanders, alerted by the flames, matched their horrified expressions.

Most witnessed the event in detached terror. A few good Samaritans stopped to help by attempting to open the doors. One person tried to break a window using a large rock found in the landscaping of a nearby government building. Their efforts against the lightly armored vehicle were met with no effect.

An intense heat began to radiate from the black town car. The people backed away and could only watch as the hands that once pounded the windows disappeared into the flames.

The second burst sent shock waves for a two-block radius. The car was ripped apart and shot fifteen feet into the air by a series of devices expertly attached to its undercarriage. The people surrounding the town car were instantly killed. Those nearby were shoved to the ground by the extreme force of the explosion.

For twenty long seconds, all of DC was eerily quiet as its citizens were shocked by the violent nature of the explosion that reverberated throughout the city.

Rescue workers, police, Secret Service, and a plethora of other government agencies quickly flooded the scene. The media followed. Live reports, from trucks with satellite antennas reaching toward the sky, broadcast the morning's tragedy to the nation.

Chapter 6

The boxes from Owen Templeton's office had already been delivered when Emily arrived. Mary, her hardworking assistant, directed her to the west conference room.

The large rectangular room showcased an expensive high-gloss mahogany table meant to signify the vitality of the firm to visiting clients. Plush, dark-brown leather chairs surrounded it. The conference room was unlike any other in the firm. Most of the firm's office was decorated with high-quality reproductions from famous artists, while the artwork hung on these walls were originals from contemporary artists.

As Emily walked toward the conference room, she saw a small congregation of coworkers gazing out the window. The smoke from the explosion no longer billowed in the background, but they remained fixated on the commotion just a few blocks away.

Emily opened the door. She nearly dropped the coffee she had purchased on the way to the office. Over fifty banker boxes littered the room, making it more reminiscent of a storage closet than an elegant meeting place. The boxes were stacked in piles across the room and covered much of the ornate table. The mismatched boxes indicated they were from multiple storage companies and included varying levels of wear.

This is going to take a while, she thought, shaking her head. Emily was glad she assigned a junior associate to help with the investigation. The tall, blond-haired, blue-eyed man sat at the crowded table with his attention on his mobile device. He sat up when he noticed her.

"Hi, I'm Mark." His eager smile demonstrated his youth.

"I know who you are," Emily replied with a grin. In truth, she didn't know anything more than his name. He had started at the firm last month. She took off her coat and draped it over one of the conference chairs. Before she started talking, Mark spoke.

"I can't believe it," he said. She looked up to see a subtle nod toward the window.

"I can't either." She stopped unpacking the contents of her work bag on the table. "What have you heard? I only learned about it at the train station. People were freaked out."

"Not much. CNN reported that the explosion decimated a car. It doesn't sound like an accident."

"I would have to agree, given the extra security on the trains. Crazy."

"I'm glad I finally get the opportunity to work with you," Mark said. "Terrance always seems to monopolize your time."

"He does keep me quite busy," said Emily with a half laugh. After a brief description of the project, they got straight to work. They began organizing the boxes by date.

The next step was to start cataloging the contents of each box to create a master directory for easy reference. The financial data would be segregated into two major categories, contributions and expenditures. Contributions would include the amount and date of the donation, along with the donor. Expenditures would include the date, amount, and purpose for the expense.

They began reviewing the documents. Mark broke the brief silence just a moment later.

"Our client is Congressman Templeton?" he asked.

"Yes, why?"

"I've seen him on TV. He seems pretty charismatic."

"I know. I met him over the weekend. I teased my boyfriend about his charm and good looks."

They continued to work throughout the morning. Mary delivered their deli sandwiches, chips, and drinks to the conference room exactly at noon. Neither Emily nor Mark looked up from what they were doing as Mary organized the food and drinks on the side table before quietly leaving the room.

Emily got a meeting reminder on her phone just after their food was delivered. "Shoot," she said out loud. "I'm supposed to meet a friend for lunch. Apparently, she's having boy issues." Before she could elaborate, Mark spoke.

"Go. I've got this covered. Just bring me something other than a sandwich," he said, looking at the food sitting on the side table. "I've only been here six weeks and don't think I've eaten anything other than a sandwich for lunch. Something different would be appreciated." He smiled.

"I'll bring something good," Emily assured him as she rushed out the door.

Emily met her friend Jen at an upscale restaurant that specialized in Southern comfort food. Jen stood across from the hostess' stand, along the wall. There were two other people waiting: a man in a black fedora and a woman with a shopping bag.

Jen tapped on her watch as Emily approached her. She worked for a government think tank. It was a high-paying job that compensated employees for their problem-solving ability. The two women had met six months earlier at a business conference and quickly became good friends.

"Sorry I'm late," said Emily. "I got caught up on a new engagement."

"That always seems to be the case with you," Jen said in jest.

"How did you get reservations on such short notice?" asked Emily as the hostess walked them to their table.

"I've got friends in high places." Jen laughed. She sat at the corner table. "Should we get a drink?"

"It's barely after noon," replied Emily. "Besides, I've got to make this a short lunch."

"That's too bad," Jen said with a frown. "I'll have a pink lemonade."

"Make that two," added Emily. "Thanks."

"Thanks for meeting me today, Em."

"Of course. I always have time for you. I've been meaning to call. What's up? Your text last night made it seem like you really needed to talk."

"I recently started dating this guy…"

"You're dating someone?"

"Let me finish. It's not going well. He was just too clingy."

"You're the pickiest person I know. You're going to die an old maid, Jen, if you don't try harder to make a relationship work."

"Look who's talking."

"What? Don't talk to me about my relationships. We're talking about you today. You reached out to me, remember?"

"My crisis is over. I came to my senses this morning," said Jen. She paused, then added, "I'm thinking about becoming a lesbian."

"That would only solve some of your problems," replied Emily as they both laughed.

"You're right. I guess I just don't have time for a relationship right now. Speaking of relationships, how's Scott doing?"

"You know how it goes. We're both busy with work. It's hard to find the balance for a healthy relationship."

"We need a girls' night out sometime soon. That'll numb some of our concerns."

Before Emily could respond, the waitress placed the lemonades at the table. "Are you ready to order?" she asked with a polite smile.

"I think I speak for the both of us," Jen said, looking at Emily. "Two fried chicken plates."

"That works for me," said Emily as she handed the menu to the waitress. "I don't think I've ever ordered anything else here."

"Why would you?" Jen said. "Let's get back on topic."

"Oh, yeah. Your boy problems," said Emily.

"No, I'm done with that topic. Let's talk about girls' night out."

"Yes. We need one desperately."

"How about Friday night? I don't have any plans this weekend. The timing would be perfect."

"I don't know. Work has been crazy, and it's not looking any better the next few weeks."

"Sorry, you've used up that excuse," complained Jen. "Besides, isn't that the exact reason why we need a night out?"

"I guess."

"Come on. We'll make it retro night. We'll start off at the night club above the mattress place."

"Is that still open? We haven't been there in forever." A smile slowly returned to Emily's face.

"Exactly. We'll hang out there for a few hours. Get some digits from guys we'll never call."

"But they'll get us drinks." Emily laughed.

"Yes, even though we out-earn them. The world's a messed-up place. I'll take advantage of it," she said with a smirk.

"You always do, don't you?"

"Of course. Mama ain't raised no dummy. So, you're in, right?"

"I guess."

"You guess? That's the wrong attitude, Em."

"I'm in. I really do need a night out," she said.

"I saw you the other night," said Jen mysteriously.

"What? Where?"

"At a political fundraiser last Saturday. I saw you talking to a rather handsome older man. I thought I recognized him, but I couldn't place him."

"The Congressman?"

"Ooh, a congressman. You slut."

"It's not like that," began Emily. "Wait, you were there that night? I didn't see you."

"I go to those events all the time. I was surprised to see you there. I wanted to talk to you but couldn't escape my conversation."

"I know the feeling. I hate those events," Emily replied.

"I know. That's why I was surprised to see you there."

"Owen Templeton. Scott works on his campaign team."

"Well, he certainly seemed smitten with you. I bet Scott is quite jealous." Jen laughed.

"Whatever. He's a politician. They're supposed to act that way. Definitely not my type. Anyway, I just found out he's my new client too."

"I knew it. He is trying to get into your pants. There are much worse-looking men, you know. He's a gray fox."

"Stop," said Emily. They laughed and spent the remainder of the brief lunch catching up.

After lunch, Emily headed back to the office with a fried chicken plate for Mark. She didn't want to leave him alone for too long. There was too much that needed to get done. The investigation required her complete attention.

Chapter 7

By later that afternoon, Emily and Mark had gone through nearly a quarter of the boxes. The contents of each had been organized and documented. She wanted to make substantial progress before her meeting with Terrance on Monday.

"How's it going?" asked Emily. Mark faced the window as he stood. His laptop rested on a stack of boxes as he worked through a box on top of an adjacent pile.

"I'm hitting my stride," said Mark.

"I'm seeing a lot of checks from individual donors, but haven't seen nearly as many from organizations, have you? I wonder if it has anything to do with the campaign finance laws and disclosure," added Emily.

"Actually," began Mark, "political donations can be categorized into two main groups, hard money and soft money. Essentially, hard money is money donated to a specific candidate, which is why we're seeing mainly individual donors. Candidates can only receive hard money directly from individuals or political action committees, and it is subject to strict limits: $2,500 per individual and $5,000 per committee."

He took a sip of water and continued, "The laws that are geared toward restricting soft money are much more opaque. Essentially, you can donate as much as you want to a political party, just not a specific candidate."

"You seem to know a lot about this subject. Please enlighten me," Emily said with a dry smile.

"There were some efforts to restrict private funding in the 1990s, but those were effectively stalled. In the end, politicians need and want money, and don't really care where it comes from."

Before Emily could respond, Mark added, "My first two years at William and Mary I spent as a political science major. You know, to impress a girl."

"How did that turn out?"

He laughed. "I know a ton about politics, but nothing about women."

"What about the money that is left over from the elections? Does that just stay with a specific candidate?" asked Emily.

"There's still a lot of gray with these war chests. Sometimes, a candidate will save leftover funds for future elections. Other times, it will go to a general political fund. After you write a check, you never really know what it will be spent on or who will spend it. It might end up funding some obscure election for a politician you never even heard of."

"Huh, I never thought of that. What about the expenditures? Have you noticed any unusual expenses?" Emily asked.

"Nothing unusual so far. Miscellaneous expenses for polls, restaurants and, of course, travel. This guy travels extensively."

"I've noticed a lot of travel expenses as well, but that doesn't seem too surprising," said Emily. "How about his personal investments?"

"Nothing crazy. He seems well-off. In addition to his publicly traded stocks, he also has a lot of investments in private companies."

"That doesn't surprise me either," said Emily. "A lot of our clients have investments in companies not traded on public exchanges." She paused for a long moment. "He does appear to be a very active investor. In one of his personal investment statements, I saw a substantial investment in Uzbekistan. Have you seen any financial activity for known tax havens like the Caymans or Switzerland?"

"Uzbekistan?" asked Mark with a questioning look. "Wait, I saw some travel expenses for Tashkent. That's the capital city, right?"

"I think so," said Emily.

"Do you think they're related?"

"I imagine they would be," said Emily. "That's certainly not a typical vacation destination. I'll show you the document I found so you can flag other similar documents."

Emily walked to one of the boxes and quickly thumbed through the pages. She knew exactly where to find the document.

"Here it is," she said. "It was over four years ago." She handed the document to Mark.

"What's that marking on the paper?"

Emily closely examined the round marking near the top right corner. It was faded, but she could see an outline of a design, reminiscent of a coat of arms.

"It looks like a bird holding a branch in its beak," she stated.

"I agree. And it appears that a similar branch is wrapped around each side of the insignia."

"Are those olive branches?"

"That wouldn't be surprising. They're common in many coat of arms designs because of the implied peace element," added Mark.

"The branches almost meet at the top, but are separated by two letters."

"Can you make them out?"

She squinted as she pulled the sheet of paper toward her face. "I think there are two lowercase letters. One is a *k* and the other an *a*. It's really not very conclusive."

"Do you think it's someone's initials?"

"Possibly," she replied when she turned toward him. "Did the Uzbekistan document you saw have the same insignia?"

He quickly found the paper and confirmed the same insignia was also stamped on the upper right corner. It was less faded than the marking on the first document, but did not yield any additional clues to its origin.

"Interesting," she said.

"What does it mean?"

"I'm not sure it means anything, but I want to take a closer look at any investment from Uzbekistan."

"For what purpose?" asked Mark.

"We need to dig as deep as we can. It would be problematic if someone found an irregularity in his finances that we didn't. Surprises are never beneficial to our clients. They pay us well for certainty."

"Do you think we'll find any *irregularities*?"

"Unlikely. We just need to ensure his personal travel expenses don't get categorized as political expenses."

"I agree," stated Mark. "I've heard of politicians that have resigned because of vacations expensed to their constituents."

"Exactly. Flag anything you think might be even remotely irregular. That includes suspicious vacation expenses, any investments in known tax havens, as well as anything related to Uzbekistan. I'll do the same. After we finish our initial review, I want to take a closer examination of the flagged items."

"Got it," replied Mark.

As the afternoon turned into evening, they devoured Chinese take-out in the conference room and ignored the sandwiches that still sat on the table from lunch. They efficiently worked in tandem until almost midnight.

Chapter 8

Emily and Mark were back in the office early the next day to continue their investigation. The Congressman's donations increased exponentially over the most recent six months as his speeches and travels reached more prominent political stages.

Like the prior day, most of the expenses reviewed either related to travel or the day-to-day operations of the campaign. Emily was relieved that they hadn't uncovered anything incriminating.

When Emily next checked her watch, she found the work day had already ended. It was half past six in the evening. She couldn't believe the day passed so quickly. She began writing a quick email to Jen to tell her she wouldn't be able to make it. Before she could finish, Emily received a text encouraging her to not cancel. Jen pleaded for Emily to make time for her friends.

She laughed to herself. Jen knew Emily better than she knew herself. She would just have to carve out some time over the weekend to review the rest of the documents.

"What's that laugh for?" asked Mark. He sat at the opposite end of the conference table.

"Nothing," replied Emily.

"Then you must be coming down with cabin fever. We've been at this for too long. I think I need a break."

"I agree. I'm meeting some girlfriends for a drink tonight."

"Good for you. You're always here. I see your office light when I leave at night, and again when I arrive in the morning."

"I know. I need to get a life."

Emily looked around the room to inventory their progress. The reviewed boxes were neatly stacked in one corner. She estimated they had finished about three-quarters of the documents so far.

"I'll come in over the weekend so we can make more progress before your status meeting with Terrance," said Mark.

"I'll do the same," Emily said as she let out a sigh. "It's a lot, but it should be manageable. I'll also take a closer look at the flagged documents."

She gathered the documents they had stacked on the glossy table. There were about fifty or so that needed further investigation. Emily quickly flipped through them. Most were trips that appeared to be personal travel. There were also documents related to the Uzbekistan investment she had identified earlier, but they didn't appear to shed any additional light on the nature of the investment.

"Just keep me updated," said Emily. "If we have any issues, I want to alert Terrance as soon as possible." Emily sat up, threw the flagged documents and her computer in her work bag, then walked to the doorway. "Let me know if you find anything important."

Without taking his eyes off the computer screen, he responded, "Sure thing. I'll let you know if I find anything unusual. Regardless, I'll send you a quick status of my progress over the weekend."

"Thanks."

"I'm glad we finally got to work together," he continued. "You're not nearly as much of a hard-ass as everyone says." He immediately caught himself and turned to look at her. "You know what I meant."

"I'll take that as a compliment, I guess." She laughed. "And you're not nearly as stupid as a typical first-year associate," she said dryly before heading down the hall to the elevator bank.

Emily checked her watch again. She had enough time to head home, change, and grab a quick bite before meeting her girlfriends at eight. She exited the building and walked briskly toward the DC subway.

The weather had cooled and the air felt wet. Emily adjusted her coat and tied the belt around her waist in a double knot. She slid the strap on her work bag higher on her shoulder. She looked up to note some of the fall leaves had already turned gray.

As she made her way down the sidewalk, a strong cigar smell permeated the air. A black sedan had its window partially rolled down as smoke blew out the window. Emily noticed someone casually sitting in the sedan, reading a newspaper.

Honestly, who reads a newspaper nowadays? When she was two car lengths past the black sedan, she heard the engine start. She saw the headlights reflect off the vehicle in front of her.

Two blocks down the street, she noticed the same black car had moved. *That's strange*, she thought. The car was still behind her, but it was stationary whenever she looked.

Emily quickened her pace, while trying not to look like she was hurrying. The pedestrian traffic increased as she neared the Farragut North Metro station. Located in one of the busiest work districts, it was relatively crowded at this hour.

Emily looked back at the street once she reached the station. A man in a black fedora hastily exited the vehicle. He appeared to look directly at her before diverting his attention elsewhere. She made her way to the main escalator that led down to the train platform. She politely excused herself as she moved through the crowd at the top of the escalator. She looked over her shoulder and could still see a black fedora in the crowd. She asked herself, *Is that the same fedora? Couldn't be. I'm just being paranoid.* She looked back, but it had disappeared. The black fedora appeared again as the man strained to look through the crowd.

Emily began the descent toward the subway platform. She pushed her way through the crowd to further distance herself from the man in the fedora. Upon reaching the platform, she looked up to see three black fedora hats dispersed throughout the escalator. "Fuck," she said out loud. A few nearby commuters threw her a disapproving look.

"Sorry," she mouthed back. She wasn't sure if one of those three hats belonged to the person following her. She didn't want to wait to find out.

The LED displays around the platform indicated that the next train would be arriving in two minutes. She scanned the platform and made her way toward a group of military men cloaked in black jackets with gold buttons and dark blue pants.

She positioned herself behind the men, with the escalator on the other side. Emily stood directly behind the tallest man, but still found it necessary to bend her knees. *I thought military guys were supposed to be taller.*

"Avoiding an old boyfriend?" the handsome uniformed man said with a laugh when he glanced over his shoulder. He offered Emily a smile. His five buddies turned to look at her. One man nudged him in an apparent attempt to encourage him to engage her in conversation.

Not the type of attention I was aiming for, thought Emily as the man slowly turned toward her with an ear-to-ear smile.

"Sort of," Emily responded. "A guy in a black fedora has been following me since I left the office. I really don't know what to do," she added with a false hint of desperation.

"Is that so?" said the man. He peered toward the elevator. "I think we can help," he said with a smile.

He reached into his breast pocket to retrieve a shiny silver case. He casually opened it and presented a business card to her. "Nolan Callahan, at your service," he said, holding his smile. "You can repay me with dinner."

"Thank you," said Emily with a surprised tone as she gently accepted the business card.

"I didn't get your name. Miss..."

"Emily," she said as the row of floor lights began to slowly pulsate, indicating a train was approaching the platform. The large, electronic sign confirmed her train was approaching.

"A pleasure to meet you, Emily. I look forward to our dinner. Come on, men," he said with a musical focus on the word *men*.

"Thank you," she replied.

As the men made their way toward the escalator, a musical chorus began to fill the platform. They presented their booming voices to the subway patrons.

Every woman that stepped off the escalator was greeted by a semicircle of singing men in uniform. It effectively brought the pedestrian traffic to a crawl as people began to congregate.

Emily glanced at his business card. It read, "US Army Chorus." She smiled to herself as the train doors opened and she casually entered the train with everyone else. She glanced back to see a sea of people applauding. The uniformed men bowed upon the completion of their song.

The arriving train was nearly filled to capacity. Emily slowly shuffled toward the middle of the car and held on to a handle attached to the seats for stability.

She exhaled as she looked at the platform through the train window. She strained to see a black fedora hat, but couldn't find any. Emily pondered why someone would follow her. *Am I just being paranoid?* she thought again. *Why would someone be following me?*

A pair of black shoes entered her peripheral vision to the right and a casual bump ensued. *I hate mass transit*, she thought. She looked up to see a man with jet-black hair and silver streaks.

The blood drained from her face. Her pale complexion searched for answers as she experienced thoughts of familiarity. *Where have I seen him?* she wondered as she backed away. She squeezed her small frame through the packed train and moved toward the farthest of the two exits.

The man never made eye contact with Emily, but she kept her gaze fixed on him from a distance. When the train arrived at the next platform, an automated voice announced they were nearing the Dupont Circle station. The train came to a complete stop under the cement coffered ceiling of the train station.

When the doors opened, the man exited the train. He never looked back. Emily watched as he strolled toward the escalators. The train began to move in the same direction the man was walking.

When her window was nearly parallel with him, he made a casual glance toward her. He pulled a black fedora from his trench coat and placed it gently on his head with finesse. Then he gave her a discreet nod from the moving escalator.

In total disbelief, Emily's right leg buckled. She was forced to catch herself against an unsuspecting woman, who quickly gave her a push back with her broad backside.

Emily clutched her work bag awkwardly in stunned silence. The train made two more stops before her intended destination of Cleveland Park.

Emily was always proud to say she lived in DC among its vibrant neighborhoods and diverse cultures. Cleveland Park was not as well-known as some of the other neighborhoods, but offered quick access to the main business district.

None of these thoughts were on Emily's mind as she rode up the escalator. In a daze, she crossed the subway station and stopped at the entrance.

Rain poured from the night sky, and a howling wind swirled around her. It felt like a storm had just passed or one was just about to begin. Emily did not know which was the case.

She frowned as she slowly walked up the five-degree incline of Connecticut Avenue. Her apartment was a ten-minute walk from the subway. The constant rain managed to penetrate her coat and further dampened her spirit.

Emily entered the marbled foyer of her aging colonial brick building and walked past the evening doorman. His eyes were firmly fixed to the basketball game playing on his cell phone. She rode the elevator to the top floor of the four-story building.

She moved her exhausted body into her immaculate two-room apartment and dropped her work bag on the floor. After only a few steps, she stopped and leaned against the wall for support. Her body slowly slid down the wall until it gently reached the floor. With her head resting on her raised knees, she began to cry.

Emily tried hard to carve out a life of meaning. She studied. She followed the rules. She worked for everything she had. Without a father, it wasn't always easy. She missed the guidance a father would have provided. When she faced major life decisions, she often thought about his perspective and what he might say.

She didn't know if she missed her father or merely the idea of a father. She needed one more than ever as she sat on the floor. The water from her rain-soaked clothes and hair began to pool beneath her.

She tried to hold back her tears, but couldn't. The harder she tried to stop, the more she cried. The tears flowed out of her tightly closed eyes and over the contours of her cheeks, and eventually dripped to the pool below.

Paranoid thoughts filled her head, but she couldn't find a logical reason why someone would follow her. "It doesn't make sense," she said to herself.

After regaining her composure, she pulled herself off the floor and wiped the tears from her face. She walked to the bathroom to wash up, but her gaze never left the floor in front of her.

In the bathroom, Emily was reluctant to look in the mirror. She felt horrible. Eventually, she lifted her head. Her reflection mirrored her state of mind.

Not able to think clearly, she sought the comfort of her couch. The combination of a stressful job, routine lack of sleep, and the encounter at the train station proved to be overwhelming. She closed her eyes and immediately fell asleep.

Light from the easterly exposed windows crept along the floor and up the side of the couch. It seemed to stop when it reached her face. Emily awoke with a disorienting gasp. She sat up and swung her legs off the couch and onto the hardwood floor. After resting her head on her hands, she gently massaged her frontal lobes. Last night's event just didn't make sense. She refused to accept that someone might be following her.

After what felt like an eternity, she got up and walked across the floor to the open kitchen that connected to her main living space. She heated some leftover coffee in the microwave and pondered what to do next.

Shit, she thought. I was supposed to meet my girlfriends last night. I need to give Jen a call.

She retrieved her brown leather work bag that she had dropped on the floor last night. She opened it and pulled out her cell phone. She had numerous missed texts and calls from the friends she had neglected to meet.

Emily saw a white piece of paper sticking out of one of the outside pockets of her bag. She lifted the neatly folded paper out of the pocket. Due to the rain from the previous night, the paper felt cloth-like in her hands. She began to carefully unfold the paper and read it aloud. "Dupont Circle, bench located at 11:45, Sunday at noon."

Dupont Circle was not only a prominent neighborhood, but also a popular park. Its shape was similar to a European roundabout.

The city was littered with roundabouts. They were constructed when the US Government first formed to confuse an invading army. Given the circular shape of the park, the *eleven forty-five* must indicate that she was to meet at a bench on the western side of the park at noon.

Emily retrieved her coffee from the microwave, but her trembling hands almost spilled it. She placed the cup on the counter before rubbing her clammy hands together. *I need to talk to somebody about this*, she thought.

Chapter 9

The Bombay Club was one of DC's hidden gems. Its dining room emulated *Old India* through its elegant use of pastel colors, ceiling fans, and thoughtful placement of greenery. The addition of live piano music and a sophisticated menu made it one of the city's most distinguished restaurants.

Emily sat alone at a corner table. She was still nervous from the strange encounter the evening before. She felt an unfamiliar emotion that had induced an almost paranoid state of mind.

When Emily decided to leave her apartment, she double- and triple-checked her surroundings. She walked more cautiously. She even looked at the traffic behind the taxi to ensure she wasn't being followed.

Scott was late. Emily's eyes wandered toward her water glass. The ice melted slowly. Beads of condensation formed on the outside of the elegant vessel, then trickled down the stem, only to be absorbed by the perfectly smoothed white tablecloth. The water formed a damp circle around the base of the glass.

Emily tried to put on a forced smile before Scott arrived at the restaurant. She debated whether or not to tell him about yesterday's encounter. She needed to talk to somebody, but her inner circle of friends had gotten smaller as she'd gotten older and spent more time on her career.

Will Scott understand, or totally freak out? She didn't know the answer. She checked her watch. He was officially late.

Before she frowned, a soft kiss tickled her neck, just above the shoulder. She immediately got goose bumps. Emily turned her head to look at him with a forced smile. She could not hide the sadness in her eyes.

"You're even more beautiful when you're upset," he said. Immediately, tears began to form in her eyes. "What's the matter?" he asked with obvious concern.

"You wouldn't believe me," she said as he took her hand. He sat in the chair across from her. She didn't know how to begin to describe her emotions or the turmoil she'd experienced. She looked momentarily into his eyes, but found herself staring elsewhere.

He was immaculately groomed and dressed. It was out of character for him. The effort to reconcile his absence on Tuesday caught Emily by surprise. She examined him more closely. His hair was slicked back. He wore a dark green knitted polo shirt with cream-colored linen pants. *Horribly out of season*, she thought.

"I'm sorry I'm late," he said.

"No, it's not that," she quietly stated. "Something happened yesterday on the way home from the office."

"Tell me."

"Someone followed me from the office to the Metro station," she said.

"That's crazy. Are you sure?"

"Of course I'm sure. Wouldn't you be if someone chased you down an escalator?"

"Wait, someone chased you down an escalator?" Scott asked as he leaned forward in his chair.

"Yes, it was horrible," Emily began slowly. She spoke increasingly faster as she continued. "I noticed someone following me after I left the office. I persuaded some military guys to intervene at the train station."

"Okay."

"They slowed him down so that I could get on the train. Then, on the train, I think he bumped into me. The same guy nodded to me after he got off at a station and the train passed by him."

"Slow down," Scott said as he raised his hands slightly. "I'm still trying to process all of this. Are you sure he wasn't just some creep trying to get your phone number?"

"Yes, of course I am! I think he was the same guy I saw when I was out to lunch with Terrance earlier in the week," she added. "I recognized the black hair with gray streaks. It had to be the same guy. It was too much of a coincidence."

"And this happened yesterday!" Scott interjected. "Why didn't you call me? What if you had been hurt?"

"I don't know, Scott, I really don't. Everything happened so quickly. I'm still not entirely sure what happened myself." Emily glanced nervously around the room, not certain what she expected to find. She knew she was just being paranoid, so she stopped.

"I'm glad you're okay," Scott said. He reached over and gave her hand a reassuring squeeze. "You're going to have to start from the beginning. I want to know every detail."

After Scott ordered a round of cocktails, she began to give a complete breakdown of the events, but didn't mention the note in her work bag or the meeting in the park. She wasn't sure why she held those facts back, but saying something about them just didn't feel right.

They ordered a second round before their food arrived. By the time she finished recounting, only the crumbs on a dessert plate remained.

"I'm glad you still have your appetite," he jested.

"Screw you," Emily said with an annoyed smile. "I'm still a bit freaked-out. What am I going to do?"

"You need to talk to the police."

"And tell them what, exactly?"

"There should be security footage in the subway station that could pinpoint the guy. They probably even have some sort of recognition software that could identify him."

"I think I may talk to Terrance first and tell him what happened. It could be related to a new engagement I've started for Owen."

"Wait. What engagement? The Owen I work with?" Scott asked in a confused tone.

Emily knew she couldn't withdraw her comment. He wouldn't believe it.

"Yes."

"What could Owen possibly have to do with this? Wait. You're working on an engagement for Owen? Why didn't you mention this earlier?"

"I don't know. I haven't had a chance to tell you about it. I just learned about it two days ago. It was supposed to be a quick engagement just to validate his finances for some big donors."

"I see. Did you get this assignment from Terrance?"

"Yes."

"Does he know that I work with Owen?"

"He didn't know that you worked for Owen when he gave me the assignment."

"How could the incident at the subway relate to your work with Owen?"

"It has to be related. Otherwise, it's just a big coincidence. I just started working on this engagement and then someone follows me around town, right?" said Emily. She paused, then added sternly, "I don't believe in coincidences."

"I'm not saying that, Emily. I really don't know what to think at this point." Scott scratched his head and let out a loud sigh.

"I don't understand why you're having such a difficult time believing me." Emily was staring directly in his eyes.

"I think you're just being a bit emotional, that's all. Let's just try to get the facts straight first."

"I damn well know the facts, Scott. It seems as plain as day, so why are you being resistant?"

"Well, we've been in this situation before. We just need to calm down."

"I can't believe you're throwing *that* in my face."

"Emily, I didn't mean it like that. I just meant that you're being overly emotional right now."

"You know this is nothing like *last time*. That had everything to do with us and what could have been." Emily's hand subconsciously moved to her stomach.

She caught herself and moved her hand back to the table. She couldn't hide the empty look in her face when their eyes met again. "I really just want to be alone right now."

"I don't think that's a good idea," said Scott. He leaned forward in his chair. "Given all that's happened, and *if* someone is following you, the last thing you would want right now is to be alone."

"I'm a big girl. Always have been." Emily remembered the day she left home to attend college at the age of seventeen. She had been in complete control of her life ever since.

With a renewed sense of confidence, she got up from the table. The waiter graciously presented the check to Scott when Emily put on her coat.

"Emily, don't go."

"It's too late, Scott."

"Listen, I'm going to be campaigning the next few days and won't be available. But we really need to talk."

Emily began to walk away from the table.

"Wait," said Scott. He tried to grab her arm, but it was too late. The waiter appeared, blocking his attempt. He was holding the black bill folder, wearing a cautious smile on his face.

"Sorry, I was just... never mind." Scott reached into his pocket. He gave the waiter his card.

Scott looked toward the door. Emily was gone.

Chapter 10

Emily woke up early, with a renewed sense of purpose. The previous night's dinner with Scott had frustrated her, but it also put everything back in perspective. She didn't need anyone's help. She was in complete control.

In an attempt to remain anonymous, Emily wore an olive-green trench coat, a hat, and black sunglasses. She glanced in the mirror before leaving. Her reflection looked like a cliché, but the discretion was necessary for her task. She aimed to arrive at the park early to learn more about the man in the hat and to identify anyone working with him. She had to know why someone would follow her.

She climbed up onto the bike she had purchased three years ago, but rarely used. She cranked the pedals and the wheels began to rotate. After a wobbly start and a dangerous swerve toward oncoming traffic, she found her rhythm and began to zip down the street.

She was nervous about the mysterious meeting. She needed some time to think about her situation. She knew of a small coffee shop located just a few blocks from the meeting point.

After locking the bike, she entered the shop. The simple décor consisted mostly of aged wood and antiqued trinkets. Hints of pumpkin and nutmeg added to the heavy coffee aroma.

Two baristas worked to satisfy a long line of customers who were either getting a lazy start on their Sunday or enjoying a second cup.

Emily ordered a double-shot espresso latte. She needed a jolt of energy to get her mind properly engaged. After receiving her order, she sat at a table next to the window. She ceremoniously blew on her coffee before taking the first sip.

She considered her decision not to go to the police, and decided it was the right thing to do. There just wasn't much to go on anyway. But her decision not to tell Scott about the meeting at the park bothered her. *Am I making a mistake?* she asked herself. She had three missed calls and two unchecked voicemails from him. She knew he would have strongly advised against this meeting, but she needed answers.

Emily gazed out the window. The overcast sky was not helping her mood.

She was confident that there was a connection between her new engagement and these events. She didn't think the man was an immediate threat to her life. *If he wanted me dead, it certainly wouldn't be done at a busy public park*, she reasoned. *But why did he want to meet? An information exchange? Maybe he worked for a political rival?*

Emily reached into her coat pocket and pulled out her phone. She launched an app she had used to record lectures in graduate school.

She intended to record the conversation for evidentiary purposes. Emily wasn't sure of her intended audience. It could be Scott, Terrance, or the police. She nervously rubbed her hands together, then wiped them on her pants to dry her sweaty palms.

She checked her watch. The meeting was scheduled to start in twenty minutes. It was time to start her reconnaissance. She casually walked out of the coffee shop and into the chilly air. She adjusted her collar by lifting it up and pulling it forward.

She walked down the street as casually as she could, but her movements made her self-conscious. *I'm too nervous,* she thought. She needed a reason to *hang out* on the street inconspicuously. Emily approached the nearest street vendor.

The homely shack used a broom stick to hold up a wooden flap. A Middle-Eastern man in a traditional headdress stood inside. Two coolers in front of the shack contained ice and beverages. Snacks hung from poles on either side of the portal. Magazines and cigarettes lined the inside back wall.

"A pack of American Spirits," Emily said as she perused the wall.

"Which kind?" asked the man.

"The yellow pack will do," she said, pointing. "Do you have any matches?"

"No matches, just lighters. Many colors," he stated with a casual wave of his open hand toward the lighters. "Pick. One fifty each." After paying the man, she discarded the cellophane wrapper in a gray metallic trash can on the corner.

Emily walked down the street toward the park. She approached Dupont Circle, but was careful to view it from a distance to ensure she wasn't putting herself in harm's way. The traffic around the park was predictably heavy for this time of day.

Despite the gray weather, the park was beautiful, with many varieties of trees. There were also a lot of people for a chilly Sunday morning. *That's a good thing*, she thought, letting out a chilly breath.

The park had an outer circle and an inner circle. Most people sat on the benches that lined the circles. A small contingency sat on blankets placed over the grass.

In the center of the inner circle was a large, elegant marble structure. It housed an oversize cauldron being held up by three Neoclassical nude figures depicting earth, wind, and fire. The water from the cauldron was channeled through three lips and gently fell fifteen feet into the pool below.

Emily was envious of the people enjoying a leisurely Sunday. She thought back to three weeks ago, when she enjoyed a casual afternoon at this very park. Her world had changed dramatically since that time.

During her stroll, she didn't recognize anyone remotely matching the description of the man from the subway. She wasn't sure if she'd recognize him anyway. Besides a fedora and black and silver hair, her memories were vague.

Ten minutes before the scheduled meeting, she turned on her recording app. She wanted to avoid raising any suspicion during the meeting.

Emily sat on a bench on the western side of the park. It was directly opposite the proposed meeting point. She planned to get a view of the man when he sat down. She retrieved the cigarette pack from her coat pocket and placed a cigarette in her mouth. The flint spark ignited the butane gas on the third strike. She lifted the flame toward the end of the cigarette and drew the smoke into her lungs.

She instantly had thoughts of her college days and the smoky bars she frequented. Then the smoking law changed, and with it, so did her habits. Immediately, she coughed and became overly self-conscious. No one else around her was smoking. A few people appeared to be annoyed when the foul smell reached their noses. *I guess no one really smokes anymore*, she thought.

Careful not to draw any additional attention to herself, Emily brought her hand down and rested it on the bench. The cigarette continued to burn between her index and middle fingers. After a couple of minutes, she dropped the cigarette and placed her foot on the ember. She extinguished it with two quick twists of her ankle.

Emily checked her watch again. The mysterious man was scheduled to arrive in just a few minutes. *What am I doing here?* she thought to herself. *This is crazy. I'm not a spy. Just leave and call the police.*

"Do you have a light?" The voice came from a man standing directly behind her right shoulder. Emily looked over her shoulder to see a man in a dark rain coat and black fedora. He held a folded newspaper under his arm.

She felt as if her attempt to gain the upper hand had been thwarted. *He must have been watching me the entire time.* She immediately retreated two feet down the bench to distance herself from the man. Her eyes then made a quick glance around to evaluate her escape options.

As if he knew her thoughts, the man began to speak casually. "I'm not here to hurt you. In fact, I'm glad that you came today. I wasn't entirely sure you were going to show up."

"What do you want from me?" Emily asked with a controlled emotion that couldn't quite hide her trepidation. She watched him with a keen eye as he reached into the top left inside pocket of his coat.

He pulled out a silver case and opened it to reveal ten cigarettes banded with an elastic strap on both the top and bottom of the case. He carefully selected one of the hand-rolled cigarettes and placed it in his mouth. He closed the case with a single motion of his hand and slipped it back in his pocket.

"Do you have a light?" he repeated.

"I don't smoke," Emily said in a cold voice. Her intent to keep a distance was apparent.

"That's okay. I have my own." He reached into his outside pocket and pulled out a nondescript white book of matches. He lit the cigarette. With a swift movement of his hand, the flame went out. He tossed the match to the ground, where it continued to smolder.

"Mind if I sit down?" he asked with a slight hand motion to the bench.

"Keep your distance, if you wouldn't mind."

"Of course," he said. His gracefulness surprised Emily as he easily hopped the bench and sat in one action. He glanced down to acknowledge that the space he had given Emily was sufficient.

He stood a good five inches taller than her, but his build and closed trench coat made him appear stocky, not tall. She had trouble determining his age. The gray streaks in his hair and the crow's feet around his eyes seemed to tell an incomplete story.

"Like I said, I'm glad you came. I just want a few minutes of your time."

"You could've just made an appointment at my office. I'm assuming you know a lot more about me than I do about you."

"That would be correct," he confirmed. "I'm afraid an appointment would have been too obvious."

"Too obvious?" Emily asked incredulously. "So instead, you follow me from the office, chase me to the train, and then plant a note in my purse to meet at this park? How is this any less obvious?"

"That was my mistake. I didn't intend to be so dramatic. I apologize," he stated in a sincere tone. "I honestly didn't expect to be spotted so quickly. Usually, I'm much more discreet."

"Usually? What line of work are you in, or aren't you at liberty to tell me? Wait before you answer that," Emily stated.

"Please, Emily." He elevated his hand slightly to quell her temper. It didn't work.

"Let's make this conversation as short as possible," she continued. "I'm really not comfortable speaking with you. If I don't get some answers, I'm going to scream bloody murder while running to that cop over there!"

Emily's voice was a loud whisper, as she pointed to a uniformed officer who had just walked into the park. She was trying not to create a scene but wanted the man to understand that they were not alone.

"Okay," he stated without looking to where she was pointing. With a quick "ahem" to clear his throat, he began. "My name is Oscar, and I'm in need of information."

"Okay," Emily said, surprised. "Whatever information you think I may have, I assure you won't be very useful. I'm just a consultant. I evaluate numbers and trends. That's it."

"We know a lot about you and your colleagues." There was an uneasy pause after the *you* that disturbed Emily.

"What do you know about me? Are you being ambiguous on purpose?" she asked with an annoyed tone.

"No," he quickly replied. "I don't know nearly as much as I would like at this point. Our *meeting* the other day was unintentional. The only reason I have come forward now, is out of necessity. Since you found out that you were being watched, I thought that you might start acting strange, which would likely bring undue attention to you and perhaps endanger your life."

"What do you mean, *endanger* my life? Are you threatening me?" Emily felt a shiver up her spine.

"I'm trying not to," he replied.

"I'm leaving. This is crazy." Emily prepared to get up, but was quickly interrupted.

"Your life is in danger." It was his matter-of-fact tone that caught Emily by surprise. "It's up to you if you really want to listen."

"I'm listening," she said as she slowly eased against the back of the bench.

"Think about what has changed in the last week," he said.

"I started a new engagement."

"Bingo," he said with a casual finger pointing for emphasis.

"But how does that put my life in danger? It doesn't make sense."

"I need to know what you'll be telling Terrance tomorrow."

"Why... we haven't even finished our preliminary assessment," Emily stated cautiously.

"I need you to finish your work and soundly conclude there aren't any issues, even if you find one." The steely look in his dark blue eyes remained fixed on Emily. He was deadly serious.

"And what if I don't?" she said. Emily was always good at reading people. A skill that served her well in her profession. But she couldn't read the man sitting next to her. There was something contrasting about him, and it made her very uneasy. Still, she tested the man with her defiant words.

"Don't risk the lives of your loved ones because of this assignment. I want you to come to me if you find anything. Capiche?"

His words resonated in her head. She didn't need any further convincing. The purpose of his request was inconsequential. The lives of her loved ones were indispensable. Besides, she and Mark hadn't found anything unusual in their search.

Oscar reached into his inside coat pocket. He pulled out an index card sized notepad. He flipped several pages over the spiral binding until he found a blank one. Emily watched in silence as he scribbled on it. Oscar ripped the page from the notepad and handed it to her.

"If you find anything, call me. Don't even try to trace the number," he added. "It would be a complete waste of time."

"I understand," she replied stoically as she looked at the piece of paper. Not wanting to spend any more time with this discussion, Emily got up to leave.

"Before you go, Miss Hendricks..." Emily turned to face him, only to be greeted with his out-stretched hand. "Your phone, if you don't mind. We wouldn't want any part of our conversation to go anywhere but between us. Wouldn't you agree? That *includes* Terrance and Scott."

She reluctantly handed him the phone. The slight tremor in her hand betrayed her courage.

"Your phone will be in your office building's lost and found." He proceeded to casually lift the phone up past his head.

A seemingly random bystander walked into her field of vision. Without breaking his pace, the man in jeans and a dark grey hoodie accepted the hand-off and kept moving through the park.

Before Emily could turn and walk away, Oscar got up and adjusted his coat. He courteously tipped his hat before walking in the opposite direction as the man in the hoodie.

A look of bewilderment reached her face. Not knowing what to do next, she just began walking in the general direction of her bike.

Chapter 11

MONDAY. 8:15 AM.

The Irishman waited patiently in a vehicle near the offices of Sufferton & Waine. To bide time, he read the *Washington Post* as his coffee cooled in the armrest's cup holder. The engine was off, but the keys remained in the ignition of the stolen SUV.

He had paid an early morning visit to a local hotel chain. Once the valet had left to park a car, he approached a businessman taking luggage out of the back of his vehicle. Based on earlier observations, he knew the valet wouldn't be back for nearly eight minutes.

He used the time to strike up a lighthearted conversation with the man to suppress any suspicion he would have about placing the keys of his expensive car in the hands of a stranger. Experience dictated there wouldn't be a problem, especially given the red vest he wore with the word "valet" plainly stated on back.

The man gladly offered him the keys to his German SUV, along with a five-dollar tip. The owner wouldn't miss the vehicle this morning. The Irishman knew the purpose of his trip and even directed him toward the hotel conference rooms located in an adjacent building.

He loved German cars. They reminded him of everything he didn't have growing up in rural Ireland. His selection of an SUV wasn't random. An SUV offered many advantages over a sedan, including better street visibility, all-wheel-drive traction, and what he needed most: height.

To mask his identity from prying cameras, he had installed tinted window shields over the front windshield and side windows after driving away from the hotel.

He had never met his target, but memorized the picture sent to him. Along with a picture, an address had been provided. For this task, the Irishman sent a couriered package to the target's apartment building. It was addressed from one of the target's team members with instructions to bring the package to work.

Unbeknownst to the target, the package included a small tracking beacon hidden under the button of the interoffice style envelope. The Irishman had smiled at his craftsmanship when he wrapped the string around the button to secure the package.

He heard a beep from the tracking device. After placing the newspaper on the seat next to him, he turned the key in the ignition.

The screen displayed a grid of the immediate area and a blinking red dot represented the target. It indicated the target had just left the nearest Metro stop and was positioned just two blocks away. He slid the transmission into drive, but kept his foot firmly on the brake. He waited.

He perfectly timed his departure from the street parking to approach the intersection as the light turned red. Pedestrians began to flood the crosswalk. As planned, his target was among them. Instead of stopping the vehicle, the Irishman accelerated. The vehicle launched into the intersection before the opposing traffic had an opportunity to move.

The target had made it a quarter-way through the one-way intersection when he looked around to spot the speeding vehicle. A blaring car horn had warned the pedestrians of the impending danger. It was too late to move out the way.

The Irishman veered the SUV to hit the target dead center. The height of the vehicle delivered its intended result. The body was hit with great force and landed in front of the vehicle, where it was then run over and crushed by the nearly five-thousand-pound vehicle. The chance of survival was minimal, at best.

In the deadly attack, two bystanders in his wake were also hit. The vehicle's grill violently propelled one man to the ground, while another launched into a crowd of people near the sidewalk.

The street surveillance cameras in the vicinity would not catch any footage of the accident. They had been expertly disabled very early that morning.

The damage to the vehicle was minimal, as expected. The Irishman sped through the downtown streets for the next few blocks before dramatically reducing his speed to blend into the general traffic flow.

He casually sipped his coffee, which was now at an ideal temperature to enjoy, then drove to a chop shop he had used before in a run-down neighborhood southeast of the Capitol. Before leaving the vehicle, he eliminated any evidence that could connect him to the crime scene.

Chapter 12

Yesterday had been a complete disaster for Emily. After her encounter with Oscar, she spent the remainder of the day in her apartment with the blinds drawn. She had tried to work, but her inability to focus made it impossible.

She picked up her phone in the lobby's lost and found when she arrived at the office. Oscar's team had expertly wiped the phone. All of her data and applications were gone.

She gave the phone to her IT contact at the firm. After telling him she had accidentally erased it, the technician indicated he would get it back to her around noon. He explained all of her emails and voicemails were located on the firm's server and would be restored. Emily felt oddly naked without the device.

Sitting in her office, Emily found herself leaning back in her chair, staring at the ceiling. She had an unfamiliar feeling of not being in control of a situation. It felt paralyzing.

She got a glimpse of her reflection in the window. The hastily brushed hair she saw in combination with her unusually wrinkled pants, painted a rather bleak picture.

She surmised that, unfortunately, it reflected her current state of mind.

She hoped to avoid Mark and Terrance this morning. She hadn't reviewed the work Mark emailed over the weekend or read any of his subsequent emails. They waited in her inbox.

With her office door closed, she worked to catch up on her assignments. Before too long, she heard a knock. She sighed before she answered.

"Come in."

"Well, there you are," Terrance said with a sarcastic tone. He looked at her. "Hey, you look like shit."

"Thanks," she replied in a more serious voice than she intended.

He stepped into her office. "Are you okay? It's only Monday after all." He smiled.

She wasn't in the mood for jokes and had trouble hiding that fact. She knew he was only trying to lift her spirits.

"Sorry, Terrance. It's been a long weekend. I'm just stressed. I really haven't had time to finish my review. Would you mind if we delay our meeting until this afternoon?"

"Sure, Emily," he said. "Is there anything you need from me?"

"No, I'll be fine."

"Remember, it's just work. Life is more important, and way too short. Let me know if you need a pick-me-up this week. I'm always up for a drink."

"Will do, Terrance. Thanks."

"No problem. The Ferris Report looks good. I just had some minor edits. After you're done, just send the draft to the client." He placed the marked-up draft on the corner of her desk and exited her office.

After sending the report to the client, Emily felt more like herself. The morning pep talk had managed to lift her spirits enough for her to get engrossed in work again. She switched her attention to the Templeton engagement. She reviewed Mark's summary schedules and made some minor edits, but was overall pleased with his effort.

Emily next began to review Mark's emails. He had some questions regarding some documents he flagged. Overall, he didn't identify any major concerns.

I'll be ready to talk to Terrance after lunch and put this whole situation behind me, she thought. Relieved, Emily was able to catch up on some administrative tasks before lunch.

Mary unexpectedly knocked on her door at exactly eleven forty-five. "Compliments of Terrance," she said softly before placing a bag gently on her desk and exiting her office.

"Thanks, Mary," Emily said with a polite smile before her door closed.

The bag was from her favorite lunch spot near the office. She eagerly pulled the sushi tray out of the bag and onto her desk. *Terrance outdid himself*, she thought as she examined the impressive array of fish.

For the first time all morning, she smiled as she mixed the wasabi into the soy sauce using chop sticks.

Emily began a more thorough review of the issues Mark had identified, then paused to send him a meeting invite for later in the afternoon. She wanted to meet with him before Terrance's review.

There was a commotion in the hallway. Emily opened her door. Two female associates sobbed as they walked down the ornate hallway. They headed toward the break room, where Emily saw a congregation of coworkers through the fifteen seamless glass panels that separated the break room from the rest of the floor. Curious, Emily followed them.

The break room was typically a lively place where people ate lunch or dinner and enjoyed casual conversation. The inspirational artwork and colorful plants seemed notably out of place with the dour expressions people now wore.

The four partners and most of the firm's consultants were present. People were either silent or speaking quietly in small groups.

Claudia Briggs stood waiting in the center of the room with a similarly somber expression. Emily had not seen her since the reception.

After scanning the room, Claudia began to speak. Her tone was much less boisterous than usual.

"We're very sorry to have summoned you all here today. As many of you have heard, there's been a terrible tragedy in our *family*." There was an extra emphasis on family when she spoke. "This morning, Mark Ryan died in an accident on his way to the office."

Gasps and moans filled the room. Even people who seemed to already know about it became emotional from the finality of her statement.

Emily felt faint. She took two small steps backward until she felt the stability of the wall against her back. She glanced across the room. Her eyes stopped when she found Terrance. He sat on a bar stool in front of the large granite island near the kitchen. His elbows were propped on the counter with his head facedown in his hands.

Claudia continued, "There are no words to describe the loss that we all feel. I know this is a trying time for everyone. As such, we are closing our offices for the remainder of the day. We have gotten in touch with his family and will let everyone know about the funeral arrangements, if you wish to attend."

After her words ended, she immediately began to console people throughout the room and offered a motherly shoulder for people to express their sorrows. There wasn't a dry eye present.

Ann, a first-year associate, sobbed. "I saw it happen across the street from me." Her words drew a few people toward her. "I didn't know it was Mark. I didn't," she reiterated with a shaken voice. "The SUV just ran the red light. It never even slowed down," she continued. "It was horrible. Two others were injured. What's wrong with people?"

I can't believe it, thought Emily, *we were just working on that engagement together*. Before she could gather her thoughts, Claudia appeared in front of her. She gently placed both hands on Emily's shoulders and looked into her eyes.

"And how are you holding up?" she asked in a comforting tone.

"I don't know," were the only words Emily found in her head. "Shocked, I guess. I really don't know what to think."

"None of us do, my dear. All we can do is pray for him and his family. We can honor his memory and hopefully move forward with our lives." Claudia gazed intently into Emily's eyes as she spoke her words. "If there's anything you need from me, please don't hesitate to ask." She reached up from her short frame and hugged Emily close before continuing to console others in need.

As Emily made her way down the hall back to her office, she heard her name. She turned to see Terrance behind her.

"Do you have a few minutes to regroup?" he asked. "I know this isn't the best time."

"Oh, I guess," replied Emily. "Let me just grab my notepad and I'll be in your office in five minutes."

"I'll get some coffee," stated Terrance before he wobbled toward the kitchen.

Chapter 13

MONDAY. 12:45 PM.

Emily stepped into Terrance's office. The grandeur of it never ceased to amaze her. From the hand-carved custom mahogany table, to the gold-plated pen once owned by President Nixon, to the first edition books that lay unused on his shelf. Every item in his office was extravagant.

Terrance was accustomed to luxury, which was apparent from the opulence that surrounded him. Emily found it strange. He didn't dress particularly well and was often disheveled or mismatched.

She especially liked the artwork on the wall. One piece in particular stood out. Emily stepped closer to admire it. It was a dark and disturbing abstract painting that depicted someone's interpretation of hell. Emily wasn't sure if it was meant to be some sort of commentary on how Terrance felt about the consulting industry or the clients they engaged.

Dante's Hell, stated Terrance as he casually walked in with two coffees. He placed Emily's coffee on the desk.

"Thanks."

"I've always liked that piece." He walked up to the painting and intently admired it. He continued his thought, "Morbid, if you really think about it. I'm sure *hell* is quite subjective, anyway," he said with a shrug of his shoulders.

Without altering his gaze, he began to speak again. "This is actually just a reproduction. An expensive one, but it's not the original. I keep that one in Charlottesville. The firm refused to pay the insurance to keep it here," he added with a laugh.

Terrance stared at the artwork for another moment before he walked around the desk. He pulled up his sagging pants with a couple twists around his round waist. He then eased back into his plush, antique leather chair that was unlike anyone else's in the firm.

"I'm really sorry to have invited you here, given everything that has happened today," Terrance said. He still appeared shaken by the morning's events. "At the end of the day, though, people depend on our work. Mark will certainly be missed at this firm."

He paused for a moment, then asked, "Are you okay to finish everything up this week?"

"Of course, Terrance. I just... I can't believe he's gone. I don't really know how to process this. I feel numb."

"I understand," Terrance replied solemnly.

Emily continued, "Mark finished most of the work over the weekend. He only identified a few minor loose ends that need my attention. He documented everything in his emails that I'll certainly pay closer attention to after our meeting."

"Good."

"I should have everything wrapped up by Wednesday. There weren't really any surprises, I'm glad to report."

"That's great to hear," he said. "That'll be one less item on our plate, and we'll be able to focus on our other engagements."

"I'll be glad to have this behind us as well," she stated a bit more seriously then she intended. She just wanted to get her life back. She wasn't accustomed to having her work and personal lives in disarray.

After the meeting, Emily returned to her office to see that her phone had been placed on her desk. *I'm sure I have some missed calls and voicemails from Scott.* She turned on the phone and continued to work.

Once her phone booted, it buzzed repeatedly, indicating multiple voicemails needed her attention. She finished her coffee and threw the empty cup into the trash.

Four voicemails—wow, Scott really did miss me, she thought. The first two voicemails were from Scott. In the first voicemail, he expressed that he really cared for her and couldn't wait to see her on their weekly Tuesday night tryst at Clyde's.

The second voicemail, he apologized for his actions and lack of compassion on Saturday night. He also said he was concerned with her well-being. She felt some remorse for leaving him the way she did that night, but knew she needed time to herself.

Emily decided she would make it up to him another time. A night at his favorite pub and tickets to a hockey game would be an acceptable apology, she reasoned.

The third and fourth voicemails were from an unfamiliar number. *Probably a telemarketer,* she thought as she hit play. The voicemail started.

"Emily, it's Mark." Her heart felt like it was going to stop. Tears filled her eyes, but she managed to keep them from streaming down her face. "I wanted to follow up with you regarding our engagement. I've noticed a few irregularities in some of the documents. I'll summarize them in an email later tonight. It's probably nothing, but I wanted to give you a head's-up anyway. Sorry to disturb your weekend."

The voicemail was time stamped at eleven after four on Sunday afternoon. She reluctantly pressed play on the next voicemail.

"Emily, it's Mark again." The connection was less clear. It was apparent he placed the call outside, given the city background noise. "I don't know what to do. Something's not right. I found some unusual documents pertaining to an account in Switzerland. After I left the office, I realized that I forgot my iPad. By the time I got back to the office, there were two guys at my cube. They didn't look very friendly. I tried to leave quietly, but they saw me. I've never seen them before, so I just took off."

"I'm kinda confused. They seemed to be looking at some of the documents I flagged. It was all very weird. I'm walking to the Metro now, but wanted to touch base with you. Should we call the police? That's what we should do, right?"

"I left a copy of the flagged documents on your desk before I left the office. They're in a manila folder. Never give the originals to a superior," he said as he laughed in an oddly upbeat tone. "I had the originals at my desk, but I'm assuming they're gone, now."

Partners were notorious for marking up originals or losing them altogether. Their propensity to lose documents was sometimes problematic for litigation engagements. It was often necessary to reproduce the originals as documentation for the work completed. *Apparently, Mark had paid attention to my advice on his first day*, she thought.

His message continued, "I'll touch base with you first thing in the morning before I do anything. It's probably some crazy mix-up."

The message was time stamped at nine thirty-seven. Emily's head spun. She tried to process everything she just learned. With her eyes closed, she buried her head into her crossed arms on the desk.

"Why is this happening?" she asked herself. After a few moments, she pushed herself up from the desk to regain her composure. *Is Mark's death related to these documents? Is Oscar somehow involved?*

Emily needed answers. There were far too many coincidences. *I'm going to figure this out*, she thought as she found the manila folder and placed it in her purse. Mark's death weighed heavily on her mind as she gathered her computer and personal items.

I'm in over my head, she thought as she reflected on her encounter with Oscar. *These people are very dangerous.*

Part II

Chapter 14

Emily reviewed the documents Mark left in her office. They were intriguing, but inconclusive. Inherently, the documents were not incriminating. They did, however, call into question certain transactions related to a Swiss bank account. She flagged similar documents from the work she completed previously.

A closer review indicated that the Switzerland account had a substantial number of deposits made to it. Each transaction was less than ten thousand dollars, which wasn't unusual for a political donation. What interested Emily was that transfers of less than ten thousand dollars often avoided the suspicion of regulating authorities. *Were they trying to hide these transactions?*

Emily systematically went through the documents. She put all of the pages with transactions in a separate stack. When finished, she had collected over two hundred pages. Each page had multiple deposits. She added up the amounts and was amazed to find it totaled over forty million dollars. *Wow!*

She found the timing of the transactions especially interesting. They were all made within a twenty-four-hour period over two years ago. *These funds were funneled into the Swiss account to avoid detection*, she thought.

She tried to make a connection between the source routing numbers for the transactions, but found none. They were from all over the world. The transactions might have been masked, but the timing stood out. *There must have been a reason they were rushed to transfer the funds over a twenty-four-hour period. This is where I need to focus my attention.*

Emily decided to leave the office just after noon. Mark's death made her paranoid that someone might be watching her and the investigation. She was careful to avoid saving any documents she had on the firm network drive.

The thought of approaching Terrance for help crossed her mind many times, but she decided against it. Owen was a high-profile client for the firm. Besides, she didn't have direct proof of any wrongdoing by their client. She needed to treat this like any other engagement, where she organized all of the facts and drew sound conclusions.

Emily sighed. Maybe it was wrong to link Mark's death to her new engagement. The car bombing near the Capitol had really shaken her. There was a good chance that some of those feelings may have affected her overall state of mind. She closed her eyes and took a few deep breaths. After she organized her thoughts, she focused on what she needed to do next.

After purchasing an overpriced latte, Emily entered a small, tree-lined park adjacent to her office building. She sat at one of the park benches across from a large, shallow fountain.

Emily pulled her cell phone out of her coat pocket. After selecting a name from her personal directory, the phone rang twice before it was answered. Being a consultant didn't always mean you were the smartest person in the room. Often, it just meant you knew how to effectively and efficiently complete tasks. Knowing how and when to leverage available resources was also key.

"Emily, darling. How the hell are you?" It was David Harvey, a good friend from her MBA program at George Washington University.

"I'm doing well, David. You know me, always working."

"I'm sorry to hear that." He laughed. "Are you single yet? You never took me up on my dinner offer last month."

"No, I'm still with Scott. He's been treating me okay. I'll see him tonight and give him your regards."

"I wouldn't go that far. Besides, he knows I'm still waiting for my chance to prove myself to you."

"Ha," replied Emily with a polite laugh. She always found his flirting odd, given his unabashed preference for men. Regardless, she always played along with the innocent ruse. "I'll definitely tell him you said hello, just to keep him on his feet," she added.

"The offer always stands." After a brief pause, he added, "What can I do for you, darling? I don't expect this is a social call to discuss our drinking days at GW."

"No, unfortunately, it's not. I'm hoping to leverage your knowledge of off-shore investing."

"I see. And you're hoping my knowledge on working with the SEC would be beneficial to you?"

"Actually, I'm hoping you could do me a favor outside of your current expertise. I would like to access your knowledge from your previous job."

"Intrigued, I am. And I have to admit it's still kind of weird being on this side of the fence. I got accustomed to developing opaque financial strategies, not uncovering them."

"That's exactly why I reached out," said Emily. "Besides, you were always the smart one."

"Oh, please. I forget. Who aced that nightmarish applied regression analysis class?" He asked in a sarcastic tone.

"Ha, you always have to bring that up, don't you?" she replied. Emily just beat his overall GPA, but he overwhelmingly bested her in the quantitative classes. "Wise ass," she added.

"Too funny. What exactly are we talking about, here? What type of investments, and where would these investments be located?"

"My client has a numbered account in Switzerland. Money has been funneled into the account. It likely holds some investments, as well. I would like to learn more about the account and the investments."

"Your client? You've been hired by this person? Why can't you just ask your client?"

"The short answer is, *I can't.*" Emily continued, "Ultimately, his investments may involve some shades of gray. I want to have all of my facts straight before I bring everything to light. The issue at hand and subject matter are quite sensitive."

"Now I'm really intrigued. Count me in," David stated.

"I knew I could count on you, David."

"Just tell that to your boyfriend. What's his name again? They always seem to come and go."

"Very funny. I'll send you an email from a new email account I opened for this task."

"A burner email address. Wow, this really is sensitive. Are you sure you're not getting in over your head?" he asked with a hint of concern.

"I'm okay. I'm just being paranoid and careful at the same time."

"Gotcha."

"Do you think you could complete your work in the next couple of days?" she asked. "I need to know relatively quickly."

"I'll do my best. It all depends on the bank. I have numerous connections, but not at every bank. You do know that this isn't entirely legal, right?"

"I don't know what you're talking about." Emily laughed.

"Good. I'll have to ask for a few favors, but I think I can help. The banking community in Switzerland is fairly incestuous. If I don't have a direct contact at a bank, one of my discreet friends might. I'll make some calls."

"Thanks, David. You really are awesome."

"I know. Listen, I gotta go, darling. I have to jump on another call."

"Okay."

"Take care." After a slight pause, he added, "Emily, I mean it. Take care of yourself. You always put other people first. It's a bad habit."

"Thanks again, David. I needed to hear that. I will certainly take your advice. And I'll take you up on that dinner offer when this is over," she added.

"Now that's what I like to hear. I look forward to it."

Back in the office, Emily stared at the ceiling. She tapped her pen against the edge of the desk in an entranced state of thought. A knock on her office door roused her.

"Come in," said Emily as she put the pen up to her lips.

"Hi, Emily," Terrance said as he opened the door. He leaned against the doorframe.

"What's up? What can I help you with?" she asked.

"Nothing, really. I was just seeing how you are doing, emotionally. I do worry about you sometimes, you know," he stated in a fatherly tone.

"I know you do. I appreciate it." She smiled at him.

"Now, when can I expect the results from the Owen engagement? He's a *congressman*, and I don't want to keep him waiting."

His over-emphasis on the word congressman signaled he was in a playful mood. "That's what you wanted? You're not concerned with my well-being at all." She laughed. "I knew I wasn't going to get off easy today."

"We need to move on to other engagements. Let's keep this machine rolling." He attempted to dance in place as he moved his arms in a forward circular motion. His *running man* interpretation looked absolutely ridiculous and made Emily laugh. He didn't have any rhythm, and his belly flopped up and down.

Still laughing, Emily said, "You really are a crazy, old guy. You know that, don't you?"

"Of course I do," he replied as he retrieved a handkerchief from his pants pocket. He began to wipe the perspiration from his forehead and smiled as he tried to regain his breath. "So, how does it look?" he huffed.

"I really haven't seen anything of any concern, Terrance." Emily decided to keep the conversation short.

"Good. So what's the hold-up?"

"I've reviewed most of the documents Mark flagged, but not all. I just want to ensure I have everything covered before coming to a conclusion." She looked away. She caught herself and quickly re-established eye contact.

"There's something you're not telling me, Emily." His serious tone matched his stoic demeanor as he leaned against the doorframe again with his arms crossed in front of him.

"No, I'm just being thorough, Terrance. Really, there's nothing there." She purposefully omitted any reference to the Swiss bank account. Her investigation was incomplete. "I just need an extra day to tie up loose ends," she continued. "The whole thing with Mark really shook me. Concentrating is a little more problematic than usual, that's all." She didn't like using Mark as an excuse, but she needed more time.

"It hasn't been easy on any of *us*," Terrance responded. With a thoughtful look, he added, "Okay. I'll hold them off until Friday. They won't like it, but we need to do our job, right?" He added a smile after his last point.

She knew Terrance was upset about Mark. It made her feel guilty. "Of course. I didn't mean to insinuate I was the only person shaken by the accident."

Emily decided that her viewpoint probably wouldn't change, regardless of what she found. The threat to her family wasn't worth the risk of speaking out. "On second thought, Terrance, you'll have my findings tomorrow. I'm sure that it's nothing."

"Emily," began Terrance, "complete your due diligence. Remember, we're the *good* guys. White hats and all." He pointed to an invisible hat on his head. "Just have everything completed by Thursday. I'll review it, and we'll deliver our results Friday. They'll wait."

"Will do," Emily responded. The extra time wouldn't change her answer to Terrance, but it might allow her enough time to investigate the Swiss account more thoroughly and at least put it to rest in her mind.

Chapter 15

TUESDAY. 7:25 PM.

When Emily arrived at Clyde's, she saw Scott right away. He sat at their usual booth with two draft beers waiting on the table. He stood up to greet her.

"Hi." Without another word, he gave her an apologetic kiss. She accepted his apology with a kiss of her own. When she sat down, he gave her a bouquet of flowers he had hidden on his side of the booth.

"I can't believe this," Emily said in a surprised tone. She placed the flowers next to her and lifted the beer to her lips. "Pumpkin ale. It's good," she added when she set her glass on the table.

"I was being an ass," Scott said.

"Yes, you were."

"Come on. Be nice. Let's make this a fresh start."

"I think I can oblige," she replied playfully. "How's everything with your boyfriend?"

"Very funny. You make fun of him, but I think he's the real deal. He's speaking at an upcoming Republican party event in New York. He's been well received by everyone he's met. It's exciting."

"Great," Emily replied with forced enthusiasm.

"I really think he might be White House material," he continued. "Seriously. I could be working in the White House one day," he added in a dignified voice.

"That's great." She found it difficult to fake a good mood.

"You're not sharing my enthusiasm. I just told you that I may have a legitimate shot of working in the White House, and your only reply is *that's great*. I'm not even going to mention Owen's speech he's giving Thursday. It's going to garner him a lot of attention. You'll see what I'm talking about."

"Sorry. It's been a long week."

"It's Tuesday. The week is just starting. I can tell something is bothering you. What's wrong, Emily?" Scott asked as he put down his beer.

"It's just that…" She paused and looked down at the table. "I don't even know how to start this conversation, Scott."

"Just tell me. Did you meet someone else?" he asked with an incredulous tone.

"Of course not," she quickly replied.

"Then, what?"

"It's the engagement I'm working on."

"The one with Owen?"

"Yes. Has he spoken to you about it?"

"No. We've been busy on other facets of the campaign. Besides, I wouldn't expect him to announce to the team that he hired a firm to independently validate his finances."

Emily was hesitant to elaborate on her thought. Scott stared at her thoughtfully as she saw his demeanor change.

"What exactly have you found?" Scott asked as he tapped his finger against the side of his glass.

"We're still not done with our work. I'm not supposed to divulge my work or results to anyone. I think that would be especially true with you."

"Let's back up a minute." Scott stopped tapping his finger and closed his eyes. Emily usually found this type of behavior entertaining, but she feared the conclusions he might establish.

"Scott."

"Hold on, Emily," he said as he concentrated. "I was just talking about riding someone's coattails to the White House and you blindsided me with the revelation that something bothers you regarding his finances. Reading between the lines, it appears you've found something. Otherwise, you wouldn't have said anything."

"I honestly don't know. We're still reviewing things."

"But, I know you, Emily." He pursed his lips and looked down. He looked defeated. As if the world he thought he knew had fundamentally changed.

"There's something that concerns you, right? You're too good at your job not to overturn every stone. If he was hiding something, even something he thought he hid well, you would find it."

"I haven't found anything incriminating, yet," she responded.

"*Incriminating* and *yet* are the only two words I heard you say. Why are you doing this? I'm going to talk to him."

"No, you can't!" she shouted in protest.

"Why?"

"You just can't. That's it. Period! Once you open this, there's no way you can close it." After a slight pause, she added, "The ramifications of such an action could be dramatic and unpredictable."

"You're just protecting yourself. What about me and my career? I've put a lot of faith into him."

"I know you have. And I'm not just thinking about my personal interests, here. I have your interests in mind as well."

"Emily," he began, "I need to speak with Owen. This is just too big to ignore. I know him. Shit, I've been working seventy-hour weeks with him for the past couple of months."

After a brief pause, he continued. "We're on to something. He's so charismatic. Everyone loves him. He can capture a room. You've talked to him before. You know what I mean."

"I just don't think it's a good idea to talk to him about this," she reiterated. "Not yet."

"You're just being dramatic. He's very reasonable. Besides, it may just be a misunderstanding or misinterpretation of the data. You said that you haven't found anything incriminating yet."

"I know what I said."

"What exactly have you found?" He picked up his beer to take a sip, but found it empty. He got the bartender's attention with a slight raise of his hand. After noting that Emily's glass was three-fourths gone, he held up two fingers.

"Scott, I can't talk about it. You have no idea who you're dealing with here." She said it more forcefully than she would have liked, but meant it.

"Emily, you have to give me something if you want my help."

"I can't say much, but we did find financial activity related to a Swiss bank account. That account may also be related to some investment in Uzbekistan."

"Uzbekistan?" asked Scott. "He's certainly never been there. In fact, he's only been to Europe once in the past few years, and it wasn't even Switzerland. Somewhere near Greece two years ago. He mentioned it in passing. The only reason I remember this is because he said he wished he had taken the time to visit the *Greek Isles*."

"We reviewed his travel expenses and never saw any travels in Europe," said Emily, more to herself than to Scott.

"Well, if you haven't found anything related to his financials, what else are you looking for?" he asked. After a quick pause, he continued. "What? Do you think this is related to the encounter in the subway?"

Emily didn't reply.

"No. That can't be it. You're serious? You think someone was following you because of a *due diligence* assignment at a boutique consulting firm? That was just some creep. I told you to talk to the police, but you never did, did you?"

Just then, Tom came to the table with two beers. "Thanks, Tom," Scott said.

Scott took a long drink of his beer and wiped the foam from his upper lip with the back of his hand.

"I'm feeling much better now," he continued. "You're just being paranoid. That encounter really shook you, didn't it?" After he finished his thought, Scott noticed the genuine concern in her face. "I'm doing it again, aren't I?"

"You're being an asshole."

"Come on. You don't have to be so harsh."

"I'm telling you that you really don't know what you're up against. I guess ignorance is bliss," she stated as she finished her first beer. She pushed the empty glass to the side and slid the new one in front of her.

"How would I know what I'm up against unless you told me?" he replied.

"Mark is dead," Emily blurted out.

"What? Wait, you mean the guy that's helping you on the engagement?" Emily just nodded. "That's horrible. What happened?"

"He was run over by a car yesterday on his way to work," she said without emotion.

"That's unbelievable. No wonder you're stressed. I really am sorry to hear about his accident. I'm sure his family…"

Emily cut him off before he could finish his thought. "It was no accident."

"What do you mean?" asked Scott as he put his glass down.

"He was *murdered*."

"Murdered? Was he into drugs or something? I'm confused. You're not making any sense here. Help me out."

"He was killed because of this case I'm working on." As Emily spoke, she slammed the glass against the table, finally saying aloud what she'd been afraid to admit to herself. The beer sloshed in the glass before splattering on the table. "He was the only one working on the engagement with me, and now he's dead."

A few drops of beer landed on Scott's hand. He wiped them away with a napkin. "That's impossible, Emily. I think you're letting your imagination and your grief intertwine."

"Why don't you believe me?"

"Because it just doesn't make sense, Emily. First you claim that someone is following you and that it may be related to Owen. Now your work colleague dies in an *unfortunate accident* and you claim it's related to Owen. It just sounds incredible to me." He paused briefly. "What proof do you have? I'm assuming none, or else you would have gone to the police." He spoke emphatically with his hands when he made his point.

"No, I haven't gone to the police. I was told not to," she said.

"By whom, Owen?" Scott asked incredulously.

"You're doing it again. Stop being a jerk."

Before he could reply, she continued. "I was approached by some mafia guy who explicitly stated that he was interested in the results of my investigation. Further, he said not to approach anyone with the knowledge of my encounter. Especially you and Terrance," she added.

"That's absolutely crazy. I'm starting to get worried about you, Emily. I know you hate politics, but this is my career. I work for politicians. I always will. You've always done better than me, but now I have a real chance at something big, something important. I think you just may be jealous that my career is reaching another level. Is that it?" He looked intently into her eyes.

"I am not making this up. I have a growing suspicion that your boss is not who you think he is." She grabbed her cell phone, bag, and coat. Before she got up from the table, Scott took hold of her forearm.

"Emily, what would you think if I made these claims against Terrance? You have to see this from my perspective."

"I would believe you." Without any further words, she removed his hand from her forearm and walked out of the bar. Scott didn't try to stop her.

She walked down the street. After two blocks, she stopped. She found herself leaning against a building, looking to a dark sky for answers. She tried and failed to hold back tears. She wiped the stray tears from her face and dried her hand on her coat.

What's wrong with him? she thought as an overwhelming feeling of loneliness overcame her.

Chapter 16

WEDNESDAY. 8:22 PM.

The next day had been difficult for Emily. She couldn't stop thinking about Mark, or the fact that the people responsible could also hurt her or her family.

Emily needed Scott more than ever, but struggled to place any trust in him. His reaction to her claims really made her angry. She tried to understand his perspective, but ultimately couldn't.

Emily's thoughts slipped back to her engagement for Owen. She was scheduled to meet with Terrance tomorrow. She had completed the summary analysis with the appropriate support and hoped it would be enough to placate both Terrance and the client.

So far, the work she had given to David hadn't panned out. They'd had a few short conversations, but his connections abroad hadn't materialized anything. He needed more time, which Emily didn't have.

All of her life, she had been stubborn. She hated to lose an argument, even if it was immaterial. But this situation was different. There was a lot more at stake than her pride.

After careful consideration, she decided to give the results to Terrance in the morning. If anything did come of David's investigation, she would either bury it or anonymously leak it to the media. *Let those people fight it out*, she thought.

How she dealt with Scott was another matter entirely. If Owen was involved in murder, Scott would have to leave the campaign. She couldn't imagine a scenario in which he would choose to stay.

Her phone rang as she entered her apartment that evening. It was her mother. With a sigh, she prepared for the conversation. "Hey, Mom. What's up?"

"Why haven't you called? I've been worried sick about you."

"Mom, I've been really busy. You know that my work schedule is hectic."

"You can always call your mom, you know."

"Yes, I know."

"When's the last time you talked to your Uncle Collin in Annapolis?"

"It's been a while." Emily's eyes gravitated to a picture on her wall. In it, she was smiling with her uncle. They were dressed in camouflage during a deer hunt a few years back.

Emily dreaded these conversations. It was like talking to a brick wall. She talked, but her mother just didn't listen. It didn't help that she didn't understand her work or why Emily even chose to have a career.

"You really should call him," her mother continued. "He's been very good to you all of these years. We've never had a large extended family, but you need to treat the ones you have the best you can. He cares about you. He says you haven't returned his calls for your annual hunting trip. What happened?"

"I've been busy, Mom. I'll call him next week. Work has been really crazy."

"That always seems to happen," her mother said with a disapproving tone. "Please make time for him."

"I will. Sorry. Did you call for any other reason than to make me feel bad?"

"I'm getting a count for Thanksgiving dinner. Are you planning on visiting?"

"Not for Thanksgiving. As you know, I usually head to a friend's house for dinner. I *will* be there for Christmas, though."

"I'm glad to hear that, Emily. It'll be nice to have the family together again. Your father would be glad."

Emily shook her head, annoyed again at her mother's attempt at manipulation. She hadn't forgotten about her father; she just didn't like talking about him. Those were her private memories. She didn't even talk about him with Scott.

"I look forward to seeing you then, Mom. I need to go. People are depending on me to get some things done."

"I understand. Call me later in the week?"

"I will, Mom. Bye."

After ending the phone call, Emily looked at the folder on top of her kitchen counter. Inside it, were the documents that summarized her findings. Everything was ready for Terrance's review tomorrow.

All she needed to do was summon the courage to lie to his face. *Well, it wouldn't be a complete lie*, she thought. She hadn't found any incriminating evidence or wrongdoing by Owen. Terrance would be pleased that the findings would be positive for their client.

In an attempt to get her mind on something other than work and her recent spat with Scott, she decided to make dinner. Emily enjoyed cooking, but rarely took the time.

She selected one of the dozen bottles of wine from the decorative rack on the kitchen counter. She uncorked the bottle from Northern Italy and set it aside.

Italian food had always been one of her specialties. She made her own sauce from scratch and was never one to shy away from trying new recipes. She never used a cookbook and refused to measure ingredients.

She opened the refrigerator and retrieved the vegetables she had purchased at the local market. She washed and chopped tomatoes, green peppers, and onions.

It always amazed Emily how such a simple action could alleviate stress. Her abundant problems seemed less insurmountable as she let her mind be taken over by the routine task. And it didn't hurt that Sonny Rollins was working his saxophone magic in the background while she finished her prep work.

Emily retrieved a pan from a kitchen cabinet and placed it on the stove. She sautéed the vegetables before tossing some fresh-pressed garlic in the pan. After adding a few generous glugs of olive oil and some dried oregano, she let it simmer.

She switched her focus to the pasta. She filled a pot with water and turned the gas heat on high. After the water began to boil, she added the freshly made pasta from the local market.

Emily poured a glass of wine and tried her best to put the events of the past few days behind her. She served the pasta in a bowl and carefully ladled a generous portion of sauce on top. A napkin and fork had already been placed next to the bowl on the island countertop.

She sat down and observed her dinner. Her stomach growled in anticipation of the meal. Emily was about to take her first bite when a nagging thought stopped her cold. It was something Scott had said. She had dismissed the thought at the time, but it kept creeping back into her consciousness.

She took three bites of her food just to appease her stomach, but knew she didn't have time to enjoy the meal. She had to devise a plan for the morning. She wasn't sure if she'd get an opportunity like this again.

Chapter 17

Everything looks very presidential, thought Scott as he admired his work. The Republican-red backdrop, the American flags, a podium that mimicked the one used in White House press conferences. His group worked for two days to prepare for the press conference. The room was in a building adjacent to Owen's campaign headquarters. Scott drafted the speech for Owen, selected the decor, and organized a small fleet of reporters from major and local news networks to cover the event. A hundred staunch supporters of various demographics were in attendance to foster a favorable atmosphere.

The first arrivals walked through the door. Junior staff members and volunteers sprang to life as they directed the guests to their seats. Scott felt satisfied everything was ready. But his conversation with Emily the night before still lingered.

She can't be serious regarding the accusations against Owen, he thought. Murder seemed far-fetched and certainly didn't fit Owen's character. His defensive response to her accusations bothered him too. A more delicate response would have been more effective in retrospect.

Emily did raise questions that needed to be answered. Why didn't Owen tell him he had engaged a consulting firm? It was likely an innocent oversight, but he needed to find out the truth for himself.

Scott walked into the room behind the drapes. Owen was seated in front of a large mirror as a makeup stylist gingerly applied a makeup sponge to the wrinkles around his eyes. Owen made eye contact when Scott approached.

"Just need to ensure I don't experience the Nixon effect," stated Owen with a laugh as he referenced the candidate's famous debate with a more charismatic Kennedy.

"Looking good, Boss," said Scott. "Do we need to go over any last points?"

"No, we're all set. Everything is coming into place. I hope you're as excited as I am." He gave Scott an encouraging slap on the back from his seated position. "Just think, this could be the start of something great," he stated with a smile.

"Your supporters arrived an hour ago, and most of the reporters we contacted have shown. We have five minutes until you're scheduled to speak."

"Fantastic! After the conference, we need to meet and re-evaluate our strategy. I expect that we're going to generate a significant buzz." His smile reached from ear to ear. Scott couldn't help but smile back. *His charisma really is infectious*, he thought.

Owen got up from his chair. He examined his appearance in the mirror as one of his assistants helped him put on his suit jacket. Scott adjusted Owen's lapel and patted him on the back as the man confidently strode toward the dividing curtain, which slowly opened on his choreographed approach.

All eyes were on Owen when he entered the room. He fed off the energy of everyone in attendance. Like a boxer parading through a crowd before a bout against an overmatched opponent with a foregone conclusion, he raised a victorious fist.

He took a deliberate deep breath upon reaching the podium. "Let's go!" he exclaimed to a cheering crowd. His confident and infectious smile was immediately greeted with a barrage of clicks and flashes.

Owen looked every bit like a president. His red tie clearly identified his party allegiance. After pausing to enjoy the well-received reception, he raised his hands to quell the crowd.

"Thank you for coming here today," he began. The crowd quieted.

"It is with great sorrow and concern that we come together today. The actions by the individual or individuals responsible for the heinous attack upon our sovereign nation need to be identified swiftly. We will not allow anyone to tread upon our freedom we hold so dearly."

The speech went beautifully. He had purposefully omitted any reference to the incumbent president, who continued his foreign tour of Asia. Owen began to detail his plan to find the individuals responsible and to further ensure the safety of the citizens of not only Washington DC, but all parts of the country.

Scott watched with great enjoyment as the cameras continued to flash. He grinned as many of the reporters nodded their approval over the substantive portions of the carefully crafted speech. The event could not have gone any better for him or Owen.

Scott knew the speech would garner much attention in the political world. His next step would be to adjust the campaign strategy to effectively leverage the new attention placed on Owen. A revised travel schedule would be necessary to accommodate the national press circuit.

I have a lot of work to do, Scott thought. *And how do I approach Owen with the accusations from Emily without losing my job?*

Scott lost his thought as Owen pounded his fist on the podium to punctuate a promise to punish anyone directly or indirectly responsible for the terrorist act committed in the nation's capital. The crowd responded with applause. Scott couldn't help but smile. He enjoyed the moment despite his fears.

A woman passed through the open doors of the building wearing a campaign T-shirt and hat. No one paid her any attention as she melted into the crowd of supporters. She purposely stood near someone who had placed a purse against the back wall. The woman discreetly snatched an office badge that partially stuck out of the purse's side pocket. She then slipped into the adjoining campaign headquarters without drawing attention to herself.

Chapter 18

THURSDAY. 9:24 AM.

The woman placed the stolen office badge in her pocket. Even though she had never been to the campaign headquarters, the woman deduced where to begin her search. In most buildings, the largest offices were located away from the entrance and toward the back of the floor.

With a confident stride, she passed the open desks used by the volunteers and the cubicles used by the organizers before reaching an array of offices. These were small offices and included a conference room with a wall map that appeared to outline key cities and dates for an upcoming campaign trip.

She continued down the hallway, to where the doorways were farther apart. She stopped upon reaching the last office and glanced behind her. With no one in sight, she turned the knob on the closed door. An explosive round of cheers and applause caused her nervous hand to relinquish the knob. She let out a sigh as she faced the door and gained her composure. When all was quiet again, she unconsciously held her breath as she slowly swung the door open.

Owen's office is surprisingly clean and free of clutter, the woman thought. A large desk faced the door at the center of the back wall. It was outfitted with an open laptop and an antique lamp. Along the longest wall were two chairs and a slightly worn deep brown leather couch. She recognized a recent edition of *The Economist* on the coffee table next to an ash tray with three stubbed-out hand-rolled cigarettes. Thoughts of a man in a park flooded the woman's head.

There were two large filing cabinets against the right wall. *That's where I'll start.* Unsurprisingly, she found them both locked. Undeterred, she scanned the room for out-of-place objects. A quick check inside a university mug and other random knickknacks that adorned the bookshelves didn't yield what she sought.

She checked the desk next. The laptop screensaver streamed random photos of Owen. She pulled the drawer knob, and it slid open.

A quick rummage through the drawers came up empty. Upon poking her finger through a tin of paperclips in the next drawer, she found it. With a smile, she pulled a key out.

She went back to the first cabinet, unlocked it, and began to thumb through the file folders. After a quick search, the woman determined the documents were not useful.

The woman tried the second cabinet, knowing she only had a few more minutes. Perspiration began to build on her forehead as she aggressively rummaged through the file folders. She saw human resource files, office lease contracts, and other documents related to the daily operations of the campaign.

"Shit," she said out loud. Frustrated, she paced the room and looked around. Her eye caught the photos streaming on his computer.

She touched the track pad to wake it. The desktop appeared. *He must have his computer on a delayed password*, she thought. It wasn't uncommon. Most people found it cumbersome to constantly enter a password and only set the password to activate after an hour or so.

There wasn't time for a detailed search. She pulled a flash drive out of her pocket, placed it in the computer, and began downloading targeted file folders. She began with the folder labeled *My Documents*. She then dragged any other folder seemingly of a personal nature to the flash drive icon.

Simple queries were performed to locate any travel and expense files on the computer, including any documents related to any countries in Europe. All of the files were saved to the flash drive. A queue was created that would take precious time. Time she didn't have. A rapidly blinking green LED on the drive indicated the files were being copied.

Next, she opened the application folder for Microsoft Outlook. She selected folders containing emails and calendar events and exported them to the flash drive.

She had never done anything like this before. It was both exhilarating and terrifying. Her heart raced. There was something here. She knew it.

A noise in the hallway disrupted her concentration. She jogged to the door and peered out. With no one in view, she began to walk back to the desk to finish her task. It would only be a few more minutes until it was complete. *This might just work.*

She was just a few feet from the desk when a familiar voice made the hair on the back of her neck stand.

"Miss Hendricks," the voice said in a controlled monotone.

She couldn't move. She had practiced what to say if caught, but couldn't recall any of it. She could only focus on the green blinking light that stuck out of the side of Owen's computer.

"Miss Hendricks," the voice began again. "Can I help you?"

She turned around with a large smile. "Why, hello, Ben. It's great to see you again."

"I wish I could say the same," he replied in a confused tone. "I saw the light on from the hallway. Owen isn't here. But you probably already know that," he added a bit too politely. "May I ask what you're doing in his office?"

"Oh," said Emily in an exaggerated tone. "I thought this was Scott's office."

"Of course. You haven't been here before, have you?" His polite smile was deafening. He began to casually peruse the office. In her peripheral vision, Emily was relieved to see the cabinet drawers were closed.

"No, I haven't. So could you direct me to Scott's office?" Emily asked in an effort to alleviate the tension and to redirect the focus of the conversation. The perspiration on her forehead culminated into a single droplet that ran down her left temple. Ben's piercing looks exacerbated her fears. She wasn't sure if he had actually witnessed the sweat or if she had just imagined he focused on it.

She felt the situation couldn't get any worse until the key she used to open the locked cabinet caught her eye. It stuck ominously out of its lock. *Shit*. When she reestablished eye contact, a furrowed brow confirmed her suspicion. He saw exactly what she saw.

"So, you're here to see Scott, Miss Hendricks?" He walked to the cabinet and slowly removed the key from the lock. As he did, his jacket opened slightly. A holstered gun caught Emily by surprise.

"You know what? Maybe I should just go. I'm expected at a meeting in just a little while. Anyway, this is obviously a bad time to stop in on Scott. I guess I wasn't thinking." *I need to get out of here.*

She found solace in the fact that there were people nearby. Voices from the adjoined building continued to cheer in reaction to Owen's speech. She wished she was among them right now. Anywhere but here.

"As long as you're here, there are some things we should probably discuss," he said as he played with the evidence in his hand.

Emily took a few steps back toward the desk. She wanted to obstruct his view of the blinking flash drive. *Please don't see it.*

"There's really nothing to talk about. Just a simple misunderstanding," she added with an uncomfortable smile.

"Miss Hendricks, I'm really disappointed that you've decided to come here today." He began a slow walk in her direction. She took another three steps back before the desk impeded her movement. She found herself cupping the edge as she braced herself against the desk.

"I'm going to ask you some questions, and I need answers," Ben said in a calm, but authoritarian voice. Her heart sank as he continued to shorten the distance between them. "Your presence here is quite unprofessional and concerning, to say the least. We have retained your services, and your firm has signed a nondisclosure agreement. Are you not aware of that?"

"What's going on?" asked another voice. Emily looked to the door with excitement.

"Scott!" she cried out in an overly boisterous tone.

The steely look from Ben indicated this wouldn't be the end of the conversation. He shot her a disapproving expression before reluctantly turning to face Scott.

"Hello. What are you doing here?" asked Scott. His confused expression belied his understanding of the situation. The tension in the room was undeniable.

"I wanted to surprise you."

"I can see that. And look, you're wearing one of our campaign T-shirts. And a matching hat. It's a bit surprising," he said as he looked her up and down. "But it works." He smiled awkwardly. "Am I missing something here?" He looked to both parties for an answer before decidedly approaching Emily.

"No. Not at all," responded Ben. "We were just talking about some specifics regarding Emily's consulting assignment. As you may be aware, we have engaged the services of her firm." Ben made eye contact with Scott when he spoke. A habit likely formed from working with people who demanded a person's full attention.

While Ben appeared distracted, Emily reached behind her back with her left hand. She found the flash drive and put her thumb and index fingers carefully around its casing. With her other fingers, she pushed against the side of the laptop. She applied just enough force to remove the drive from the computer without making a sound.

"I was vaguely familiar that her firm was engaged to do some work for Owen," stated Scott. "Is this a conversation from which I should be excluded?"

"We're done," said Emily. "I was explaining to Ben that everything is in order. They will have our results tomorrow, as promised by Terrance."

Emily pushed off the desk to meet Scott in the middle of the room. Her left hand grazed her back pocket, where she deposited the drive.

"We're very appreciative of your services," said Ben as he walked behind the desk to examine the computer. He looked up to make eye contact with Emily when he spoke next. "I'll be in touch with you soon."

"I'll walk you out," said Scott in an apparent attempt to diffuse the tension. Emily saw an angered expression cross his face after he turned away from Ben. Without any further words, she followed Scott to the door. Before exiting, she looked back to see Ben's unwavering gaze. *This expedition is going to have significant ramifications*, she thought.

Scott didn't speak a word as they walked down the hallway, past the cubicles, and finally to the front door. He opened it for her as they exited to the street.

"What is wrong with you?" he asked incredulously.

"I don't know where to start," she admitted.

"This has got to stop. *I... I—Jesus Christ!* What was that in there?" he asked as he pointed his entire arm toward the building.

"Scott, listen. I can explain."

"I don't even want to hear it, Emily. It's obvious your careless actions have everything to do with our conversation yesterday."

"Yes, it does. But there's a clear reason I'm here." Before she could continue her thought, Scott cut her off.

"What's this? Is this a work badge?" Emily didn't say anything as he pulled a badge that was partially exposed from her front pocket. "You took Barb's office badge? Com' on. This is getting out of control."

"If you would just listen for a minute."

Scott raised his hand in protest. "Emily, stop." He lowered his head and intentionally exhaled before continuing. "I think we need some time apart. It seems like you're intentionally trying to sabotage my career. I'm not even sure it's repairable at this point," he stated as his head shook in disappointment. "They won't trust me again. In this world, *trust* means everything."

"I'm sorry," she said. Emily reached out to him, but he stepped back. "Please be careful. I know there is something going on here."

"I love you, Emily, but you're crazy."

His words caught her by surprise. Scott was always very careful and deliberate in his word choice. "I've never heard you say that," she replied.

"You've always known I have felt that way. I'm just not good at saying it. Don't change the subject. I'm very angry right now. I'm going to have to perform some serious damage control. I'm serious when I say that we need a few days apart. I need to clear my head."

"I understand," Emily said. Before she could say anything else, he quickly turned around and disappeared into the building. Her gut felt wrenched with guilt. She tried to push the emotions aside as she realized the detrimental situation she had made for herself.

Flustered, she tried to regain her composure by taking a few deep breaths. She checked her watch. The meeting with Terrance was scheduled to begin in just over an hour. She exhaled before raising her hand to hail a taxi.

Chapter 19

THURSDAY. 10:45 AM.

Back in the office, Emily's heart still raced after her ad hoc investigation at Owen's campaign headquarters. The encounter with Ben made her uneasy. Unpleasant thoughts on how he could ruin her life filled her head.

It is unlikely that Ben would contact Terrance, she thought. If he did, she wasn't sure how she'd respond. She debated telling Terrance about her illegal attempt to uncover the truth. If he found out that she purposely withheld information, it would be problematic.

Her life was beginning to spin out of control.

It was nearly eleven. She had just enough time to organize her thoughts before the meeting. Mary stepped in the doorway of her office before she had a chance to begin.

"Terrance is looking for you," she stated unenthusiastically. "He asked me to let him know as soon as you got back."

"Thank you, Mary." Emily was annoyed. This wasn't the start she anticipated for her meeting. Before Mary left, Emily quickly spoke again. "Would you mind delaying your notification to Terrance? I wanted to gather some items for the meeting." Emily really just wanted some additional time to gather her composure.

"Sorry," replied Mary in her soft voice. "I already notified him you were back in the office." With an apologetic shrug, she turned around and exited as quietly as she entered.

Emily gathered her documents and headed toward Terrance's office. His door was open, but he faced away from her. The back of his chair partially obstructed her view.

She presumed he was engaged in his thoughts. Trying not to disrupt his concentration, she gave a polite knock on the door before sitting at the closer of the two chairs in front of his desk.

Terrance began to speak. Emily looked up, expecting their meeting to begin. It did not. She realized he was on the phone. He wasn't aware she had entered the room and swiveled his chair toward the window. She could now see him, but was outside of his field of view.

Emily decided to stay seated and took the time to organize the documents she had brought with her.

"Yes, I hear your concerns. Uh-huh. Yes. I'm in the same boat. You'll know everything I know, soon." The voice on the other line was barely audible to Emily, but she could make out a few curse words. "I can't control everything," Terrance interrupted. "The damage will be minimal."

Emily adjusted her position in the chair. She cringed when it squeaked. Terrance casually swiveled his chair toward her, and their eyes met. With a polite smile, he adjusted the demeanor in his conversation.

"Yes, everything is as expected. I need to go. We'll catch up later." Without waiting for a response, he placed the phone on the receiver.

That must have been Ben, she concluded. Surely he told Terrance everything. She felt a cold sweat coming on.

"Sorry about that," said Terrance, calmly. "Clients need to be managed or they can be quite unruly. They seldom see things the way we do, wouldn't you agree?"

"They only see things our way if we provide the answer they're expecting." She gave him a confident smirk.

"Exactly. Which is why our first question to them is always, *What do you think the answer is?*" He laughed. "Grab your coat. Let's get some lunch." He stood up and lifted his jacket off the hook on the back of the door.

"What about our meeting?"

"That's what we're going to talk about. You're ready to talk, right?"

"Of course," stated Emily. "What about the documents, should I bring them?"

"I don't think they're necessary, do you?"

His response surprised her. He typically liked to review everything related to the engagement. *The Devil is in the details*, he often said.

"We can get by without them," she finally said. "I'll just drop these papers back in my office. I'll meet you at the elevator."

When the elevator door closed, Emily turned her head toward Terrance. "What's the latest on Lisa. Is everything okay?"

He kept his eyes fixated on their reflection when he responded. "It's not looking good. Her brother is in a coma."

"A coma! That's terrible."

"It's inexplicable. She's totally innocent. She doesn't deserve this. No one does."

They stood in silence for the remainder of the descent to the lobby. When they exited the building, Terrance's usual driver stood patiently next to a black town car.

Terrance didn't have a driver's license. He had never driven a car. Everyone in the firm knew that, but no one knew why, not even Emily. She, like most people, just accepted it as one of the many eccentricities Terrance possessed that added to his mysterious charm.

"I take it we're not going local?" she said.

"No, we are not. I've got a craving."

The driver held the door open as they entered the vehicle. When he appeared in the front seat, his eyes gravitated toward the rearview mirror.

"BlackSalt."

"Yes, sir," replied the man as the car pulled away from the curb.

"BlackSalt," repeated Emily. "What's the occasion?"

"Their clam chowder is amazing."

They sat in silence for most of the drive. The restaurant was located just off the Potomac River on the west side of DC. Its reputation more than compensated for its undesirable location.

They arrived before the major lunch crowd and were seated in the corner of the main dining area. The restaurant perfumed a mixture of lobster and charred cedar planks.

Suddenly hungry, Emily perused the menu. Everything looked appetizing to her.

"A vodka and Fever-Tree," said Terrance to the waiter when he approached the table. "And the lady would like…"

"I'll have the same, please."

Terrance made his food order without referencing the menu he politely handed the waiter.

Emily ordered the lobster bisque. She found the lingering smells too tempting. She also ordered the crab cakes on Terrance's recommendation.

After the waiter left, Emily made a reference to the ordered drinks. "Is this going to be one of those days?"

"No. I just think you need to take the edge off."

"I'm fine, Terrance."

"I don't see it that way. You haven't been yourself lately. I just want to be sure everything's okay. You can talk to me, really."

"I know I can." Emily again thought of confessing. She deliberately pinched the tip of her tongue between her teeth.

"Well, let's talk. Business first. How were the results?"

"We didn't find any red flags," Emily stated. "We first reviewed the contributions to Mr. Templeton's campaign. We summarized the donations by donor and whether they were an individual or organization. We did not identify any suspicious or unusual activity with his donations."

"Okay, good," responded Terrance.

"We next reviewed all of the expenses. Staff, travel, meals, events, et cetera. We classified them as best we could and found them to be consistent with his campaign and travel schedule. Again, nothing unusual stood out."

Terrance looked at her intently before speaking. "There's something you're not telling me. I can feel it."

"How?" Emily laughed.

"I've been in this business long enough to know when someone is skirting around key issues. Being able to read people is an important skill."

"You've said that before." She tried not to break eye contact. If she had, it would have been an obvious sign she was hiding something. Terrance had often preached that sentiment when prepping for a material witness interview. If they look away, keep digging, he would say. Emily felt she wasn't intentionally trying to hide key facts. Her work was just incomplete.

The conversation reached a natural pause when the waiter delicately placed the drinks on the table. Emily was glad to have a brief break. It gave her time to think. She glanced at a distorted image of herself in a water glass.

"Well, come out with it, then." When she found his eyes, he smiled. "Don't procrastinate. Let's get everything we know on the table."

He did notice. She had no choice but to offer additional information. "We did note some unusual account activity abroad, but they didn't indicate anything of significant concern."

"What do you mean, unusual account activity abroad?" Terrance asked. "Please elaborate."

"By unusual, I mean we noticed significant funds that were transferred into a bank account in Switzerland. We weren't able to get specific details on that account."

"Okay," said Terrance. "Any other details available for that account?"

"It appears there were numerous transactions of amounts less than ten thousand dollars."

"Hmm," interjected Terrance. "Those amounts would likely not raise suspicion of the banking regulators."

"Exactly," she agreed.

"Could they be political donations? The denominations might suggest as such."

"Definitely not. These transactions were done over the course of twenty-four hours and totaled over forty million dollars."

"Well, they're not political donations, and they're not really enough to be a large-scale money laundering scheme." As he spoke, he gently tapped his finger on the side of the table before adjusting his glasses.

"No, you're right. I don't think it's money laundering, but it's enough money to raise attention to our client."

"I agree," stated Terrance with a thoughtful expression. "Did you uncover anything else?"

"We did see an investment in Uzbekistan."

"Uzbekistan?"

"I know. I thought the same thing. That country is really not on too many people's radar. It just stood out because of its location."

"Do you think these two are connected? Uzbekistan and the money in the Swiss account?" He looked to her for answers.

"I'm really not sure. I don't have all of the facts. Besides, both of these happened a couple of years ago. As such, we don't think it's an issue. We have this labeled as a specific question to Mr. Templeton, but there aren't any regulations regarding investment limitations. He'll obviously have to make his investment portfolio public, but he's not required to disclose any liquidated investments."

"Of course," stated Terrance.

"As such, our investigation is complete. We should be able to move on."

"Not so fast," Terrance said. "I'll relay our results to Ben. Email the files to me. I want to see how much dirt we can dig up on the Uzbekistan investment. Also, see if we can uncover anything regarding the Swiss account."

"To what end?" His enthusiasm for the additional investigation surprised her. But it comforted her to know that Terrance was in pursuit of the truth.

"If we can uncover something potentially damaging to Owen, then someone else could as well. Let's be proactive and make sure we serve the best interest of our client."

"What about our deadline?"

"I know we said we'd get back to them this week." He adjusted his glasses before finishing his thought. "I'll take the heat from Owen's team. Don't worry about that. Finish your work and get back to me on Monday."

"Got it, Boss," said Emily.

"You're glad this one's over, aren't you? Or at least almost over," he added with a grin.

"Yes. This one was a bit too personal for me, considering that Scott works on Owen's campaign team."

"As I said before, I didn't know that when I gave you the assignment."

"What a crazy coincidence. It is a coincidence, right?"

"Of course. I had to check with the client when I found out. I needed to ensure it wouldn't be a problem for them. Apparently, the Congressman is quite fond of you."

"Very funny."

"You left quite an impression on him. He's a good friend to make."

"That's all I need, a psycho stalker politician. Every girl's dream." She laughed. It felt good to laugh again.

She looked at Terrance. He had a special knack to make his employees feel appreciated. She briefly reconsidered her decision not to divulge her recent encounters in DuPont Circle and the campaign headquarters, but stood strong in her resolve.

"So, how is Scott?" Terrance asked as he took a small bite of his key lime pie.

"I don't know," replied Emily. "I thought women were supposed to be the complicated ones."

"Sorry, didn't mean to pry." His fork hovered over his plate before he filled it with his next bite.

"No, it's fine. Just a bit of a hiccup. We're both so focused on work. It's just not easy when both of our schedules are so demanding."

"I'm sure you'll figure it out."

Emily's guilt finally got to her. She couldn't stand withholding information from Terrance. He had been instrumental in the success of her career. "Terrance," she began.

"Yes?" he responded. He rested the fork on his plate as he made eye contact.

"I do have to confess—"

"Save it, Emily. I know. I received a call today."

Emily put on her best *poker face* to hide her embarrassment.

"I always expect you to go the extra lengths to finish an engagement. However, I have never asked you to do anything you weren't comfortable doing. I certainly didn't expect you to infiltrate Owen's office." He put an extra emphasis on the word *infiltrate* when he spoke.

"Why didn't you say anything earlier?"

Terrance laughed. "I'm still trying to picture you in a Sherlock Holmes cap while you searched for clues." He made a motion with his hand as he pretended to look for clues with an imaginary magnifying glass.

"Oh, be quiet," responded Emily in a playfully defiant tone. "It was nothing like that."

"Well, are you going to tell me about your adventure?" asked Terrance with a grin.

Emily began to recount the event. She conscientiously inserted smiles as she spoke and purposefully omitted the portion related to the flash drive. She wasn't ready to tell him everything.

In the back of her mind, she began to plan her next move. The files and calendar events collected at Owen's office would need to be scoured for evidence. Emily was looking for a specific piece of information. One of Scott's comments on Tuesday still rang in her head. It would require some investigation to learn if there are a link between Scott's comment and Owen's use of international tax havens.

Chapter 20

THURSDAY. 10:33 PM.

Emily sat at the kitchen counter. With her computer in front of her, she connected the flash drive that stored the data from Owen's computer. She hoped her efforts weren't in vain.

She searched for details related to Owen's travels abroad. On Tuesday, Scott had mentioned a specific trip Owen had made two years ago. It made her think of the financial crisis in the Republic of Cyprus around that time.

So far, the only solid evidence against Owen was a bank account in a known tax haven, Switzerland. If she could learn more about his international accounts, it may provide insight regarding any illegal activity. She knew Mark's death wasn't an accident. Her investigation may even provide a direct link to his death.

Emily opened Microsoft Outlook and directed the program to use the files from the flash drive. It was immediately evident there were at least five years of emails and calendar events. She suspected he wouldn't personally keep organized records of his travel schedule. His assistant likely kept detailed calendar records to facilitate the hectic travel schedule.

She started with simple keyword searches for *Cyprus*. The small Mediterranean country located near the Greek Islands was a well-known tax haven.

The *Wall Street Journal* had featured an article on the Eastern Mediterranean country highlighting the mandated fifty-percent levy on all foreign accounts. It was unprecedented and created financial havoc for the country. There was great panic amongst foreign account holders, who scrambled to withdraw funds before the levy was imposed.

Was it a coincidence that Owen was near that country around that time? Emily didn't believe in coincidences.

Her first few queries to his email account didn't yield any results. Emily began to review his calendar events, starting two years back, around the time of the Cyprus tax levy. Owen's travel schedule was predictably busy around that time. His position as a congressman required significant travel between DC and his home state of New York.

"Larnaca?" Emily asked herself as she pointed to the name on the computer screen. In July of that year, Owen had an international flight out of Dulles Airport. She read his itinerary out loud, "Dulles to Heathrow, then *Larnaca*." Emily wasn't familiar with that city. After a quick Google search, she learned it was the largest airport in Cyprus.

Emily perused his calendar events to determine the specifics of his visit. Anything that might help her know more about his trip. She saw a meeting scheduled the day after he arrived at the capital of Cyprus, Nicosia. *The capital likely housed the headquarters for the country's prominent banking institutions*, thought Emily. His calendar didn't indicate who he was scheduled to meet.

Emily switched her focus to the two email accounts on his computer. She queried the capital, Nicosia. Two emails immediately returned. They both originated from the same person, *Stan Murphy*. Emily revised her query to only include emails from Stan.

Five emails resulted. She read them in chronological order and immediately identified a sense of urgency in the communications.

The first email from Stan was in response to an email Owen sent regarding the status of the funds. Apparently, he learned about the potential levy in the media. He questioned Stan on why he had not informed them of the levy and why he hadn't returned his calls.

The repeated use of the word *we* in the emails confirmed that Owen was not the only account holder. Stan stated that the funds were still held with the bank, but he was trying to liquidate the account before the levy was imposed. He assured Owen that he had the proper measures in place.

The subsequent emails were quite short. Owen stated that he had lost confidence in Stan's ability to effectively manage the investments. He wanted to personally facilitate the transfer to another account.

"It has to be related to the Swiss account," she said to herself. The email chain ended after the two men agreed on a hotel rendezvous in the capital city.

Emily performed other keyword searches related to the major cities in Cyprus, but they didn't yield any results. Keyword searches using any mention of a Cyprus or Swiss bank account ended similarly.

She tapped on the keyboard. She needed to know more about Mr. Murphy. A series of Internet queries yielded a lot of information about his investment successes and failures in defunct mines abroad. He appeared to be a fairly well-known investment manager.

There seemed to be a significant amount of bad press related to claims of improperly investing funds. Thoughts of another *Madoff* entered her head. *Except this guy got what he deserved*, she thought after reading one of the articles regarding his disappearance in Tashkent. She noted the day of his death was only one day after his meeting with Owen in Cyprus. *I don't believe in coincidences.*

His body was never found, but more than one article mentioned the possible involvement of a Russian criminal organization. The implications of murder were abundant and clear. He was not a well-liked individual.

Emily knew who could fill in some of the blanks. David might be familiar with Mr. Murphy, given his background. If not, she thought, he might know of someone who is.

She sent him an email asking if he would have time to talk tomorrow. He would know how to find information on Mr. Murphy's investment portfolio. She knew of one other person who might be helpful. He had been in the banking industry his entire career. Emily was reluctant to reach out to him, though, given their history.

Her investigation went late into the night, but other searches were fruitless. She caught herself from dozing a couple of times. Eventually, she succumbed to much-needed sleep as her head found a comfortable position against her crossed arms on the counter.

The sound of a ringing phone jolted Emily. Disoriented, she looked around. With her eyes closed, she fumbled her hands inside her purse positioned on the stool next to her. She found her phone tucked in one of the pockets before clumsily drawing it to her ear.

"Hello?" she asked in a groggy tone without opening her eyes.

"We need to talk," said the voice on the other line.

Chapter 21

FRIDAY. 7:56 AM.

"Who is this?" she asked.

"You won't believe what I've found," said the voice.

"Who is this?" she asked again as she repeatedly blinked her eyes to gain consciousness.

"Emily, wake up! It's me, David."

She widened her eyes. "Yes. Yes. I'm here. Sorry, long night."

"I'm sure you'll live," he said sarcastically.

"Hey, I'm glad you called." She felt her body waking. She recalled her work from last night. "Did you receive my email?"

"Yes, I got it. We can talk about it when we meet."

"Why can't you just tell me now?" asked Emily.

"I heard back from my contact abroad."

"And...?" A shot of adrenaline hit her body. David had her full attention.

"I was able to get some visibility on the investments. You owe me big time. I had to pull a major favor with this guy. I think I have a date with him the next time I'm in Zurich."

"Very funny."

"I'm actually not kidding. Listen, we really need to talk about what I've found. I don't want any electronic or paper trails that lead back to me. Understand?"

"You're starting to scare me. What did you find?"

"It would be best if we could meet in person. And I'm not trying to scare you, but there are some very recognizable names affiliated with that Swiss account."

"In addition to Owen?" she asked in a questioning tone.

"Yes."

"Can you be more specific? I need to know."

"I can't talk right now. I've been at the office since six. As I said, let's meet to discuss this further."

"Okay. How about meeting in forty-five minutes at the park near my office? Does that work for you?"

After a pause, he responded, "Make it twenty. I'll switch one of my morning meetings to the afternoon. I'll be there. Bye."

Before she could respond, the call ended. Emily's mind churned as she thought about the investigation.

Who else is affiliated with the Swiss account? There has to be a connection between the Swiss and Cyprus accounts.

There was more to uncover. *There had to be a reason Mark was killed,* she thought. After placing the phone in her purse, she looked in the mirror and tried to smooth the wrinkles on the work clothes she still wore from yesterday. Seconds later, she gave up, put on her coat, and quickly headed out the door.

Emily got to the park a few minutes early. She was eager to get the information from David.

She nervously walked around, trying not to think of worse-case scenarios involving Owen. *David's probably just being dramatic*, she thought.

Emily tried to clear her mind. She looked around. The leaves that clung to the trees were dying and beginning to succumb to gravity. She closed her eyes and slowly inhaled the cool air into her lungs. It smelled of fall and reminded her of childhood, when she would jump on the leaf piles in her backyard. Simpler times.

She exhaled and checked her watch again. It was almost eight thirty. *He's late*, she thought. *David is never late.* She pulled out her phone to call him, when he appeared across the street. He was crossing the street as he headed toward the park.

She was about to raise her hand to catch his attention, but noticed something unusual in his demeanor. He repeatedly mouthed words to her as he crossed the street. She tried to read his lips. On his third attempt, she thought she understood what he said: *I'm being followed.*

His mouthed words caught Emily by surprise. She recoiled into a small crowd of people walking through the park. She raised the hood on her raincoat to shield her face, but kept her eyes trained on David.

He turned his right fist around, which was clenched. With his forearm showing, he slightly unclenched his fist to reveal a wadded piece of paper. He immediately closed his fist again and casually sipped his coffee with his other hand.

Intrigued and confused, Emily ensured David stayed in full view. She didn't see anyone following him, but kept her distance.

He took another sip of his coffee, this time with both hands. When he lowered his free right hand, she saw him stretch his fingers. He rubbed his thumb against his fingers in a deliberate gesture before he opened his hand again. She couldn't see the crumbled paper any longer.

Emily looked in the vicinity behind David. She wanted to see if she could identify the person following him. She expected to see Oscar, but didn't recognize anyone.

David veered slightly off his route and no longer headed toward Emily. After he deposited his coffee cup in a trash receptacle, he stopped and deliberately wiped the palms of his hands as if they were dirty. *The paper must be in the coffee cup*, she thought.

She decided to wait before retrieving the piece of paper. Someone else might have witnessed his charade. David walked toward the park exit. He nervously adjusted his glasses.

A black man with an English cap appeared directly behind him. His pace matched David's, step for step. Emily stopped. She could only watch. She didn't recognize him from her Dupont Circle encounter with Oscar.

She wanted to warn him. Her mouth opened, but no sound came out. She was paralyzed with fear.

The man with the cap casually bumped into David. Emily witnessed their eyes meet and saw fear in David's eyes.

After the apparently innocuous bump, the man casually changed direction and blended into the crowd. She tried to follow his movement, but quickly lost him.

She refocused her attention on David. He began to stumble, grabbed his chest, and then quickly dropped to his knees. He looked around and appeared to be confused. He reached out to a woman passing next to him. Before she could respond, he toppled to the ground.

His face crashed against the cold cement. One of the lenses of his round, European-style spectacles cracked from the impact.

"David!" yelled Emily when her voice returned. She started to move toward him, but a crowd had circled around him. Not wanting to draw attention to herself, she stopped. She looked around for the man in the English cap, but she didn't see him. She was afraid to approach her friend.

A person bent down to aid David. "He's having a heart attack. Give him space!" He looked up at the crowd. "Somebody call an ambulance!"

"Oh my God!" said another person. David's body appeared to go limp. His body then convulsed three times before it stopped.

His eyes remained open as his body lay dead. The crowd grew tense. A few people began to cry. One sought the comfort from a complete stranger. Others stood in silence with their hands covering their open mouths.

The only movement in David's body were the rhythmic motions applied by someone trying to resuscitate him. She knew it was too late.

A bewildered Emily stood in silence. The egregious act mortified her. She knew there was nothing she could do for David. *I've done enough already*, she thought. *If it wasn't for me, he'd still be alive.*

The crowd around him continued to grow. She heard an ambulance approach the park. The medics attended to David as the crowd stood around his lifeless body.

When it was apparent he wouldn't be revived, people began to leave. They would continue their day, but David would not.

She fought back her tears as she tried to regain control of her emotions. She wiped the tears away with a mixture of anger and disbelief. *At what point do I go to the police?* she thought. *If Scott doesn't believe me, why would the police believe me? What could they even do?*

She made up her mind to gather as much information as she could before going to the police. *I hope I don't regret this decision.*

Emily picked up a piece of paper from the ground so she would have a reason to approach the trash receptacle. Upon opening the lid, she peered inside to find that it contained mostly used coffee cups and discarded newspapers.

David's cup had a lid on it. She found an empty bag in the trash. She grabbed all of the cups with lids in view and placed them in the bag. There were fourteen cups in total. *One of them must hold the note*, she thought.

After taking a seat at a nearby bench, she began to systematically remove the lids. She found the note inside the fifth cup she tried.

With the crumpled note in her hand, she perused the park for traces of the man in the English cap. He was nowhere to be found. Emily opened the note and read its contents.

I need a computer to understand this note.

After throwing the bag of empty cups back in the trash, she walked toward the park exit. She paused to watch the medics cart David to the ambulance. His body was draped with a white blanket. She fought back her emotions as she struggled to keep her composure.

"I can do this," Emily stated to herself. She pulled out her phone.

"Sufferton & Waine. This is Mary. How can I help you?"

"Mary, hi, it's Emily. I'm really not feeling well today. If anyone asks for me, please let them know that I'll be back in the office on Monday."

"I certainly will, Emily." She then added, "You don't sound like yourself. I hope you feel better."

"Thanks. I certainly don't feel like myself today," said Emily before ending the call and quickening her pace. She didn't want to linger in the area any more than she already had.

Chapter 22

FRIDAY. 9:12 AM.

Emily's hands trembled. David's death felt surreal. After leaving the park, she turned off her phone. Her choices were limited.

She felt overwhelmed and completely out of her element. The thought that the deaths of Mark and David were attributable to the Owen engagement would have seemed unfathomable if not for what she had just witnessed in the park and the voicemails from Mark.

Moments ago, she had made the decision to go forth with her rogue investigation. Since leaving the park, Emily began second guessing her decision. It made the most sense to speak to the police, but she didn't know anyone in the department and was wary of whom she could trust.

She began to aimlessly walk as she gathered her thoughts.

She found herself in front of a building she had seen innumerable times in movies and on television. She backed away to view it from a distance. The odd architectural choice always perplexed her. The square concrete block windows seemed more reminiscent of a library at a nondescript university than of a powerful agency in the heart of the nation's capital.

It sat directly between the White House and the Capitol Building. *I imagine some conspiracy theorists would claim its location wasn't random*, she thought.

After viewing the building, Emily realized there wasn't any obvious indication that it was the headquarters for the Federal Bureau of Investigation other than a small sign over the main doors. She passed in front of the building, but didn't approach the entrance.

She didn't know the best method to bring her claims to the FBI, but it seemed the most logical authority to approach. She didn't think the local police would be much help. Besides, claiming a congressman was involved in a murder plot might end up with her being institutionalized. The FBI would likely be more willing to listen and certainly better equipped to investigate such a claim.

As Emily continued to think, she found herself standing in the center of the Naval Memorial. It was bustling with vacationers commemorating their visit with photographs.

She frequently ate lunch there with coworkers. The circular memorial included a world map etched into a mass of gray two-tone granite. The darker tone indicated the vastness of the water throughout the globe, whereas the lighter tone represented land.

Emily's footing was firmly planted in the darker of the two granite tones. Lost in thought, she glanced around the memorial. The sun reflected off the water that slowly trickled down a seven-step circular staircase water feature which surrounded the map.

Her mind focused on the most appropriate words to support her accusation that her coworker was murdered. She knew if she wanted to get their attention, she would have to elaborate on what she'd found. The voicemails from Mark would provide some evidence.

She also had the flash drive that contained not only the client files in her investigation, but also the contents of Owen's personal computer. And then there was the coffee-stained note from David. She still didn't understand his cryptic message, but surmised that it likely contained enough information to start an investigation.

A light reflected from one of the fountains and caught her eye. She put up her hand to shield herself from the nuisance. Once Emily's eyes adjusted to the changing light, she saw *him*.

On a bench ten yards away, sat someone she had met just once before. Their ominous conversation still lingered in her head. The hand gesture she used to block the light had brought attention to her. The man with gray streaks looked in her direction. Their eyes locked for only a moment. *This can't be happening*, she thought.

Her mind raced as she tried to piece together a plan. *These people won't stop. They will either destroy my life or end it.* She had to get out of there. *He must have followed me from the park.*

As she backed away, she inadvertently bumped into someone taking a picture of his girlfriend, causing his camera to drop to the ground.

"I'm sorry," she said in a tone that didn't sound the least bit remorseful.

He flashed her a queer look as he bent to the ground. "The lens cracked!" he said after a quick examination. His girlfriend, who had been posing moments before, joined him.

"I'm... I'm sorry," Emily reiterated. She didn't have time to apologize. She started to walk away. The man she bumped tried to grab her arm.

"You're going to pay for this," he said. "This is an expensive camera." His voice rose in obvious anger.

Emily dodged his initial attempt, but the man firmly grabbed her arm the second time he reached for her. With her momentum impeded, she looked toward the man from the park. He had erased half the distance between them.

Her options were limited, and she feared what would happen if he reached her. The image of David's death flooded her head. She looked up at the man with the grip on her right arm and acted swiftly.

She reached over with her free hand to grab the man's expensive camera. Before he had time to protest, she lifted the camera out of his clutches and tossed it five feet in the air in one quick motion. The rash action caught him by complete surprise. He let go as he tried to catch it with both hands.

Emily spun away from the man. The motion of her body caused the man to fumble the camera, and it smashed to the ground. This time, the impact damaged more than the lens. He scrambled to inspect it.

"You bitch!" yelled his companion.

"Hey!" said the man with his attention fixated on the damage. "It's broken."

Emily didn't hesitate. She ran. The ruckus drew plenty of attention. She looked behind her to observe Oscar slow his pace.

Whatever plan he had for her had been thwarted by her actions. Surely, he didn't want to draw attention to himself while the crowd focused on her.

Her actions were being monitored more closely than she had realized. *How can I go to the authorities now?* Emily continued to run. She zigzagged through alleys and side streets for over five blocks in an attempt to lose anyone trying to follow.

Emily knew her life would never be the same.

Chapter 23

Emily leaned against the building in the alley with her hands on her hips. Her chest heaved as she tried to catch her breath. She was confident she lost Oscar. *Why would he follow me?* It was obvious that her life was in danger.

Now she needed to determine her next action. She tried to think about her situation objectively. She had spoken to David this morning. Oscar's people had obviously learned of his inquiries in Switzerland. They must have had him under surveillance.

That meant Oscar knew David had contacted Emily, which is why he had followed her to the Naval Memorial. The thought of someone following her scared her immensely and had serious implications. It meant she could not go home again because they would be looking for her there. She was on her own now.

Emily decided to change her patterns. She would need money to remain autonomous. After a quick stop at a nearby bank, she walked out with three thousand dollars in her purse. Without reliance on credit cards and with her cell phone turned off, she could eliminate any obvious paper or electronic trails.

Next, she needed to solve the puzzle of David's note. She didn't know how helpful it would be, but she needed to know what he had been trying to protect. What he wrote was completely useless on its own.

She sat in one of the nondescript cafes in Chinatown. It was only a twenty-minute walk from the park where David had been murdered, but it allowed her some anonymity. With three hundred dollars less in her pocket, she opened the laptop purchased at a pawn shop a few blocks away. Two prepaid cell phones sat unpowered in her purse. She would only use them when absolutely necessary.

Emily took out the piece of paper from David and smoothed it with her hands on the table. She flipped the paper over to examine the back. It was a receipt from the shop where he purchased his cup of coffee.

He must have known he was under surveillance, she thought. Emily's stomach tightened with guilt as she thought about his selfless act.

Written haphazardly on back of the receipt were two pieces of information.

The first was an email address. Emily was unfamiliar with it. The second contained a series of letters and numbers. *Likely a password, given that it included a capital letter, a number, and was longer than eight characters.*

Emily assumed that the email account housed the information gathered from David's Swiss contact. She pulled up the website for the email account and entered the login name and password from the receipt. An error message indicated the username and password did not match. She tried the password with different letters capitalized. Still nothing.

Emily tried every possible variation of the password, but received the same error. She tried the personal and email addresses listed in her phone directory. Nothing worked. She banged on the table in frustration. She took a sip of her coffee and tried to think. While typing lightly on the keyboard, she had an epiphany.

David knew he was being watched. He would likely conclude that his email accounts were compromised. He was smart. Very smart. His actions indicated he was protecting the data given to him. *He wouldn't leave it exposed on his email accounts or computer*, she reasoned. *He would hide it.*

"Cloud storage!" she said more loudly than she had intended. They would allow him to store information easily and securely from anywhere. "David, you're way too smart. I'm going to miss you, darling," she said to herself.

There were countless cloud storage options. Emily reasoned that David would have chosen one of the more well-known companies. After a few attempts, she found the account for the username and password. The website loaded. *That's exactly what he did.* She grinned. Emily successfully accessed his cloud storage account.

The next step would be to determine what he intended her to find. The cloud storage account contained over twenty folders with names that indicated the contents of each folder.

The categories ranged from various jobs he held, his undergraduate and graduate schools, and apparently some hobbies, given the titles. Nothing stood out. *Had he not had a chance to upload the information to the storage site? I hope I'm not going on a wild goose chase.*

Systematically, she opened the folders and searched the contents. The folders contained sub folders that housed a wide range of file types. *This isn't going to be easy.*

She went back to the main screen again. If I'm right about David, he would be deliberate in the placement of his documents, she thought.

Staring at the file folders, no specific one stood out. She opened the *Photography* folder, thinking that David never mentioned any such interest to her. It contained photos of his travels. While he seemed to have an artistic eye for photography, it was a dead end.

Reflecting on her relationship with David, she refocused her attention to the folders related to his graduate program, where they had met. The program's curriculum was neatly categorized into various sub folders. A few stood out from the rest. They were titles from classes she didn't immediately recognize. She investigated those folders, but didn't find anything of interest.

Emily reviewed documents contained in his *social* folder. She spent a fair amount of time getting to know him at happy hours and recruiting events. She again didn't find any document of interest. She decided to refill her coffee so that she could take a quick break and clear her head.

After many fruitless searches, Emily looked at her watch. It was nearly two o'clock. She was hungry, but not in the mood to eat. She let out a sigh as she reflected on her relationship with David. *There's something I'm missing,* she thought.

A random thought entered her head. David overused a certain phrase when they spoke. It was habitual and she hardly noticed it after a while. She went to the main page on his cloud storage account and typed two words. *Nothing.* She typed the same two words but without a space between them. She tapped the return key in anticipation.

She felt a rush of blood to her head. Her query resulted in a single folder labeled *Darling*. She opened the folder and her heart sank. *This can't be it.* There were three scanned documents with nondescript names.

She opened the first PDF file. An image in the upper corner of the file caught her attention. It was unmistakably the same insignia she saw stamped on the Uzbekistan investments.

She reviewed the document thoroughly. The low resolution indicated it was a scan. It contained an investment summary that listed all of the assets held in the Swiss account. The assets included various publicly held stocks and private stocks and totaled over forty million dollars.

One of the private stocks, Muruntau Gold Deposit, stood out from the rest. An Internet search indicated it was located in the Kyzylkum Desert of Uzbekistan. The region contained some of the largest gold deposits in the world.

There's my Uzbekistan connection!

The second document listed all of the historical transactions associated with the account. It included the purchase and sale of various interests in public and private stocks.

The third document, much like the first two, included the same insignia and account number. However, this document also included other account numbers. The main account number had twenty-one digits, while the other account numbers had only nine. From previous work engagements, she knew international bank accounts typically had thirteen or more digits. US bank accounts had nine.

Emily couldn't believe she had the documents in her possession. She needed to tread carefully with the information they contained. A plan of action began to materialize in her mind.

First, she needed to match the bank account number from these documents to the documents provided by the client. Emily had a hunch the twenty-one-digit account from the PDF document would match the account number she saw earlier in the week. This would necessitate a trip to the office. She didn't want to go back there, but it was unavoidable.

Next, she needed to reach out to the one banking acquaintance she had hoped to avoid.

Brent Gambel.

He wasn't the nicest person in her network, and was probably a complete alcoholic by now. However, he possessed two qualities that she needed. The most important was his banking knowledge. He worked at a major bank and had access to databases they could use to identify the individuals who owned the US bank accounts.

His other quality was his predictability. It was Friday. He hung out at the same bar every Friday night. This week would likely be no different. He typically left work around five thirty and was at the bar thirty minutes later to enjoy the happy hour specials.

Emily had gone on a couple of dates with him a few years back. His interest in her was unrequited, and their brief relationship had ended quickly, but also awkwardly. They hadn't spoken since. But now Emily desperately needed his help. The identities of the account owners might shed light on Owen's involvement. *Maybe a drink would calm my nerves*, she thought.

Before she left the coffee shop, Emily inserted a flash drive into the computer. The evidence uncovered today didn't tell the complete story, but it began the foundation for her investigation and needed to be preserved.

She copied the three documents to the same flash drive that held the files from Owen's computer. Before placing the drive in her pocket, she stared at it. "Is this really worth being killed over?" she asked herself. She thought about Mark and David. And the answer was clear.

Chapter 24

After Emily paid the driver with cash, she exited the taxi and stood in front of a dive bar in Adam's Morgan. The street bustled with groups of people seemingly wandering between the plethora of drinking establishments in the trendy part of town. A few people lingered outside the bar to converse with their friends. It was a typical Friday evening in the city.

Emily entered the subterranean bar and surveyed the room. Nothing had changed since her last visit. The nauseating scent of stale beer that permeated the air indicated the place was still in desperate need of a major cleaning.

She did note a major change in the patrons. The alternative crowd was now seemingly outnumbered by people in professional attire. *I guess some things do change*, she thought.

Stepping up to the bar, Emily ordered an ale before looking for Brent. He wouldn't be hard to find. After sipping her beer, she walked through the crowd and toward a pool table at the far end of the bar.

She stopped when she saw him. He chalked his cue stick while eyeing the table for his next shot. Brent loved to play pool. There were many high-end pool halls in the city, but he much preferred this place. The competition was unusually good, and the beer was cheap.

Emily sat at a table just outside of his line of sight to observe him. She enjoyed having a few minutes to herself to drink her beer. When Brent lined up a shot on the eight ball, he faced her. Their eyes met.

He smirked before confidently sinking the black ball with a bank shot. He grabbed the winning cash off the edge of the table, told his competitor the table was his, and casually walked toward Emily.

"*Jesus, fucking, Christ.* Look who decided to make an appearance in my part of town." He wasn't drunk, but Emily could tell he had a buzz. It would be necessary to feed him a few more beers to get what she wanted from him.

"Hey, Brent, how are you?" He hadn't changed much since she had last seen him. Tall, handsome, with thick, dark brown hair. Most women would be envious of his hair.

"Much better now," he said as he leaned slightly to greet her with a kiss on the cheek. He casually pulled the chair out and eased his nearly six-foot wiry frame into the rickety seat.

Brent leaned back and eyed her. After a few moments, he spoke. "To what do I owe this pleasure? I thought you hated this place."

"I do hate this place," confessed Emily after her eyes darted across the room. "Can we just drink a bit, first? I need some time to decompress."

Brent didn't immediately respond, then said with a dry smile, "You don't have to twist my arm. It's been a while since I've had your company."

"Don't get any ideas. This is strictly business." Then she added, "Although, the beers are welcome."

He drank what little beer remained in his glass in one gulp. "I'll get another round." Brent got up and strolled past a half dozen small tables before disappearing into the crowd.

When he returned, they sat drinking beers at the small, wobbly table for over two hours. They played a couple games of pool as they began to get reacquainted. Emily had always enjoyed the game and had spent her fair share of happy hours playing it with coworkers.

"So what really brings you here? It's good to catch up, but I know you're not here to shoot pool." Brent spoke with his hand habitually clutched to his glass.

"What do you mean?"

"You've scanned the room and looked over your shoulder a dozen times. Something's up. You always were a poor liar."

"I know. I'm trying to get better at it." Emily used to pride herself on the ability to play by the rules and succeed in her career. The recent events were conditioning her to shield facts and hide her true intentions.

"That's a strange aspiration. Seriously, strange."

"A lot has changed since we last saw each other."

"I guess it has," said Brent as he took more than a generous gulp of beer before setting his glass back on the table. "I get the feeling that you're evading the question. Do I need to ask again?"

"Always to the point, Brent. You certainly haven't changed."

He responded with a half-hearted shrug and a placid grin.

"The bottom line is, I need a favor," said Emily.

"That much I knew. By the way, the beers are on you tonight. I have a healthy tab at the bar."

"Fine."

"You're still evading the question," he said with a smile.

"Okay, I'll cut to the chase. I need help identifying the owners of a bank account."

"Is this legal or illegal? It doesn't really matter to me either way," he stated with an even tone. "I just want to know how deep you're into this mess and how much of a favor it's going to be."

"I'm not in any trouble, thank you very much. And I certainly don't need a lecture on legality from you," she added. "I just need information."

"Okay," he responded with outstretched hands. "Don't get your panties in a bunch."

"You know, I really don't miss that expression," Emily stated with a twinge as she looked down at the table.

"Well, stop lying to me. I know you're trying to get better at it, but don't try it on me. It just won't work."

"Stop talking to me that way! You're so fucking condescending!"

"Should I just leave now? This isn't going to get any easier. You came to me, remember? I think I at least deserve the truth."

"Fine," said Emily with a slight tone of resignation. After a long pause, she said, "One of my clients may be doing something illegal."

"Is that really supposed to be a revelation? It would be surprising if one of your clients *wasn't* doing something illegal." With a pause and a shrug, he added, "Go on."

"We found a Swiss bank account that had US bank routing numbers associated with it. We're assuming that the routing numbers will lead us to the individuals that own the account."

Emily was being intentional with her use of *we* and *us* in her language. She didn't want Brent to know she was essentially a one-person crusade.

She approached her discussion with Brent using the tactics taught by one of her past professors. He had preached the flow of information should be one way, if at all possible. Allow the flow of information in, but obstruct the outflow. If these rules were followed, one would likely have an advantage in a negotiation.

"I'm with you," said Brent as he polished off another beer. "How many digits were contained in the bank accounts?"

"Nine."

"Okay. That would indicate a US bank account. That's good. It's much easier for me to identify domestic accounts. Any information on international accounts is much more difficult to obtain."

"I knew you could help."

"It's not that simple," he stated, shaking his slightly raised index finger for emphasis. "There may be nested accounts with complicated ownership structures. Wealthy people are particularly good at hiding money, whether it be from the government or their spouses," he quipped. "Where there are deep pockets, there are lawyers and consultants," he added with a half-laugh.

"Ha-ha. I know. Everyone hates lawyers."

"And consultants. Please don't forget the consultants. No one knows what they do, but their fees are outrageous and often unjustified."

"Okay. You can stop now."

"Sorry," he said after he sarcastically cleared his throat. "How much money is in the account?"

"Over forty million."

"Not to be flippant, but that's all? That may be a lot of money to you or me, but in the spectrum of wealth, that's not very much."

"I know. It's not about the money."

"Honey, it's always about the money."

"In this case, it's not," said Emily as she tapped her finger on the table to help make her point. "At least, I don't think so," she added thoughtfully.

"Hmm, interesting... not sure I buy it. Go on, though."

"What's more important is who owns it."

"Why?" asked Brent.

"Politics. They own something they're not supposed to own."

"What do they own?"

"Investments hidden in tax havens."

"What do you mean?"

"They own stocks or interests that are housed in international accounts, where they don't pay taxes on the gains."

"So what?" replied Brent. "A lot of people use tax havens."

"These interests could be toxic for their political careers."

He made a facial expression and casually nodded as he processed her words. "And who exactly do you think owns this account?"

"One is my client. But, apparently, there's a consortium of owners. I've only been able to see a small part of the puzzle. We need visibility on the account owners to help us understand everything."

"A Consortium," said Brent in a questioning tone. "Sounds serious. Tell me more about this Consortium." He gave her a childish smile.

"This is not a joke. Come on, I need you to be serious for a moment."

"Sorry. I couldn't resist."

Emily's experience as a consultant had trained her to identify irregularities in data and create a complete picture with limited information. Her instincts told her there was much more than what she initially saw. *The deadliest icebergs lie beneath the surface*, Terrance often said.

"What exactly do you need from me?" Brent asked.

"I need someone to go with me to my office."

"I don't follow. Shouldn't you have access to your own office?"

"Yes, I do, but it's not that simple. There are people monitoring my movement."

"Okay, this just got considerably scarier. You know that I'm a banking guy, right? I had some ROTC training in college, but I'm certainly not a *bad ass*."

"I just need someone," Emily stated in her most feminine tone.

"God, you're pulling the *innocent female* card. That's really not fair. Besides, you're really not much of a debutante."

"Fuck off," Emily said with a playful smile.

"Exactly my point," Brent stated, laughing.

"Are you going to help me or not?"

"Don't you have a boyfriend to play this role? You are seeing someone, I assume."

"Yes, but it's complicated."

"That seems to be the theme of the night, *complicated*."

"He's not available. Let's just leave it at that. So, are you in?" she said with a large, embellished smile.

"What's in it for me?"

"I got the beers tonight, is that not enough?"

"No," replied Brent as he slowly shook his head back and forth. "Not even close." He presented an empty glass.

"*Pleeeeease*," she said, drawing out the word. "Besides, I know you're going to do this in the end. You'd feel horrible if something happened to me."

"I'd feel even worse if something happened to *me*," he jested. "Fine, I'll do it. Just please stop batting your eyelashes. It's really disturbing."

"My femininity is disturbing to you?" she said with her hand on her hip, still trying to accentuate her inner female.

"Whatever you're doing now," he said with his finger rotating in a circular manner while pointing at Emily, "needs to stop. I'll do anything to make this stop."

"Fantastic! Now you need to sober up. We're taking a trip to the office early tomorrow morning. We need to go when there won't be anyone there."

"Early in the morning? Fine. I'll sober up after the next round," he said, then got up from the table to retrieve two more beers.

"Sounds good to me," said Emily. She lifted her half-empty glass to her lips. It weighed a ton.

Chapter 25

SATURDAY. 4:50 AM.

Emily spent the night in Brent's bed, while he retreated to the couch. She woke up feeling surprisingly well-rested. She typically disliked the morning, but today was different. Her determination to know the truth was like a drug fueling her.

Emily quietly entered the kitchen. She toasted some bread and brewed a pot of coffee. The smell appeared to wake Brent, as she heard him fumble off the couch and gradually appear in the kitchen of the one-bedroom apartment.

"One of those smells good," he said sarcastically as he scratched his head. "What time is it, anyway?"

"It's almost five," she said as she poured some coffee into a cup and handed it to him.

"Thanks. I guess I'll have some toast too." He took a knife and scraped off the slightly burnt top layer before smearing it with a generous amount of orange marmalade.

"How are you feeling?" she asked.

"A bit groggy, but I'll be fine after some coffee. Are we really going to your office today?"

"Yes. As soon as you're dressed."

"I was really hoping this was a ploy to get into my pants," he quipped as he took a bite of the toast.

"Just eat your toast. I'll get ready." Emily wanted to ensure he was focused and didn't get sidetracked. *It should be a quick trip*, she thought.

Before she left the room, she turned around. "Thanks, Brent. I do appreciate you coming along. It helps having someone with me. A lot has happened over the past week."

"Sorry I'm such an ass. I really do care, though, which is why I'm going with you." The sincerity of his comment surprised Emily.

Brent's apartment was located in Arlington, just across the Potomac River from downtown Washington. The sky was pitch-black when they left. *The sun won't rise for another two hours*, she thought as the taxi crossed a bridge that led to DC.

She thought of Scott as the cab passed by Clyde's in Georgetown. She hadn't reached out to him since she turned off her phone. *I'll call him tonight when he's back in town.*

The taxi dropped them off two blocks from the office. As expected, the streets of Washington were empty. To Emily's relief, there weren't any cars parked on the block in front of her office building.

She knocked on the glass door. The doors were locked on the weekend and required a key card to open, but she didn't want to leave any evidence of her trip. An older gentleman with white hair greeted her.

"Can I help you?" he asked through the glass door, before he adjusted his glasses. "Oh, hi, Miss Hendricks."

He opened the door. "I usually work the nights and weekends. It seems like we always have the same schedule," he added in his Southern Virginia drawl.

"Thanks, Carl. I forgot my key card. Can you get me into the office?"

"The weekend security guard knows you by name?" whispered Brent. "You need to work less," he added in his regular voice.

Shut up, Emily mouthed to Brent as she waved him off with the back of her hand.

"I'm really not supposed to, you know. But rules are meant for other people," Carl said as he laughed slowly. He was always nice to her and often mentioned how she reminded him of his granddaughter.

"And I assume he's with you," Carl added in reference to her companion.

"Yes, I'll sign him in. He's a client on an important case," she said with a quick wink to Brent.

"Sure thing, Miss Hendricks." Carl rummaged through a drawer and pulled out a key card with her firm's logo on back. "From the lost and found," he said and handed it to her. "It's been here all week," he continued. "Someone found it on the street, just in front of the building. I notified HR, but no one's been by to pick it up. I'm assuming he won't miss it today."

"Thanks, Carl. You're a lifesaver," she said as they walked away. Emily touched the key card to the elevator bank. She hesitated before turning the key card over. On the back side, she saw Mark's picture. As she waited for the elevator door to open, she clenched her eyes shut and let out a small sigh. She still hadn't accepted his death.

"Always nice to see you, Miss Hendricks. Enjoy the rest of your day," Carl said as he picked up a book from behind the desk. He removed the bookmark and began reading, oblivious to the outside world.

In the elevator and lobby, Emily made a concerted effort to avoid facing the security cameras. It was likely a futile effort, but she was compelled to try.

Emily stepped out of the elevator and suddenly had an overwhelming urge to flee. She willed herself forward without showing any signs of hesitation to Brent.

"Nice digs," he blurted. "What do you do for a living again? Maybe I should give you a second chance."

"Seriously, shut up," Emily said. "Just follow me. I want to get out of here as quickly as possible."

"I don't want to be here either," he replied as they walked down the hall toward Emily's office. Once there, he leaned against a wall while she flipped through a stack of documents.

"I don't mean to butt-in, but you seem to be making quite a mess. What are you looking for anyway?"

"I'm not sure," she said. Emily looked up to meet his eyes before she spoke next. "I just know I must have missed something before."

"Honestly, we're here because of a hunch? What, are you a detective now?"

His comments were a reminder why their relationship never found stable ground. "Your sarcasm isn't helping. Just give me a few minutes to think," she said without looking up from the desk. "The kitchen is down the hall and past the elevator bank. Take whatever you want."

"Food? Works for me." He headed to the kitchen.

Emily welcomed the silence. She systematically went through the files in her office and placed any document that warranted further investigation in a spare laptop bag she kept in her office. She was dismayed with the small number of documents she collected.

Next, she paid a visit to Mark's desk. His voicemail had stated he housed the original documents there. She found a neat stack of documents related to the engagement on the corner of his desk. They appeared to have been undisturbed since his death. She placed them in her bag.

Emily needed to access the electronic information contained on the firm's network too. All of the files in the conference room had been scanned to the client folder. A fresh look at the files might reveal some information she had previously missed.

Emily didn't have her laptop, but the administrative assistants had desktop computers. Emily knew the exact computer to try first.

She walked directly to one of the cubicles in the corner of the building. It was located in front of the row of partner offices on the south side of the building. She sat down and turned on the computer.

She looked around the neutral-gray walls of the cubicle. They were plastered with pictures of a small, gray Scottish Terrier. The dog was dressed in raincoats, Halloween costumes, birthday hats, and other ridiculous outfits. Many of the photos included the dog's owner, Clair. "What's wrong with people?" Emily said to herself when she saw a photograph of Clair and the Terrier wearing matching Christmas sweaters.

When prompted for a password, Emily typed the name of Clair's dog, "Wiggles," with only the first letter capitalized. *Animal people are so predictable*, she thought after the computer instantly unlocked.

Emily inserted her flash drive and began transferring the entire Owen engagement folder. The "time to complete" icon indicated the transfer would be completed in just over six minutes.

Emily was performing a cursory review of the documents Mark flagged when she heard a loud bang from the break room. She instinctively lowered herself to the ground. The commotion got louder, and Emily retreated under the desk. She reached up to turn off the computer monitor.

Emily heard signs of a struggle, but couldn't make out any distinct words or sounds. A moment later, she heard footsteps of someone running down the hall.

"Leave me the fuck alone!" said a voice. It sounded like Brent's, but she couldn't be certain.

"Stop or I'll call the police," said another voice. She strained to listen, but the voice was too faint to recognize. Emily heard the struggle continue in the hall. She felt the cube shake after a loud thud, along with glass shattering. The commotion abruptly ended.

After what seemed like an eternity, she heard a voice. "Emily, let's get out of here!"

Upon hearing Brent's voice, Emily got up from under the desk and turned on the monitor. *Still ninety seconds to go.* "Just a minute," she replied.

"Stop. You're crazy. You're a consultant, not the FBI. Don't be stupid. Let's go."

Emily peered around the corner to see a motionless body on the floor at the far end of the hallway. A pool of blood circled the head. Brent held a marble vase in his hand. There was a shattered mirror resting on a sharp angle against the wall with shards of glass on the floor.

Emily cautiously approached the scene. She stopped when she saw the face of the man lying on the floor. She put her hand to her face. "Shit! I know who that is."

Chapter 26

SATURDAY. 6:54 AM.

Brent stood in the hallway, adjacent to the body on the floor. Emily fought to process what she had just witnessed. This was her place of work and not some random street corner. Everything about it felt unreal, like a nightmare from which she couldn't awaken.

"I clocked him!" Brent said in a surprisingly boastful manner. "I really did! I was running, he was following, and I just picked up this vase from the table." He paused as he played the act out for her. "I swung it behind me as hard as I could, like this. He ran right into it!"

"Jesus," replied Emily, more to herself than in response to him.

"His head crashed directly into that mirror," said Brent with a gesture toward the wall. "What the fuck?" Emily could see the self-realization of his actions materialize in his head. "What do we do now?"

"I don't know," stated Emily stoically. She continued to stare at the body just a few feet away.

"What do you mean, *you don't know?*" Brent was shaken up and becoming anxious.

"I just don't know. Let me have a minute to think. Let's both calm down."

"Who is this guy?" Brent asked as he regained his composure. He bent down to examine the body further. The face was half covered in a pool of crimson. The blood continued to drip slowly down his cheek toward the ground.

Even if she hadn't seen his face, the custom-tailored Italian suit would have been enough. "I know him," she admitted. "He works for Owen. He's his right-hand man, Ben Nelson."

"He's your client?" asked Brent with an incredulous expression.

"He works for my client."

"Who exactly is your client? You mentioned something about politics last night. Owen—wait, Owen Templeton?"

"Yes."

"The congressman that's been all over the news since Thursday. That's your client?"

"Yes."

"This just keeps getting worse." He looked again at the body. "What was he doing here?"

"I don't know," she replied. "I really don't," she added after Brent furrowed his eyebrows.

"Why would he attack me?"

"I don't know," she said. "Did he have a gun?"

"What do you mean did he have a gun?" said Brent.

"He had a weapon the last time I saw him."

"That doesn't provide me any comfort." He reached down to the body and opened the suit jacket to reveal a semiautomatic pistol. "And there it is. Wow," he said as he let out a large breath of air from his lungs. He withdrew his hand from the man and rubbed the back of his head while he surveyed the scene. "We're in a lot of trouble."

"Let's try to keep our heads. It sounds like you acted in self-defense. Tell me exactly what happened."

"He came in the break room and asked if I'd seen *Emily*. He obviously thought I worked here. I told him I hadn't seen you and began to walk away. He approached me again in the hallway."

"And that's it?" Emily asked.

"No, let me finish. He came up to me and I panicked. I told him I didn't work here and he reached out to me. I didn't know what he wanted. I caught him by surprise, and we just started to wrestle in the hallway." Brent spoke with overly emphatic hand gestures as he described the scuffle.

"He's strong, but I was able to get free and he chased me. Did I do the right thing? I mean, by hitting him with a vase?" Brent glanced at the vase, which he still clutched in his hand.

"Of course. I would have done the same thing." Emily told him what she thought he needed to hear.

The body on the floor twitched. Emily flinched. "He's moving. We need to get out of here!" she exclaimed. She backed away from the body and bumped into Brent. Clutching Brent's arm for support, she added, "I'm glad he's okay, but we can't linger."

"I'm with you," said Brent as he bent over to put the vase on the ground. He wiped off his fingerprints with his shirt sleeve before standing up.

Emily watched his act. When their eyes met, he added, "Just in case. I really don't want to go to jail. I'd be somebody's bitch in less than twenty-four hours. I wouldn't do well in jail." He mumbled the last sentence to himself.

Emily grabbed the flash drive from the computer and her work bag before they retreated down the hall. They exited the floor through the stairwell located near the elevator bank to avoid anyone else who might be around.

Only one exit didn't have an alarm. Brent cautiously opened the door that led to the lobby. He peered out in both directions. "Coast is clear," he stated. As they approached the security desk, Carl looked up from this book.

"One of your coworkers is looking for you," Carl began. "He said he's working on a case with you, but forgot his key card. I called your work extension, but you didn't answer. I assumed you were in a conference room or something, so I sent him up. I hope that was okay."

"It was. Thanks, Carl," she said as she hurried past him. She didn't want to get caught up in a conversation.

"Enjoy the rest of your weekend," he said as she exited the building.

They made their way down the street and ducked around the corner. Emily looked behind them. She didn't see anyone following. The sun still hadn't made an appearance, and they had no place to go. She stopped to get a better look at her companion.

"Are you okay?" she asked.

"I think I'm all right."

"Let's clean you up." Emily took out a tissue from her purse. She lightly wet it with her tongue and began carefully wiping Brent's face.

"I said I'm okay." He tried pulling away, but Emily tugged him closer.

"You can't go around with blood on you," she insisted as she kept wiping.

"Shit, I have blood all over me. It's not even mine."

"Don't worry. It's just a few dots. You'll be okay," she said with a small smile. "Thanks for coming with me today. I don't know what I would've done if I'd been there by myself."

Brent offered an awkward smile. "No problem."

"If you weren't so fucking stupid, I'd kiss you," Emily added with a stoic expression in an attempt to diffuse the severity of their situation.

"Come on, be serious." The smile slipped from his face. "I didn't just kill someone, did I?"

"You saw him. I think he'll be okay, but with one hell of a headache," she said with a laugh.

"I totally clocked him," he said. "I can't go home now, can I?"

Emily knew Brent had just realized the totality of his actions. "No, I don't think you can," she replied.

"When you mentioned you were in trouble, I had no idea it was this serious."

"Neither did I," said Emily. "I'm not sure I believe me. Even now, everything seems surreal." They both began walking down the street, distancing themselves from the altercation at the office.

"Where do we go from here?"

"I need to get in touch with Scott." She stopped walking and pointed directly at Brent. "You need to finish your work. We need to understand who owns those accounts."

"I'm really in this mess, huh?"

"I need you, but only if you want to be here. I completely understand if you don't. I won't hold anything against you if you go to the police. I mean it." She looked directly into his eyes, waiting for an answer.

"No, I can't leave you." Brent's eyes drifted momentarily to the ground. He stepped toward her slowly. "But I'm not going to lie, this isn't my forte."

"Mine either." She laughed as she playfully patted him twice on his cheek.

"So, what next? Where do we go now?"

"We need to split up."

"That doesn't make sense. I said I'm not leaving you."

"You have to," Emily replied with a sense of urgency. "Listen. I turned off my phone and withdrew money from an ATM to stop them from electronically tracking my movements. You should do the same. If we're smart, we'll be okay."

"Are you sure you're not an FBI agent? You seem to know what you're doing."

"I just value my life, and I'm not taking any unnecessary chances," she replied. Brent gave her a disapproving look. "Besides the risks I've already taken," she added.

"Okay. I'll head to a buddy's house and use his laptop. I know a way I can access my work databases remotely and with complete anonymity. It might get me in some trouble, but it's a little too late to worry about that." He let out an awkward laugh. "How do I get a hold of you if your cell phone is turned off?"

"I think email would be best." Emily reached into her purse to retrieve a pen and paper. She wrote down two nonsensical email addresses she reasoned they wouldn't have a problem creating later. She copied both addresses to the bottom portion of the paper.

She ripped the paper into two and handed him one. "Here you go. You take the top email and I'll take the bottom. Memorize them and destroy the paper. We don't want any connections to one another," she said.

"Wow, this just got real. Very real."

From the expression on his face, Emily knew he needed some additional words of encouragement. "Be efficient, but be careful." Emily looked directly into his eyes as she spoke. "We want to find who owns these accounts. When we have concrete proof, we'll go to the media. Once there's a public record, there's no way they can stop it. Then, we'll be safe."

"Why can't we approach someone now?"

"We could, but no one's going to believe us, or even listen to us, unless we have proof." The conviction in Emily's statement almost convinced her the plan was that simple. Almost.

After they parted ways, Emily stopped and leaned against the wall. She needed to catch her breath. She bent over and began to hyperventilate.

What the hell am I doing? "Stay focused," she said to herself as she let out a deep breath. "This will all be over soon. It'll be okay." She didn't believe her own words.

Emily took another moment to compose herself. She adjusted her untucked shirt with a quick tug on the hem and repositioned her purse strap. Once ready, she began to walk with her head down.

Her next move needed to be calculated. Too much had already happened outside of her control. She needed to regain the high ground. She told herself again that everything was going to be okay. Her world felt like it was falsely held together with hope.

Chapter 27

SATURDAY. 4:38 PM.

Emily had spent nearly the entire Saturday in the lobby of a boutique hotel. She attempted to blend with the other people enjoying their weekend, but felt severely out of place.

She had focused the bulk of her attention on the documents retrieved from her office, but also reviewed the other materials she possessed from a fresh perspective. She tried to make sense of everything. There was a lot to digest.

Emily reached a breaking point and decided to pack her bag. She needed to be ready to go. With her bag on her shoulder, she pulled out one of the two disposable phones to dial Scott's cell number. He didn't answer, and she didn't leave a message.

Emily checked her voicemail messages using her personal cell phone. She had three unread messages. The first was from Scott, dated yesterday afternoon.

"Hey, Emily, it's Scott. I haven't heard from you in the past couple of days. I'm sure you're busy at work. I'm still out of town, but will be back on Saturday. Give me a call so we can get together. I think we need to talk about the other day."

The second message was from Terrance, dated two hours ago. "Hello, Emily. I heard that you weren't feeling well on Friday. I just wanted to see how you're doing. I'm at my country house and won't be back in DC until Monday night for a shareholder's meeting. I wanted to touch base with you on the Owen engagement. Give me a call with an update. We need to wrap this up. I hope you feel better."

Emily wanted to tell him the truth. She just didn't know how. She valued Terrance's friendship and knew he would try his best to help. People who worked for him appreciated his loyalty and often returned it without restraint. She'd seen numerous instances where he sided with an employee though it had caused friction with a client. *He certainly would side with me, right?*

The third voicemail message began to play. The time stamp indicated the voicemail had been left only thirty minutes ago. She selected the play icon. "Emily, it's Scott again. I thought that you might have lost your phone or something since I haven't heard from you in a few days. I've tried calling a few times, but you never pick up. I hope you're not mad at me. If you're ready, let's talk. Give me a call when you get this message. I'm at work now, but will be at Clyde's tonight even if I don't hear from you. I need some time away from work. I'll be watching the game. Hope to see you there."

She erased the last message from Scott, but kept the first two. If someone was monitoring her messages, they would likely be doing so intermittently, she reasoned. *Hopefully, it'll be safe to meet up with him,* she thought. She just told herself she would be very careful.

She turned off both phones and exited the hotel. If someone was trying to find her, they would be able to locate her from one of the calls she made. Emily began the thirty-minute walk toward Georgetown.

She sat at a coffee shop across the street and a few doors down from Clyde's. Emily checked her watch for the tenth time in twenty minutes—quarter to seven. The hockey game tonight was scheduled to start in fifteen minutes.

Scott should be walking by any time now, she thought. He always took the same route through Georgetown. His office was only a fifteen-minute walk away.

Emily kept her eyes fixed on the sidewalk in front of the window of the coffee shop. It looked like it was going to rain again. The white, billowy clouds from earlier in the day had turned into a gray overcast sky. She wore a dark brown jacket purchased at a thrift shop near the university campus in an attempt to throw off anyone who might be looking for her.

Emily picked up the coffee cup and cradled it in both hands. The hot liquid warmed her fingers. She blew gently on the dark black liquid while steam slowly rose out of the cup. She resisted the urge to check her watch again.

Across the street, she recognized Scott's coat. The camel hair stood out amongst the sea of black coats. He walked directly under a streetlight in the direction of the restaurant.

She waited a few minutes before following him. She half expected to see either Oscar or the black man who killed David.

Satisfied no one was following him, she buttoned her coat and threw her purse over her shoulder like a messenger bag. Then, she strategically draped the hood of her coat to partly cover her face and zigzagged through the traffic to the other side of the street.

As expected, the restaurant was busy, but not at capacity. Emily looked around, but didn't see Scott. Their usual table was occupied by university students. She saw Tom tending the bar. He wore his typical starched button-down shirt with a plain black tie tucked into his shirt just above the belt. She approached him.

"Hey, Tom," she said with a forced smile.

"What's up, pretty lady? What are you doing here on a Saturday evening? Here to catch the game?" He spoke without making eye contact as he worked behind the bar. He tapped a draft beer handle to stop the beer flow just before it reached the top of the glass. He set the glass aside to allow the foam to settle.

He then grabbed a glass from under the bar and placed it over another glass he had on top of the bar. Tom lifted both glasses in tandem and shook them vigorously before separating the glasses and pouring a cranberry-colored liquid into a chilled one. He placed both the beer and the martini in front of two smiling patrons at the end of the bar.

"Sorry," said Tom after he made his way back to Emily. "What can I get you?" he asked as he placed another three drinks on a tray that was quickly whisked away by an attractive waitress.

"An IPA, if you wouldn't mind. Hey, have you seen Scott?"

"No, I haven't. But we've been busy. A bunch of college football games today, and now we have a big hockey game tonight against Pittsburgh."

"I was supposed to meet him here. I thought I saw him ahead of me on the street."

"Check the main restaurant. Maybe he couldn't get a seat here." Tom placed the drink in front of Emily. With a sincere smile, he added, "On the house. Nice to see you on a Saturday."

"Thanks, Tom," she said as she took her first sip. Emily scanned the room. There were a couple of free seats at the bar, as well as an empty booth. *He would have chosen one of the seats in this room*, she thought.

Emily perused the restaurant side of the establishment. There were two dining rooms, interconnected by a hallway, which also housed the restrooms. The kitchen was located at the far end of another corridor.

Emily walked back to the bar and scanned the room again. *Shit, something isn't right*, she thought. Feeling apprehensive, she shifted her weight from her right to left leg.

Something caught her attention at the corner of her eye. It made her momentarily lose her breath. She wanted to scream, but instead found the fortitude to steady herself by leaning against the bar.

Emily lifted her glass slowly. She looked into one of the elegant mirrors that acted as a backdrop for the bar. She saw the man again. Her spirits were crushed.

The pint glass slipped slightly in her hand as her perspiration mixed with the glass condensation. She tightened her grip to prevent it from falling. Emily gingerly set the pint glass on the bar with white-knuckled hands.

It was the man from the park. The one who killed David. His image was etched in her brain. From his vantage point, he could see anyone enter the bar, as well as anyone coming from the restaurant side. Emily was trapped. *He definitely saw me*, she thought.

He wasn't there when she first entered the restaurant. Emily was certain of that. He had the same English cap he wore the other day. *What is he doing here?* She thought. *Where is Scott?*

She picked up her beer and took a small swig to appear as if she was casually waiting for someone. She placed her drink on the bar.

Emily knew she had one advantage, and only one. He didn't know she recognized him. If he knew she had seen him at the park, he wouldn't have been so cavalier in his surveillance.

When Emily noticed a lull in ordering, she raised her hand to gain Tom's attention. He strolled over to her and silently acknowledged her half-full beer before handing her a menu. "Let me know when you're ready to order," he told her as he smiled.

He was about to walk away, when Emily grabbed his hand. The sternness of her grip must have surprised him. He turned to her and opened his mouth, but before he could say anything, she spoke.

"Wait," she said a bit more desperately than she intended. She tried not to look at the guy at the end of the bar. He would be watching her.

"Are you okay?" asked Tom inquisitively.

"Yes, I think so. Listen, Tom." Emily chose her words carefully. The man would be watching her. She knew he was dangerous and had no margin for error if she wanted to get away from him. "I don't know how to say this," Emily continued. "You have to trust that what I'm saying is true."

"I'm listening," said Tom as he shot her a concerned expression.

"The black man at the end of the bar is following me." Before Tom looked, she gave his hand a reassuring squeeze. "Don't look. Please."

"Okay," replied Tom with a drawn-out reply. "Is he a creep?"

"Worse. He killed a friend of mine and now he's after me."

"What?" His eyes indicated he didn't believe her.

"It's true. I'm not crazy," Emily added after Tom furrowed his eyebrows. "Trust me, please."

"Let's say I do," Tom began with a slightly skeptical tone. "The most logical move would be to keep him here and call the cops." He spoke plainly and convincingly. Emily derived his cool demeanor would have served him well in the military. "Are you on board with this plan?"

"No," Emily calmly protested. "That won't work. It's... complicated. He's *dangerous*, and I need to get out of here quickly. That's all you need to know." By the look in his eyes, Emily knew that she was losing him even more. "Please, trust me. You've known me a long time. I'm not a flake."

After a brief hesitation, he spoke. "No, you certainly are not. I never really understood your profession, but I understand it even less now. What do you need from me then?"

"I need a distraction so I can get out the back door. I'm assuming there is one, right? A back door."

"Of course," replied Tom slowly. "Just go down the long hall and exit through the kitchen. The door will be obvious. Are you sure this is what you want? I can handle myself." Tom patted his left arm confidently. Even though his white shirt covered his arm, an outline of a tattoo was evident through the thin fabric.

Tom continued, "I could confront him. He won't go anywhere until the cops come. This is DC, they'll be here in two minutes. It'll all be over quickly."

"Tom, he's too dangerous. I don't want you to get hurt. If you do what I ask, I'll be able to escape. I'm going to the proper authorities, trust me," Emily lied as she looked convincingly into his bright blue eyes.

"Scott would kill me if something happened to you," Tom pleaded.

"Tom, I'm going to do this with or without you. This is the only way, I promise. I wish there was an alternative. We're arousing suspicion. Are you in?"

"Fine. But I'll do the distracting my way," he said with conviction. "Are you ready?" he asked before he let go of her hand.

"Yes, I am," she lied again.

"I'm doing this against my better judgment." He gave her a perplexed expression. Like he was trying to figure out who she really was.

"I'll be fine," Emily said. She hoped she wasn't wrong.

"Keep an eye on me. You'll know when it's time." He took a paper napkin and quickly jotted down his phone number. "Call if you need anything. I mean it. Good luck," he added quietly.

Chapter 28

Emily leaned against the bar and uncomfortably shifted her weight back and forth as she waited for a sign from Tom. He filled drink orders and chatted with patrons. He appeared oblivious to the talk they had just a few minutes ago.

Time seemed to stand still. She did her best to casually watch the football game. She suppressed every urge to glance at the man at the end of the bar. Instead, Emily found herself watching Tom's actions behind the bar.

He showed up suddenly and placed a new pint in front of her. Before she could say anything, he winked. He proceeded to the end of the bar.

"Oh my God, I'm *sooo* sorry!" she heard Tom exclaim. Emily couldn't help looking over, as did most of the other people seated nearby. Tom began to mop up the beer spilled on the man with the English cap. "Here, let me help."

Tom then walked around the bar with a towel in hand toward the man. When he reached Emily, he gently tapped her waist as he squeezed by another patron standing near her. That was her sign.

Emily heard the mysterious guy speak for the first time. "No, that's quite all right," he protested in a thick Irish accent as Tom wiped his trousers and chair with the towel.

Emily walked away from the main bar. She tried not to draw attention to herself as she quickened her pace toward the kitchen. She got to the end of the room, where her exit was halted.

An elderly man in a wheelchair clumsily drove into the wall of the narrow entryway between the bar and dining area. He attempted to get out of the way, but inadvertently blocked the entire passageway. Emily couldn't go around him. She was stuck.

Tom continued his poor job of cleaning up the spilled beer. "I'm so sorry," he said again. He purposely placed himself in front of the guy to block his path. "The next round is on me," he added in a cheerful voice.

Emily couldn't help but look back at the bar. It was a mistake. The man stood while Tom continued to wipe the beer. She made direct eye contact with him.

There was no doubt to Emily he knew his cover was blown. The coldness of his stare sent a chill down her spine. The trained assassin had her directly in his sight. His expression reflected all of her fears.

Emily knew the man would act quickly, and she panicked. The old man apologized as he tried to move out of her way. She didn't have time to wait for him.

"I'm so sorry," Emily blurted as she placed her left foot on the seat between the man's legs. She lifted herself onto the wheelchair as she stepped on the armrest with her other foot.

People stared at her in absolute disbelief of her crass actions. Emily's plight continued when a bystander grabbed her torso to prevent her from climbing over the wheelchair. "Miss, stop what you're doing," spat the obstinate woman.

Emily ignored the woman's plea as she continued to climb over the wheelchair and managed to get free of her grip. "Sorry," she said to the confused man. She inadvertently kicked the woman in the face as she propelled herself awkwardly over him.

Emily's attempt to land on her feet failed when the woman made one last attempt to stop her and managed to get a hold of her ankle. Emily slipped from her grip, but fell headfirst toward the floor. She felt the wind get knocked out of her as the weight of her body compressed her lungs. She forced herself up from the floor. Unable to breathe, she stumbled down the hallway.

She heard the two men arguing. With a glance to the bar, she witnessed a partial view of the physical confrontation between Tom and the man in the English cap. Tom obstructed the man's path when he tried to pass the bartender. The man's motions were swift and direct when he punched Tom in three different places. One to his windpipe, one to chest, and last to his groin. Tom instantly collapsed to the floor and out of her vision.

The commotion seemed to immobilize everyone in the restaurant. It allowed her to more quickly make her way to the exit, but she knew it would do the same for the man in pursuit.

A waiter carrying a tray of plates stood in her direct path. Emily offered him an apologetic look before she deliberately pushed the tray up in the air with both hands. The dishes crashed to the floor with a loud noise as they smashed into pieces on the hard floor.

She looked back again to see the man in the English cap land in the hallway with a thud. He had jumped over the agitated man in the wheelchair, who was now waving his fist at the man. Unfazed, her pursuer pushed off the floor and onto his feet with surprising agility.

Emily opened her mouth to scream, but nothing happened. The air had not yet returned to her lungs. She disappeared into the kitchen. As she ran past a wall of neatly stacked plates and glassware, she pulled the entire wire rack shelf over.

Everything crashed to the ground and smashed into pieces. Her action caught the kitchen staff by surprise. No one made a move to stop her.

Emily slammed into the long, metal bar of the back door with all of her strength. It burst open and crashed against the outside wall with a loud bang.

She ran like hell out of the alley, using a small passage through a cluster of nearby buildings. It led directly to the main street of Georgetown, a half block down from the restaurant.

Emily headed toward the university campus, where she could blend in with the college population. She ran a quarter block, before something caught her attention from the corner of her eye.

She stopped. A man sat in a black sedan just two cars in front of her. A lit match illuminated the injured face of Ben Nelson. He grinned at her before extinguishing the match with a wave of his hand through the open window. It landed on the sidewalk, where it continued to smolder.

Ben stared at her as he took a hit of his cigarette. He waved his index finger to her as he blew the smoke from his lungs.

Emily told herself to run. Before she gathered the courage, the lights inside the vehicle turned on. Someone was slouched like they were unconscious in the back seat. She gasped when she recognized the person.

It was Scott.

"What's going on here?" she said to herself.

The car door opened and Ben walked toward her. "Emily, it's time for us to talk. This is beginning to get out of hand." He wore a hat, which partially covered the large bandage on the left side of his head.

"Stay away from me!" she yelled. "I don't want this anymore."

"Neither do we, but you just won't stop. How many more people need to get hurt because of your actions?"

"My actions?" she said incredulously.

"Yes, your actions," he replied.

There were people on the sidewalk, but none of them paid much attention to their conversation. Emily knew Ben would be reluctant to touch her with so many potential witnesses. Or at least she hoped.

She saw the man in the English cap enter the sidewalk from the alley she exited just a few moments ago. She stepped away from him, even though he was still a quarter block away.

"I see you've met *the Irishman*. A nice chap, as long as you remain on his good side." Ben smiled. "Get in the car. We'll have a nice chat, like adults."

"I'm not going anywhere with you. I've seen what you do. You won't get away with what you've done. You're a murderer," she added defiantly.

"Child, you really don't know everything. Get in the car so we can discuss this like civilized beings. It was a mistake to disappear like you did. You had some people worried. It was necessary to take precautions," he added with a nod toward Scott. "The ramifications will be extreme if you refuse." Ben made an obscure hand gesture at the Irishman.

Before Emily could react, sirens began to blare in the distance. She looked up to see blue lights approach the restaurant from both directions. *Someone must have called the police*, thought Emily, relieved.

She looked to the Irishman, but he had already disappeared. *He has a knack for that*, she thought.

"You'll be hearing from us, soon. Check your voicemail. I know you do." He grinned. "And watch your back. You won't be *protected* forever," he said ominously. "I'm sure the next time we speak we'll finally have your full attention." He got into the car and was quickly out of sight.

Emily didn't have time to think about what Ben had just told her. A crowd formed around the restaurant. She began to walk away.

Her head was dizzy from all of the emotions she felt. Her world had just fallen apart, and she had no idea how to fix it. *Why would they have Scott? What was their plan?*

So many questions needed answers. Answers she did not have. She was certain of one thing. She had struck a chord with her enemy. They were scared of something she possessed. She just didn't know what. She needed to re-examine everything and tread carefully.

Part III

Chapter 29

The Irishman surveyed his preparation with appreciation.

The condo owner's wallet, full of cash, had been placed on a narrow side table, adjacent to the front door. A decorative silver tray sat next to the wallet. On it, were a set of keys, some lose change, and a cherry-flavored Chapstick from the owner's pant pocket.

When he had arrived, the condo was surprisingly well kept. He had since redecorated. It now showed signs of a struggle between two acquainted people.

He proceeded to the living room to examine the evidence. Two couch pillows were haphazardly placed on the floor. A picture frame, which had been meticulously centered on the wall, was now crooked. The smallest details would be scrutinized.

In the kitchen, an open bottle of the condo's finest wine sat on the counter. The cork remained attached to the opener and sat next to the bottle. Only one-third of the wine remained.

Some of the wine had been poured into two wine glasses. The glass with lipstick had been purposefully smashed against the dining table to mask the lip pattern and to stain the beige shag rug under the table. The second glass, covered with fingerprints from the owner, had been delicately knocked over, but remained intact on the table.

A third wine glass with a generous pour lay on the counter away from everything else. He picked it up and walked toward the bedroom. He stopped in the hallway to view the pictures of well-known cities in France and Italy.

He recognized one of the photos taken in Montpellier. Pleasant thoughts of a dinner with a past lover in a subterranean restaurant came to his mind. He lifted the wine glass to his lips to take a small sip. He savored the taste and briefly closed his eyes while the memory danced in his head.

He entered the bedroom. Confident everything was in place, he found a comfortable position on a leather chair in the far corner. A motionless body lay on the bed.

His attention was drawn to the unusual artwork over the bed. It was a tastefully painted nude abstract of a woman without any distinguishable facial detail. The woman appeared to be lying on her back as she stretched her right arm away from her body and seemingly toward the body on the bed.

The Irishman crossed his left leg over his right as he focused on the beauty of the brush strokes. He took another sip of the wine before checking his watch.

After a few more minutes, he witnessed the body exhibit a slight movement. The Irishman casually enjoyed another sip of wine before setting the glass on the dresser. He approached the bed and positioned himself at the edge. He bent to his knees.

The body stirred again, but didn't wake. *Patience is a virtue*, thought the Irishman as he concentrated on his task. He picked up a boning knife he had placed on the nightstand earlier. He was most appreciative of the knife selection in the kitchen. Having the proper tools made his job more enjoyable.

The Irishman held the blade next to the back of the body, just below the left shoulder blade. He was careful not to touch the body.

The body moved once again. This time there was significantly more muscle movement. The body began to stretch as it woke up from its drug-induced slumber. He readied himself.

When the time was right, he expertly pushed the knife into the back, using only a third of his strength. The sharpness, coupled with the narrow blade, allowed it to penetrate the body with little resistance.

"Ahhh!" screamed the man in severe pain. He instinctively rolled over onto the blade, and it ripped open the wound.

The Irishman said nothing. He calmly got up from his position and stepped away from the bed. His work was nearly done.

The man screamed a second time. It was not as loud as the first scream. The heart, which had been partially punctured from the initial incision, was already failing. The weakened organ could no longer pump blood through the man's body.

He slowly crawled off the bed, trailing a river of blood from the gaping wound. After making it only three feet toward the door, he stopped.

Unable to move, the dark red substance pooled around him. The Irishman picked up a cell phone, which had been previously placed on the dressing table. He unlocked it using the man's four-digit pin number. He pressed three buttons and then *dial*. The phone rang four times before it was answered.

A concerned woman began speaking. "9-1-1 emergency services. Please state the nature of your emergency."

There was no answer as the Irishman carefully placed the phone in the hand of the man on the floor.

"Hello?" said the operator again. "Please state the nature of your emergency." After a brief pause, she added, "I can hear someone breathing. Please stay on the line."

After another pause, the operator continued speaking, "I will use the location services on your phone and alert paramedics of your location. They will be there soon. Please hang on."

The man's breaths became increasingly shallow, before they finally stopped. His eyes remained fixed on his cell phone, staring blankly at the background picture of him and his girlfriend at a New Year's Eve party.

The Irishman watched the crime scene create itself with immense satisfaction. He didn't need to worry about placing DNA or hair fibers at the scene. Given the level of intimacy between the would-be accused and the victim, it wasn't necessary. The blood and struggle created the story necessary to achieve his desired result.

While the operator continued to comfort the dead man, the Irishman collected his wineglass and quietly exited the bedroom. He walked down the hall and stopped when he reached the entryway.

After a small gulp, he placed the empty wineglass in a Ziploc bag and put it in a hand-crafted leather work tote. He carefully removed the blue surgical gown he wore and placed it in the tote. The tote was then placed in a FedEx box on the floor.

The Irishman viewed himself in a full-sized mirror in the entryway. He adjusted his nondescript blue jacket and removed the hair net from his head. He looked out the peephole before opening the door. Satisfied, he picked up the box and stepped out of the condo.

He removed his blue surgical booties and gloves, placed them in the box, and closed the lid. He casually strolled down the hallway as a blend of music and television echoed throughout. Instead of using the elevator, he opened the door to the stairwell. He knew most Americans would use the elevator, even in a four-story building. While in the stairwell, he removed his jacket, turned it inside out, and put it back on to expose a FedEx delivery jacket. He exited the building through the small loading dock that led to the alley.

There were many security cameras located throughout the building. He paid them no attention. The hard drive used to record the video had been removed earlier that day when he asked the doorman for assistance loading a couple of boxes from the curb.

He walked to his vehicle two blocks away. The Irishman placed the box in the trunk of the stolen car and slowly drove away. He was careful to obey all traffic laws. An ambulance passed his vehicle from the opposite direction. He put on his turn signal before disappearing from the crime scene.

Chapter 30

Emily showed up at Jen's unannounced just after midnight. She could have stayed at a hotel, but she wanted the comfort of a friend. Jen allowed her to stay the night without hesitation. She didn't even question Emily's ruse, an argument with Scott.

Emily woke up in the same clothes from the night before. She rubbed her temples as she lay on the couch in deep concentration. Mark and David's deaths weighed heavily on her mind. As did her guilt.

"Well, look who's up," said Jen as she entered the room carrying two glasses of orange juice. She handed one to Emily. Her designer nightgown seemed perfectly suited for the upscale Woodley Park condo.

Jen had a similar build and complexion to Emily. Their friends often teased that Jen was just a prettier version of Emily, but with blue eyes instead of brown.

They did have contrasting styles in fashion choices, though. Emily dressed for a professional office environment. Jen dressed in high fashion, which was evidenced by her two-hundred-dollar belts and four-hundred-dollar snakeskin shoes.

"Thanks, Jen," stated Emily. "That looks great."

"Em, it's just orange juice," she said with a small laugh. "I'm afraid this is all I have to offer." After a brief pause, she added, "I'm hungry. Want to get something to eat? There's a great brunch place just a few blocks away."

"I wish I could, but I really need to get going."

"We haven't even had a chance to talk," Jen said in a motherly tone.

"Thanks. I appreciate the offer. Things with Scott will work themselves out. I'm sure of it."

"It's not a burden. I could actually use the company."

Emily felt awkward. She was hungry, but she didn't want to involve Jen or burden her. Too many people had already been hurt.

"Jen, I wish I could, but I really need to get going."

"Where are you off to?" asked Jen inquisitively. "Is it for work?"

"No, I'm taking a few personal days."

"That doesn't sound like you at all, Em." She laughed.

"No, it doesn't, does it?" admitted Emily as she pursed her lips.

"I get it; you need to clear your head. When you missed girls' night the other Friday, I was worried. You're making me even more worried now. You can talk to me, you know. I'll listen."

"Why is everyone trying to be my mother?" Emily asked more emphatically than she intended. "I really don't need help."

Jen sat down on one of the two chairs across the couch from Emily. "Listen, I'm not trying to be your mother. God knows we all have one, and none of us needs another."

They both started laughing. "Jen, thanks, but I really think I need to be alone. There are just some things I need to deal with, personally."

"I understand, I really do. But you're a friend in need. I'm not busy at work. In fact, I have about three weeks of vacation I need to use this year or I'll lose it. Taking a day off for a friend in need actually helps me out too. It's a match made in heaven." She made her point with an exaggerated gesture toward the ceiling with her hands.

"Absolutely not, Jen." Emily was reluctant to draw Jen into her dangerous new world. She needed to get out of the apartment. "Listen, Jen—" she began.

"Stop right there, Em," said Jen. "I will not take *no* for an answer."

What did I do to deserve such friends? Thought Emily. She had never seen Jen so caring, and attributed her actions as being empathetic to her own out-of-character demeanor. Jen had never seen her like this before either. She smiled at her friend, which was immediately reciprocated.

"Well?" asked Jen. Her face indicated she was ready to listen.

"I don't know where to start."

"I'm all ears," she said.

Emily's head raced with thoughts. She reluctantly decided to tell Jen what had been happening to her. Knowing there was no good way to broach the subject, she just blurted words out. "I'm in trouble, Jen. Serious trouble."

"Okay, it can't be that bad," replied Jen.

"I'm serious. It's dangerous to be around me." She reached for Jen's phone, which lay on the coffee table in front of them. She turned it off and placed it back on the table.

"This is a side of you I haven't seen, I must admit."

"A lot has changed. I've changed. I've seen things that just can't be unseen."

Jen reached out her hand to comfort her, but Emily pulled hers away. Acknowledging her action, Jen made direct eye contact. Her expression changed. "You know I care, Emily. We may not be best friends, but we are friends, aren't we?"

"Of course. I just don't want you to get hurt."

"I'm not going to get hurt."

"David is dead."

She was surprised at the lack of emotion in her own statement. She reasoned her empathy had been dulled by all she'd been through. *Who am I?* The thought only stayed with her for a fleeting moment before she refocused on the conversation at hand.

"David from your grad school?"

"Yes, that David."

"What happened?"

Emily hadn't told Brent about the murders. He didn't need to know. But everything had changed now. She needed someone to help her think through her dire situation. She hoped it wasn't a mistake to open up to Jen. She trusted her friend's judgment and always thought her demeanor was well composed. Emily needed her strength more than she wanted to admit.

"I'm in way over my head. You remember that consulting engagement for Owen Templeton?"

"Of course. You mentioned you were working for the congressman at lunch last week. You're not sleeping with him, are you?"

"Hell, no," replied Emily indignantly.

"You're not pregnant, are you?"

"Stop. I told you I'm not sleeping with him. I haven't even seen him since the reception."

"What's the issue then?"

"I've uncovered evidence outlining a relationship between Owen and other individuals with investments in tax havens outside of the country."

"And?" asked Jen, furrowing her brow.

"It would be quite damaging to his presidential bid," replied Emily.

"How damaging is your evidence?"

"Very. Brent is helping to uncover who has direct ownership of the investments. He has access to some channels I don't. I had to reach out to him."

"Brent? Who's that?"

"He's an old acquaintance."

"You've never mentioned him before."

"We went on a couple of dates a while back. It never went anywhere."

"Okay," she replied as she appeared to process Emily's revelations. "What does this all mean? How does David's death figure into all of this?"

"David was murdered because of me." Tears began to form in her eyes. She fought them back. "I saw it happen."

Jen reached over the table to comfort her. This time Emily reciprocated by extending her arm. Their fingers briefly interlocked before Emily withdrew her hand to wipe away the tears.

"He was killed right in front of you?"

"Yes, but the killer didn't see me. His nickname is the *Irishman*. He's from Ireland, obviously. He's black with dark emerald eyes. I'll never forget his face. *Ever.*"

"How do you know his name? Have you spoken with him?"

"He followed me to the restaurant where I was supposed to meet Scott. He didn't know I would recognize him. That's the only reason I was able to escape. I showed up at your house that same night. *Last night*," she added for emphasis.

"This is crazy," said Jen. "What did Scott say when you told him?"

"I haven't told him everything. When I tried to tell him, he grew defensive and we just argued. I mean, he works for Owen. What did I expect? He doesn't know about David's murder, though. I was going to tell him last night."

"Who else have you told?"

"It gets worse. They have Scott and want me to back off. I don't know what they're going to do to him. It's a living nightmare." She elaborated on her encounter in Georgetown.

"What's there to debate? Just give them what they want," said Jen plainly.

"Listen. They killed my friend. They kidnapped my boyfriend. What do you think they'll do to me? Even if I comply, I don't believe I'll ever be safe. I'm just a loose end to them."

"I hadn't thought of that," said Jen. She tapped her finger thoughtfully on her lap.

"Make sure you keep your phone off," said Emily. She reached across the table to check Jen's phone was still off. "They were tracking me in DC. If they figure out you're involved, they'll track you as well."

"If they figure out I'm involved?" asked Jen as she glanced at the phone resting on the table. Her calm exterior appeared to be cracking.

"My only logical action is to finish the job. I have a lot of the puzzle pieces, but not everything. The evidence from Brent might be the final piece. I think it will link everything I've uncovered, but I won't know until I review it."

"What about Scott?"

"I don't know." Emily's eyes began to well up again. This time, she successfully kept her tears at bay.

Jen took a deep breath, then exhaled. "What can I do to help?"

"I can't ask you to get involved in this mess."

"You showed up at my doorstep as a friend in need. I'm not going to turn my back on you. We'll figure it out, *together.*"

"Jen, this is too dangerous. My life is in danger. Your life will be too. I don't know what's going to happen. I haven't even figured out my next move."

"Have you gone to the police?"

"I was going to go to the FBI."

"The *FBI?*"

"Yes, I thought they would be more helpful than the police."

"Yeah, I would think the same," she replied. "You said you were *going* to go. What stopped you?"

"One of Owen's henchmen spotted me at the Naval Memorial. I'd seen him once before. I had to run."

"You spoke with this man?" asked Jen. "Did you get a name?"

"Oscar."

"What did he look like?"

"Mid-fifties. Tall, with a heavy build. Gray streaks in his hair. Both times I saw him, he wore a black fedora. He was confident and intimidating."

"What did he say?"

"Jen, you don't have to help. I'm telling you, these people are dangerous."

"You've already said that more than once. I get it. But I'm still in. So, what's next?"

"We need to meet up with Brent," said Emily after a pause. "We'll then put the puzzle pieces together."

"I think I follow..." Jen added in an uncertain tone.

"I'll need to link the work from Brent with mine. Understand? I want to make sure that we have everything in order before reaching out to the media."

"The media?"

"I want to hurt these people," said Emily. A look of determination permeated her face. "What they've done is reprehensible. They need to be stopped. I'll use the information as leverage for Scott's return. Once they release him, I'll send what we've uncovered to major media outlets. They won't be able to undo it."

"That's bold."

"These people are monsters."

"Of course," agreed Jen. "I just haven't seen this side of you before."

"Why do you say that?"

"You've always been confident, but now you have an edge. It's surprising, that's all."

"I want to get Scott back."

"Of course. And it sounds like the right thing to do. I don't suppose it's going to be as simple as you make it sound, though."

"Probably not. But we have to try. Thank you for listening. And for believing." After her last word, a brief sigh escaped her mouth.

"Em, Scott will be all right. We'll get him back. Meanwhile, we can't trust anyone."

"Am I making a mistake by not going to the police? Be honest."

"Honestly? Probably, but we're in too deep now, and I don't know if they would believe you. Us."

Emily was surprised by her friend's use of *us*.

"How do we get a hold of Brent?"

Emily pulled the laptop out of her purse. After logging into the email account, she looked to Jen. "We created email accounts for communication. We didn't want to use any of the accounts we already had in case they were being tracked."

"Smart. I like it," she said with a nodding smile.

There still weren't any emails from him. "Nothing." Emily started typing. "I'll request a meeting." Her email was short. It listed the name of a coffee shop and a time.

"What if he doesn't show up?"

"He'll be there."

"And if you're wrong?"

"Then we're in serious trouble." *Like we aren't already,* she thought.

Chapter 31

SUNDAY. 1:29 PM.

The coffee shop was a short drive from Jen's condo. At Emily's direction, Jen parked her red Mercedes across the street. They sat in the car, watching the establishment.

Emily checked her watch. It was the designated meeting time, but there was still no sign of Brent. "He's not coming, is he?" Jen asked nervously as she looked out of the window.

"Let's give him time. He's usually late."

"That's another way of saying he's unreliable. What happens if he doesn't show up?" Jen tapped on the steering wheel to no apparent rhythm. Her attention remained fixed on the street in front of the coffee shop.

Emily didn't know the answer. "He'll show up. He has to."

"But what if he doesn't?" Jen insisted.

"We'll adjust our plan and go forward. We'll figure this out."

"You better be right. You've placed a lot of importance on his work."

"I know," said Emily. "I certainly hope it hasn't been a mistake."

Two cars passed their vehicle.

"I think that's Brent!" she cried. "In the grey car."

They intently watched. The grey car parked down the street from the shop. They didn't get a clear view of the individual that went in.

"Let's go find out," said Jen. She reached for the door handle.

"Wait. We don't know who could be following him. We need to exercise caution."

Jen made eye contact with her before examining the vicinity. "You're right. We should be careful."

Emily focused on the cars that immediately followed. A total of three cars passed within thirty seconds. Two were occupied by families.

The third car parked near the coffee shop. A middle-aged gentleman walked into a convenience store on the corner. After a couple minutes, the man walked out of the store, lit a cigarette, and drove off.

"I've been watching the door," she said to Emily. "No one walked in after him."

"Good. It doesn't look like he was followed," stated Emily. "But you never know. It didn't take long for them to figure out David was involved."

"Do you think it's safe to go in now?"

"I think so. But not both of us. I'll just go." Before she exited the car, she looked at Jen. "Maybe you should just go back to your condo. I'll get a ride from Brent."

"You're scaring me, Em."

"I don't mean to," Emily said.

"What should I do if something happens to you and Brent?" asked Jen. "Where are you keeping your evidence?"

"If something happens, live your life. Just let it go. These people are dangerous. I shouldn't have involved you in this mess in the first place. I'm sorry."

"Don't talk like that. Everything will work out. I'm not going anywhere. I'll wait for you."

As Emily approached the coffee shop, she lifted the hood to her coat to ward off a chill in the air. She walked cautiously, but confidently toward the coffee shop.

When she entered the store, she was immediately apprehensive when she didn't see Brent. Only five people were visible. An elderly man reading a newspaper, and some college students individually focused on their laptops.

A police officer walked away from the counter with a steaming cup of coffee. He gave her a secondary glance before easing his chubby physique into an oversize leather chair. Thoughts of the other night at Clyde's flooded her mind. *Where is he?*

Emily was about to walk out when she heard a door open. She looked over to see Brent exiting the restroom. She expected the worried expression he wore on his face to dissolve when he approached her. It only worsened.

"Brent, I'm glad you made it." She smiled at him. "When I didn't hear back from you, I thought you didn't get my message. I was worried." She reached out to embrace him, but the hug wasn't reciprocated. He gently pushed her to arm's length before he began to speak.

"I'm so sorry," he said.

"What is it?" Emily replied in a confused tone. She looked around, half expecting to see a familiar foe. "Did they get to you?" she asked. She took a step back, confused.

"You don't know, do you?" He spoke with saddened eyes.

"Know what?"

"We need to get out of here. It's not safe." He looked in the direction of the police officer. Brent gently put his face to hers and began kissing her. Emily attempted to protest, but he pulled her closer. His tongue reached hers for a brief moment. "I'm sorry," he whispered.

"Stop it. What's your problem?" she asked.

He reached down for her hand and embraced it like a lover would. "Don't talk," he said quietly in her ear. "We need to leave casually. Follow my lead."

Brent led them toward the door. She couldn't help but look over at the blue-clad man sitting in the chair. He had her in his direct vision. His head was angled toward his shoulder as he spoke directly into the radio attached to the front of his bulletproof vest.

"Brent," she said when the man lifted himself out of the chair.

"I saw it," he replied.

"Excuse me, *miss*," said the officer. Emily ignored him.

"Stop, police!" yelled the man. She heard a snap of a button being undone. With a quick glance back, she saw the officer standing with an un-holstered gun pointed in their direction.

The people in the room watched in stunned silence.

Emily felt Brent pulling her arm as he quickened his pace.

"I'm coming," she replied as he pushed the door open and began to run.

Emily signaled to Jen stationed in the car across the street and behind them. Jen appeared to understand their predicament as the powerful engine rocked the hood when it started.

Emily followed Brent as they ran down the street. The shop door opened behind them as the police officer gave chase. The man defied his physically unfit appearance with a quick sprint. The distance between the two parties shortened despite Emily's head start.

Jen's Mercedes sped past them. The car whipped into the entrance of an alley and screeched to a halt thirty feet ahead. Emily looked back to see the officer huffing, but still gaining.

"Forget your car!" Emily spat to Brent. "Into the alley," she said with a motion of her hand.

"Who's that?"

"Just go!"

They ran into the alley and leaped into the open passenger door of the coupe. After Emily jumped over the arm rest and into the rear seat, Brent closed the door.

Jen didn't wait for the passengers to get situated. She immediately jammed the gas pedal to the floor. Gravel shot behind the vehicle before the tires gained enough traction to launch the car down the narrow alley. Jen barely managed to avoid trash cans and telephone poles as she swung the steering wheel from side to side.

Emily peered over the bouncing rear seat to see the pursuer bent over with his hands on his knees at the entrance of the alley. He then moved his left hand toward the black device attached to his shoulder.

"He stopped," said Emily. "But I'm pretty sure he called for backup."

"What was that all about?" asked Jen. "Why are the police after you?" She looked directly at Brent.

"Just keep your eyes on the road," he replied. "And they're not after me. They're after *Emily*."

"What?" asked Emily in a bewildered tone. "What are you saying?"

Chapter 32

"Where are we going?" asked Jen as the red Mercedes exited the alley and randomly turned right. She maintained her aggressive driving to quickly exit the vicinity.

"Just drive!" barked Brent.

A voice came from the back seat. "I'm more concerned with why the police are trying to arrest me," Emily said. She reached forward to grab Brent's left shoulder. "Talk! What aren't you telling me?"

"We need a destination," interjected Jen. "The longer we're on the streets, the more chance we have of being spotted. Bright red cars are not very discreet."

"I agree," said Brent. "We need to leave DC. The police will be looking for *all* of us now. Shit," he added in frustration. "How am I going to explain this to my company? I'm a fucking fugitive, now." He banged his fist on the armrest.

"I know you both are frustrated," said Emily. "But I need to know what the hell is going on. Brent, tell me. Did they plant evidence?"

"This isn't about evidence," replied Brent. "Something bad has happened. That's all I'm going to say. Don't ask me to elaborate. Please."

Emily's mind raced. Before she could say anything, Jen spoke.

"Destination, people. I just saw a cop car."

"Is it coming after us?" asked Emily, looking out the window.

"I don't think so, but we might not be as lucky the next time. Where are we going?"

"Annapolis," stated Emily.

"Huh. Okay. That's where your uncle lives, right? Will he be there?"

"No, he lives in Los Angeles. But we can use his condo. He's rarely there."

"Won't the people looking for us go there?" asked Brent. "It seems an obvious place to check."

"I thought about that," explained Emily. "Technically, his ex-wife owns it, but she lives in New York. Given that it's in her name, it won't be on anyone's radar. Probably."

"Makes sense. We need to swing by my place, first," said Jen.

"Absolutely not. We're going straight there."

"We need clothes. Don't be silly, Em."

"It's too risky. The cop might have gotten your license plate number. We'll have to make do with the clothes on our backs."

The three occupants sat in silence as the coupe sped effortlessly on the highway. Emily had time to reflect on everything that had happened. Every foundation of her life had been turned upside down. Her job, relationships, and identity were all compromised. She needed time to regroup. She didn't know how it could get any worse.

Her world was about to forever change.

Chapter 33

The car arrived at the Annapolis condo late afternoon on Sunday and pulled into the driveway. In the space between the buildings, Emily could see the sun reflecting off the Atlantic Ocean. The icy burst of air gave Emily goose bumps when she exited the car. After quickly unlocking the front door, she disappeared from view.

Moments later, the one-car garage door opened and Jen pulled her car into the port. Once the garage door was closed again, Emily reached into the trunk to get her bag. Jen and Brent followed her into the condo.

"Wow, this place is amazing," said Jen as she walked into the immaculately maintained kitchen. "This is my kind of condo," she added, running her fingers across the exotic granite countertop.

The condo's main feature was its view. Jen slowly walked through the kitchen and the adjoining breakfast area before stopping at the wall of windows. They stretched along the entire width of the condo.

Spread before her was a panoramic view of the harbor. To her right and down two steps, the room opened up to a two-story living room, which shared the wall of windows.

"My aunt always had great taste."

"Why aren't they together anymore?"

"Two law careers were difficult to overcome. Geographically, it was impossible. He practices contract law in LA, and she's a bankruptcy attorney in New York. They tried using the condo as a weekend getaway, but the relationship was already doomed."

"Too bad, I always liked Annapolis."

"Me too. I used to come here during the summer with my parents."

Jen looked to Brent. "I'm Jen."

"Brent," he replied with a loose handshake.

"I need to understand what happened, Brent," said Emily. "You said something bad happened. What is it?"

"It's Scott," stated Brent.

"What about Scott?" asked Emily. After a brief pause, she added, "Wait. I never told you about Scott's abduction. How did you find out about that?"

"He was abducted?"

"Yes," she said as her voice trailed off.

"Oh, shit," said Brent. "This is worse than I thought."

"Just tell me what you know! Stop pussyfooting."

"I need a computer," he said.

Emily reached into her bag, withdrew the computer, and placed it on the granite countertop in the kitchen. After logging in, she turned the computer toward Brent. He quickly brought up the *Washington Post* website.

"I'm sorry to be the bearer of bad news." He swiveled the computer toward Emily. He attempted to embrace her for support, but she brushed him away with her forearm.

Her jaw slackened when she read the headline. *Man Found Murdered in Arlington Apartment.* "This can't be right," Emily said, shaking her head. "Are you sure it's—" She stopped talking when she read his name in the article.

Tears welled in her eyes. She paid them no attention as she continued to read. *Murder. Bedroom. Knife.* The words she read brought her world crashing down. "No, this can't be right. They have him! I saw Scott in the back of a car yesterday. He was alive."

"I'm so sorry," replied Brent.

"He's alive. This isn't right. They must just be trying to get my attention," she thought out loud. "This is all just a smoke screen."

"Emily, read the entire article," said Brent.

Momentarily lost in thought, Emily refocused her attention on the article. *Searching. Person of Interest. Girlfriend.*

"They think I had something to do with his murder?"

"It's on the local news too," added Brent. "They know who you are, Emily. They may not have mentioned your name, but it would've been easy for them to figure that out. It's not safe to go back."

Jen stood with her back against the kitchen wall, watching the interaction between the two. She opened her mouth to speak, but didn't.

"No, no, no!" screamed Emily. She grabbed a nearby Waterford crystal vase and smashed it on the countertop. The sound was deafening as crystal shards shot from the point of impact. She put her hands up to her face and began to sob. *This can't be happening.*

"Emily," said Jen as she approached her.

"Now you have something to say, after just standing there like an idiot?" Emily knew her comment was unfair, but didn't care. Her devastation felt insurmountable.

"Emily, you're bleeding." She motioned toward a wound on Emily's arm.

She moved her hands away from her face. She didn't feel anything, but saw blood. There was a two-inch gash just below her wrist. The crimson liquid flowed from the open wound and down her forearm, before it dripped off her elbow and pooled on the marble floor.

"Let me get that," Jen said kindly. She opened a kitchen drawer and pulled out a towel. Emily didn't respond as Jen plucked a large shard of glass from her wound. She applied pressure with a towel to stop the bleeding. After a few minutes, she dressed the injury from a medical kit Brent found in a bathroom cabinet.

Emily addressed them as Jen finished wrapping the cut. "What am I going to do now?" she asked.

No one had an answer.

"It's over. Why fight?"

"Emily, don't talk like that," began Jen. "We'll figure something out. I know everything seems hopeless, but it'll get better. I promise."

"You can't promise that. No one can. It's looking very bleak right about now. Just look at what they've done. I'm outmatched."

Emily walked toward the back door.

"Where are you going, Emily?" asked Brent.

"I need some time." She gave them a sincere expression. "Just please give me some time by myself."

She ignored their protests and walked out onto the deck. She grabbed the railing with both hands and stared ahead. The beautiful harbor view mesmerized her. In deep thought, she contemplated the situation she was in. *If only* she weren't so obstinate in her pursuit of the truth. *If only* she would have looked the other way when she had the chance. *If only* she hadn't involved innocent people. *If only* she just gave in now. *If only…*

With the wind at her back, she wrapped her arms around herself to fight off the chill. Emily closed her eyes and raised her head to the sky. She welcomed the distant sun on her face.

She couldn't give up. She had come too far. Mourning the deaths of her friends wouldn't bring them back. There would be time for that later. The truth needed to be brought to light.

She began to organize the facts in her mind. There was a crooked politician. "Imagine that," she said to herself. And there were two key accounts. *This is most important*, she thought. One in Cyprus that had been forced to close because of a financial meltdown, and one in Switzerland. The funds from the Cyprus account had been transferred to the Swiss account in small denominations to conceal the transfer.

Owen met with someone to oversee the transfer, Stan Murphy, who was now dead. *I need to know the identity of the Swiss account holders*. Once their names were known, the connections would become clear. It was time to review everything Brent had done.

The pieces were all there. They just needed to be assembled.

Chapter 34

Emily escaped the cold weather and entered the kitchen. Upon checking her watch, she realized she had been outside for over half an hour. Neither Brent nor Jen were in the room.

The condo had three floors. The main floor housed the garage, kitchen, and living room. The office, a full bathroom, and a small storage room were all located in the basement. Two bedrooms and another full bathroom occupied the top floor.

Emily heard the water from the shower in the basement. She walked down the stairs and knocked on the door.

"I'm in here," came a male voice from inside. "Just be a few minutes."

"Okay," replied Emily. She peeked her head in the office, but no one was there. *Where's Jen?* She went to find her friend.

As she walked up the stairs, she heard talking. Emily first thought that Jen had turned on the television.

But the sound she heard wasn't the television. It was Jen's voice. *She's on the phone?* Emily stopped a few feet before the bedroom door. She leaned toward the open door to listen.

"I told you, she's not here," Jen said. "I just checked on her, she's on the back deck. She seems rather distraught over the whole situation." There was a pause. Emily assumed the other person spoke.

"Yes, I know," continued Jen. "I couldn't talk earlier. This has been the first opportunity I've had to call. I'm taking a big risk calling now. She'll be back any minute now." There was another pause. "I told you she doesn't suspect a thing."

The blood drained from Emily's face. Her mind began to race. Jen was a *trusted* friend. Someone she confided in. Jen had always demonstrated an interest in her career. *Maybe it was an unhealthy interest.* She recalled the many times she showed up at networking events. She always just assumed they ran in similar circles. *How could I have been so oblivious?*

"I'll keep the two of them distracted until he gets here," Jen said. Emily slowly stepped backward. Feeling the floor with her feet, she found the top step of the stairs. She placed her other foot on the next step down.

There was a deafening creak. Emily's pupils dilated. *Maybe it wasn't as loud as I thought*, she reasoned. She heard nothing but distinct silence from the bedroom.

After a moment's pause, she took another step down. She briefly looked behind her to ensure she had a proper foothold for her descent. When Emily looked back up, she saw Jen's piercing eyes staring directly at her.

"Em, you're back. How are you feeling?" she asked with a look of genuine concern.

Emily didn't know how to respond. She could no longer trust the person standing before her. She feigned a smile.

"I'm feeling better, thanks. Brent's out of the shower too," she lied. She wanted to buy as much time as she could. The thought of Brent's presence might make Jen more cautious.

"Is he? Already?" Jen responded. "I thought he just stepped into the shower."

Emily wanted to run. She knew the condo was no longer a place of refuge. The Irishman was likely on his way. Jen's cold demeanor betrayed her artifice. *She must know that I heard her conversation.*

Jen began to speak again. "How's that wound?" She took a few steps toward her with outstretched arms. Emily's initial instinct was to retreat, but she found the fortitude to stand her ground. She braced herself.

A sound came from downstairs. It was just the water heater kicking on—she'd heard it many times before. Jen's attention momentarily shifted to the sound. Without a second thought, Emily launched herself at the other woman.

She found her target completely surprised. Emily connected an effective open-hand punch to Jen's jaw. As Jen fell back, she managed to grab Emily's arm. She pulled with all of her strength to heave Emily over her shoulder as she crashed into the wall.

"You bitch!" yelled Jen when she performed the acrobatic maneuver.

Stunned, Emily found herself in an awkward position against the wall. She tried to stand up, but was quickly pulled to the ground. "Why are you doing this?" Emily blurted in a distressed voice.

"You really don't know, do you?" replied Jen.

Emily managed to break free from Jen's wrestling grip. She kicked the woman's face and crawled a few feet away on her hands and knees.

On her knees, Jen paused her pursuit to clean the blood dripping from her nose. She briefly examined it before wiping it on her pants.

"Who else is involved? I can't trust anyone, can I?" questioned Emily.

"I really didn't want to do this," stated Jen. "I really liked you. I did."

"You've been involved since the beginning?" Emily took two staggered steps backward. She paused just before the top step. She felt vulnerable and completely exposed.

"They'll get to you too."

"I don't even know who they are? Tell me!"

"Oh, but you do."

"But why, Jen? Why are you doing this?" asked Emily.

"Ambition is a drug," Jen replied stoically. "My family died when I was young. I never had anything growing up. You wouldn't understand because of your idealism. Grow up. The real world is a cruel place."

"You were never my friend, were you?"

"I grew to like you, but you were a project. I mean, even the way you dressed..." After a brief pause, she added, "Now, at least you're presentable." Her smile was devilish.

Emily realized she did not know a thing about the person who stood in front of her. Their entire relationship was an illusion.

"Is this about Owen? You said you were there that night at the reception, but I didn't see you. Were you spying on me?"

"Oh, honey, it goes much deeper than you realize."

"But I just started the Owen engagement, and we've known each other for six months."

"How do you think you got the engagement?"

"No, that can't be," said Emily, confused.

"Your whole life, you've been compliant. Excelled at school, done what you've been taught. At work, you were successful, but always stayed in line. Very analytical, but straight and narrow. Perfect for this engagement. At least I thought."

"I was selected for this engagement?"

"Hand-selected." Jen inched closer to Emily.

"But Lisa was supposed to work on this engagement. Not me."

"Yes, she was." Her last word sent a chill down Emily's spine.

"Her brother is in a coma. You couldn't have had anything to do with that."

A smile crossed her opponents face. Jen moved even closer, while Emily continued her retreat.

"You're evil," spat Emily.

"You have no idea how conniving I can be. You really don't know anything about me."

"Stop. Please stop." Emily nearly lost her balance when she reached the edge of the top step. She had nowhere else to go.

"All I need to do is buy time," said Jen. "He'll be here anytime now. I've never met him. I don't want to meet him. My job is simple. To keep you occupied," she added. "I don't like to get my hands dirty. Now look what you've done." Jen motioned to her bloodied face.

Emily reached out to Jen and grabbed her wrist. She jumped down two steps while retaining a firm grip. Her action caught Jen by surprise. Jen seemed to fly over her. Fumbling with her hands, Jen managed to reestablish a link with Emily as she fell.

They were now entangled. Their bodies crashed awkwardly down the stairs, where they continued to wrestle and tumble until they reached the bottom.

Jen's head made the strongest contact with the marble floor. She was momentarily dazed. Emily took advantage of her good fortune. She leapt on top of Jen and put her forearms around Jen's throat and squeezed.

Jen thrashed her body in an attempt to free herself. She kicked wildly and pushed both of them against the front door.

"Stop!" yelled Jen in a muffled tone. Emily still had a firm grip around her throat. "Stop," she said again, in a gentler tone. "You're going to kill me if you don't stop."

Emily wasn't a killer. She lessened her grip before pushing Jen away from her with a two-handed thrust to her back. She watched as Jen coughed on her hands and knees. Her hair flowed down to the marble floor as she heaved to catch her breath. She looked up and their eyes met.

Emily saw a hatred in the woman that she had never seen before. Jen let out a quiet laugh.

"You're so predictable," she spat to Emily. "I'm going to kill you," she stated in an ominous voice.

Jen lunged at her with great ferocity.

Emily attempted to step to the right at the last moment, but couldn't evade her attacker. Jen made contact with her stomach as the two crashed into the floor-to-ceiling stained glass window, next to the condo's front door.

Emily's head whipped back and struck the window. The force of her head caused the tempered glass to spider, but it didn't break.

Dazed, Emily didn't see the fist strike the right side of her head, just above the ear. She stepped back to put some distance between them. It didn't work. Jen grabbed a fistful of hair.

With a tennis grunt, Jen pulled Emily toward her. Like a bull toward a matador, Emily couldn't help but charge straight ahead. Jen sidestepped Emily's out-of-control forward motion and landed a violent blow to Emily's back with her elbow.

Emily crashed to the hard floor. She momentarily lost her breath, then barely found the strength to roll away as Jen dove toward her.

Emily needed to escape. The Irishman would surely be here soon. She wasn't prepared for another encounter with him. He would be ready this time.

The one advantage she had was naked in the shower. If she could get Brent's attention, they could both overpower Jen. Emily got to her feet. She made two long strides before she was tripped.

"Brent," she said in much lower voice than she intended as she once again crashed to the floor. On her back, Emily looked up to see Jen's face. She was coming straight at Emily.

"You need to be stopped," said the enraged woman. She reached for Emily's throat with both hands.

Emily managed to redirect Jen's hands and forward motion with a thrust of her hands, using a technique she had learned from a rape defense in college. Jen fell hard on the floor next to her. Her head hit the marble floor, causing a slapping sound.

Jen appeared to be dazed again. Emily climbed on Jen's back and placed her right forearm under the woman's throat. She took her free hand and pulled the forearm toward her body with all of her strength. This time she didn't let go. Jen thrashed. She tried to plead for her life, but couldn't speak coherently.

Emily closed her eyes and tried not to think about what she was doing to a person she had considered a good friend until just a few minutes ago. She surprised herself when she whispered in Jen's ear, "Don't call me predictable, you bitch."

Emily could feel the strength drain from Jen's body. She kept the grip as the body went limp.

A loud crash on the marble startled Emily. She let go of the body and pushed herself to the door. She expected to see the Irishman.

She looked up to see Brent standing in the doorway. He had one towel around his waist and another wrapped around his head like a turban. It was obvious the scene in the foyer caught him by surprise. A shattered water glass lay at his feet.

"What the fuck?" he asked, looking at the chaos. A bewildered expression clung to his face.

Chapter 35

SUNDAY. 5:08 PM.

Brent stood wide-eyed and slack-jawed in the doorway while Emily crouched against the front door, trying to catch her breath. Her head was buried in her arms. Jen's body lay on the floor between them.

"Are you crazy?" asked Brent. In one motion, he ripped the turban from his head and threw it to the ground. He rushed toward the body that was sprawled, facedown, on the white marble floor. He bent to his knees and checked her pulse.

"She's dead," he said to Emily as he turned to face her. "Why?"

"Jen was one of them," stated Emily as her voice cracked. Her head remained buried.

"One of who?"

"One of the conspirators! She was helping them." She finally looked up to establish eye contact. "I caught her on the phone."

"So you killed her? Are you insane?"

"She attacked me," said Emily as she slowly picked herself up off the floor. "She was intent on killing me. I swear. I've never seen anyone so angry before."

"None of this makes sense. We need to call the police."

"We can't."

"We have to call the police, Emily."

"No! Don't you see how this looks? I've been framed for Scott's murder... and now my 'best friend' is dead. We need to finish this," Emily pleaded to Brent.

"This is getting way out of hand. You just murdered your friend!"

"She's not my friend!" spat Emily with an intensity she didn't intend. "Apparently, she never was."

"This is not you, or us," he said, pointing at the lifeless body.

"They started this. We still need to figure out who they are," she insisted.

"Emily, it's over. I'm done."

"No, Brent." He started to walk away. "Okay!" she said desperately. He stopped to turn around.

"We can't go on." He stood there in the foyer, practically pleading. "I can't go on."

"Fine. But first we have to get out of here. Fast. He's coming."

"Who's coming?"

"The Irishman! Jen said he's on his way."

"Why didn't you say that first?" Brent quickly disappeared from the room.

Emily looked at the body on the floor. This was the second dead body she had ever seen. The first was still fresh in her mind from last week. She looked into Jen's open eyes. She didn't recognize her as the woman who once claimed to be her friend.

After stepping around the body, she found Brent in the basement bathroom. His pants were already on as he pulled a shirt over his head and down his long torso. He didn't say anything as he quickly put on his socks and shoes.

"We're doing the right thing," Emily said quietly.

"Are we? What do we do about Jen?"

With a guilty conscience, she said, "There's a freezer near the storage closet."

"Emily," Brent responded. "That's horrible."

"We can't leave the body here. For many reasons," she added. "The neighbors would certainly complain about the smell, for one."

"Stop." He closed his eyes. "Let's just hurry. I really don't want to be here when *that guy* gets here."

Neither of them uttered a word as they dragged the body down the stairs. They took out miscellaneous meats and other frozen foods to make room for the body. The freezer wasn't small, but they needed to contort the body to make it fit.

They began to gather the items taken out of the freezer to bring upstairs. Brent broke the silence. "Most of this meat is venison," he said, looking at the hand-written labels on the vacuum-sealed packages. "Does your uncle hunt?"

"Yes, he hunts in the fall. He ships most of the meat to family and friends, but leaves some here. Why?"

"Does he own a gun?"

"Yes. He has a hunting rifle in a locked cabinet in the office," she said, pointing to the room they had just passed down the hallway.

They placed the frozen bags on the ground before walking into the office. Emily flicked the light switch. There was a decorative wood and glass cabinet against the wall on the opposite side of the room.

Brent walked toward the desk and began rummaging for a key. He looked up to witness Emily throw a chair into the cabinet.

"We don't have time," she stated as she stepped over the glass fragments and pulled out a hunting rifle. She handed it to Brent before retrieving two boxes of ammunition. She then opened a box located on the bottom of the cabinet. An automatic pistol lay inside a snug foam frame.

Emily slid the pistol in the back of her pants. She grabbed an extra clip and a box of ammunition for the pistol before standing up.

"Nice look," stated Brent as he gazed at her.

She checked her watch. "We've already spent way too much time here. Let's hurry up." They went upstairs, collected all of their belongings, and headed for the garage. On the way out, Emily grabbed Jen's purse and placed the pistol inside it.

"Where are we going?" He tried to walk to the driver's side, but Emily cut in front of him.

"I'll drive," she said. "We'll head South."

"Where, exactly?"

"I'm not sure. Since we're north of DC, our pursuer might expect us to continue in that direction."

"Okay," he said with a nod. "Not the most convincing argument, but there's logic to it."

"I agree it's not the best thought out plan, but it's all I can reason at this specific moment. Do you have any other ideas? I'm open to suggestions."

"No. My family isn't an option and my friends, frankly, wouldn't believe me."

"Tell me about it."

"Are you sure you want to head through a state where you're wanted for the *murder* of your boyfriend? Not only are these psychos looking for you, so are the police."

"They're looking for Emily, not Jen," she said with a smirk as she presented herself with a wave of her hand. "I've got her wallet, ID, clothes, and car."

"Wow, you're scary. You really have changed."

"Given the circumstances and my desire to live, I'll take that as a compliment."

"I guess you should. I'm with you. South it is. If we head far enough, at least the weather will improve."

The engine started with a growl. She had to give it to Jen. She always liked nice things. When they reached the street corner, a gray sedan slowed before turning down her uncle's street.

Their eyes met for only a moment, but it was a moment Emily wouldn't forget. She immediately recognized the man. Worse, she could tell that he recognized her. She pressed the gas pedal, and the car promptly accelerated down the street.

Chapter 36

The car sped down the Annapolis street as Emily gripped the steering wheel intently. "Slow down!" said Brent. He held the door handle for support. "Why are you speeding? We don't want to draw the attention of the authorities."

"That car we just passed. That's him."

In a panic, Brent looked over his shoulder to get a glimpse of the car. The sun had begun setting and was only a sliver on the horizon. It nearly blinded him as he looked toward it. "The gray BMW?" he asked.

"That's the one. It's a three-series, so we should have the advantage."

"How do you know it's a three-series?"

"I know my cars. My dad was an enthusiast. This car has a premium engine. The car he stole was likely a base model. That gives us an advantage. We'll need it."

"The more I find out about you, the less I know you," he said. "So, you're trying to outrun him?" He checked his seat belt to ensure it was properly secured.

"I'm all ears if you have a better idea?"

"I'll go with yours."

"Okay. Hold on!" Emily slowed the vehicle for a sharp turn, then firmly pressed the accelerator again. She drove to the best of her ability, but the gray sedan began to shorten the distance between them.

The winding roads of Annapolis made speeding difficult. The advantage they held with a faster car was minimized. The Irishman was slowly gaining.

"Where are you heading?"

"To Route 301."

Brent checked the navigation screen. "Okay," he began. "You'll want to take a hard right up here. There will be a brief straightaway for about two football fields."

"Sports analogies. I hate those."

"You like sports. Hey, I'm just trying to help."

"You are helping," she responded without taking her eyes off of the road. "By the way, most sports I merely tolerate, but I like hockey."

"In that case, you'll go down about eight hockey rinks. See, that's just not very descriptive."

"Fine, stick with football, but just keep talking!" She braked, spun the wheel to the right, and accelerated down the street. "Where to next?"

He referenced the map. He followed a path with his finger. "How are we doing with gas?"

"We're fine. We need to lose him, though. Remember, he's an assassin. We're a consultant and a banker." She couldn't help the awkward snort she let out.

"You didn't just do that."

"Oh, yes, I did. Focus," she barked as she glanced in the rearview mirror. She was able to speed through a straightaway. The gray sedan was about a half mile down the road. "Where's the nearest city center? We need other cars to provide cover if we want any chance of losing him."

"Agreed." After a few turns, running a red light, and a bridge, they approached downtown Annapolis.

"Do you see him?" yelled Emily.

"He just got to the bridge. Awesome driving."

"No dancing on the tables."

"What?"

"An old boss of mine used to say that. It means, don't celebrate. Just do your job." She continued the aggressive driving until she saw an alley. She jammed on the brakes, but not hard enough to leave skid marks.

"What are you doing?" asked Brent.

"We can duck in here." She drove the car into an alley, went halfway down, then turned left into a loading zone. She killed the engine.

"Are you sure he didn't see us?"

"We're about to find out." She hopped over the front seat, pulled the rifle out from under the jackets, and tossed it to Brent. She reached into Jen's bag in the footwell of the rear seat to pull out the pistol.

The sun had set, and it was now dark outside. They sat motionless as they watched for any movement in the alley. No headlights appeared.

"I think we lost him," stated Brent after five minutes. He took his finger off the trigger.

She reached over and pressed a button on the rifle. "The safety was on," she said. "You've never fired a gun, have you?"

"Sorry, I don't hunt deer with my uncle."

"Let me give you a lesson." She reached out with her hand and gave him a stern look.

"Fine," he said as he handed her the rifle. "I guess I could use a lesson. The last time I fired a gun was at a pumpkin on an Indian Guides retreat."

"Indian Guides?"

"Yes, Indian Guides. It's a Boy Scouts alternative that focuses on nature activities."

"Wow." Emily chuckled. "You don't know me? I think the truth is, I really don't know you."

"Shut up," he said with a half-laugh.

"Okay, Tonto, here's what you do." Emily picked up the rifle and demonstrated how to release the safety, cock the rifle, and reload the ammunition.

"Looks easy enough," he said.

"Now you need to practice." She was about to give him the rifle, but a headlight appeared down the alley.

"Get down," she said, lying down on the back seat. She focused her attention on the window. She cocked the gun and released the safety. They waited. "Do you see anything?" Emily asked.

"I can't see anything, but I'm not showing my head. This was a bad idea. We're sitting ducks. Give me the pistol. I think I can handle that weapon." She handed it to him over the vehicle's armrest.

Officer James Frank of the Annapolis Police Department scanned the side streets and alleys from his cruiser. He wasn't happy to be working the night shift, but as a rookie, he didn't have much choice. So far, tonight, like most nights, had been uneventful.

The area had a reputation for being a hot spot for unscrupulous behavior. Prostitutes conducted their business, often with the endless supply of young sailors from the Naval Academy, in parked cars near the campus.

He had just finished his search of one alley and now slowly perused the next. He stopped his police cruiser after spotting a late-model red sports car parked in a loading zone. The condensation forming on the windows

caught his attention. Without the air circulation of a
running vehicle, moisture typically formed after just a few
minutes. He'd seen it dozens of times over his short
tenure.

After contacting the central office to report his
location, he hit a button on the center console. Instantly,
a series of blue and red lights began to dance off the alley
walls. In a ready position, he cautiously exited his car.
Alcohol was often a contributing factor to this behavior
and usually made the situations much more dangerous to
control.

The police officer approached the car, employing the
techniques learned at the academy. With a hand firmly on
the grip of the gun, he gently tapped his metal flashlight
on the driver's window of the expensive car. He could see
an outline of someone seated in the front passenger seat,
but his vision was impaired by the condensation.

"*Police*," he yelled in his official booming police voice.
"Roll down the window."

After a few moments' pause, the driver's side window
lowered. He peered into the seat, but it was empty. He
switched his focal point to a man seated in the passenger
seat. Before he could address the man, a voice emanated
from the back seat.

"Sorry, Officer," began a female voice from the back
seat. "We were just, uh..."

The beam from his flashlight illuminated a shirtless
female occupant in the rear seat. The woman had covered
her breasts with her hands.

"I see, ma'am," he replied as he flashed the light
around the cabin of the vehicle. The clothes strewn
around indicated an obvious tryst, but something seemed
out of place. "What's your name, ma'am?"

"Jennifer Myers. Look, this is so embarrassing. We're just old friends, trying to... um... reconcile," said the woman with a shameful smile. She raised her left arm to block the blinding light from his flashlight, exposing her right breast.

His intuition was confirmed. She wore a large, bloodstained bandage around her arm. The seepage indicated that it was a recent injury. The swelling on her face had yet to turn into a bruise, but would certainly change color by the morning. She had signs of a classic domestic abuse victim.

The officer trained the flashlight on the male occupant. "Sir, don't move," he stated coldly. "Ma'am, are you all right?" he asked as he moved the light away from her face, which he knew would allow her to read his facial features.

"Yes, why?"

"How did you sustain those injuries?"

"Officer, I'm not injured."

"You have a bandaged wrist, with what appears to be a serious laceration. You have additional injuries to the face, with some swelling. It appears to be a recent altercation, given the redness. I'm assuming the *gentleman* in the front seat is at least partly responsible."

"Officer, I've known him for years. He's not like that, I assure you," added the woman. Her response was typical for a domestic abuse victim. He had extensive training dealing with these situations, and they were by far the most dangerous.

Protocol dictated he had to call for backup before proceeding. He removed his hand from his holstered weapon to press the button on the radio attached to his vest. It was dead. He pressed it two more times. The unit appeared to be working, but it communicated through his cruiser to the central office. *The issue must be with the car's radio*, he thought.

He had to proceed without backup. His hand moved back to the grip of his pistol for security.

"I'll need you both to exit the vehicle. I need to search it for contraband and alcohol. You've given me probable cause. I see your lips are stained red. Have you recently been drinking wine, or is that blood? Either way, something is wrong here."

"I had a glass of wine earlier in the evening," replied the woman.

"Please exit the car, ma'am. I'm not going to ask you nicely again."

The man in the front seat began to speak. "Officer, this appears to be a simple misunderstanding." He began to move in his seat.

The officer un-holstered his weapon and trained it directly at the man. "Don't move," he said in a stern voice. "I will not hesitate to arrest you for lewd behavior or disorderly conduct. Do I make myself clear?"

"Yes, sir," replied the man.

"Good, now keep your hands where I can see them," said the officer. He'd been in this situation before and it was important to take command. He switched his attention to the woman.

"Ma'am, you can exit the car now." He watched her intently as she opened the rear door on the driver's side and stepped out. He didn't protest when she covered her breasts with a crumpled shirt from the back seat.

"Stand over there, ma'am," stated the officer as he stood behind the door. He pointed toward the back of her vehicle. "That's good enough," he said when the woman was parallel to the rear bumper. He stepped around the open car door and strategically began illuminating the cabin of the vehicle.

Chapter 37

Emily stood in the cold with only a crumpled shirt covering her chest. It provided an insignificant relief from the elements. A drizzle began to fall softly from the sky.

Those were the least of her concerns, as the police officer began to take a more thorough review of the contents in the vehicle. To her relief, he had switched his attention from the back seat, where the weapons were hidden, to Brent.

She rehearsed what she would say once the officer located the weapons. They would be difficult to explain. Their coats covered them, but it would only take a rudimentary search to find the guns. *Especially to a person that appeared to run everything strictly according to the letter of the law*, she thought. *Everything is going wrong*.

Per the request of the uniformed man, Emily remained standing near the rear door on the driver's side. The contents of Brent's pockets were laid neatly on the dashboard. The officer holstered his weapon as he began his investigation. With a flashlight in his left hand and Brent's driver's license in the other, he asked the seated man questions to ascertain his sobriety and relationship to the half-naked woman.

"How many drinks have you had tonight?" he asked Brent.

"None, Officer."

"Have any funds exchanged hands tonight?"

"I'm not a hooker!" spat Emily. She tried to keep his attention on the relationship and not the contents of the vehicle. "Brent is my boyfriend, and we are attempting to reconcile our relationship." She intentionally used Brent's forename to demonstrate familiarity to the officer. She hoped it worked.

Emily was immediately blinded by the high-powered flashlight. It annoyingly alternated between her left and right eyes.

"Ma'am, please stay put and keep your mouth shut."

"Yes, sir," she responded. She couldn't help but smirk when he continued to question Brent.

"Please answer the question," the officer said sternly to Brent. "Have any funds exchanged hands?"

"No, Officer. As Emily stated, we're trying to work on our relationship. I admit we could've picked a more romantic spot. That's my fault."

His words made Emily cringe.

"I thought her name was *Jennifer*," stated the officer. He shined his flashlight in Brent's direction as he tried to get a better read on the man's facial expressions.

"Sorry, Officer. I'm nervous and was just thinking about my ex-girlfriend."

"I hate that woman." Emily spoke up to play along with the ruse. "That's not the first time you've made that mistake," she added, sounding believably annoyed.

"I'm not buying this relationship, folks. Sir, please step out of the vehicle."

Just then, there was a noise just in front of Emily. A small rock bounced off the front metal wheel rim. The sound of the rock contacting the metal was unmistakable.

The officer's demeanor immediately changed. "Sir. Stop. Stay in the car," he said to Brent. He closed the door before Brent was ready. The door nearly clipped his leg. Brent looked toward Emily with a confused expression.

The officer walked around the front of the car to see the source of the noise. "Ma'am, what are you doing?" he asked Emily. He illuminated the ground around her with his flashlight. "Any illegal substances will warrant your arrest," he added firmly.

"No, Officer. I've just been standing here," she admitted with confusion. Her eyes switched to Brent, who gave her a disapproving look with a furrowed brow.

"Ma'am, keep your attention on me and not on your friend," said the officer. He took three long strides toward her and shined his flashlight directly in her eyes again. His face was about eight inches from hers. "Ma'am, I'll ask you only one more time, what did you discard?"

Before Emily could respond to the officer's inquiry, a deafening blast emanated from just behind her right shoulder. The officer's face appeared to explode in front of her.

The backlash from the explosion caused a mixture of blood and brain matter to splatter her face. Emily's head twitched from both the sound and wetness of the explosion.

The event left her emotionally paralyzed.

For Brent, everything appeared to stand still for what felt like an eternity. The only visible movement stemmed from the red and blue lights that continued to move across the alley's brick wall. The only sound he heard was the engine of the police car.

After a minute of silence, he cautiously retrieved the pistol from the back seat and exited the vehicle. He held the weapon awkwardly as he crouched in front of the car. He expected gunfire from the darkness on the other side of the police car.

Nothing came.

He continued his crouched stance as he slowly inched to Emily's side of the car. A dead body lay before him, still clutching his police-issued weapon. The officer's face was no longer recognizable.

The body appeared to have collapsed straight back, as if it were tipped over like a board. The flashlight had rolled out of the officer's hand, and its bright beam was directly pointed toward the unblemished gold band on the officer's ring finger.

The smell of gun smoke permeated the air as Brent summoned the courage to step around the body and approach Emily. She hadn't moved.

The crumpled shirt slid from her hand to expose one of her breasts. With an open mouth, she stared to the nothingness in front of her, where the officer's face had been just moments ago.

"Emily," said Brent as he gently put his arms around her. "Emily," he said again as he held her face. This time his words were much more stern. "We have to leave. Now."

It was obvious there were only two real choices given their situation. The first option would be to stay there and explain their complicated situation to the police. The second option was to run.

Brent closed his eyes. He exhaled in frustration, opened his eyes again, and looked at his friend. At the end of her dangling arm, she loosely held an unfamiliar pistol. They certainly hadn't brought it with them and the officer still clutched his weapon.

There were no longer two options. Talking to the authorities would be impossible with Emily's fingerprints on the murder weapon.

With no other choice, he gently eased Emily into the back seat of the Mercedes. He used his shirt to wipe the blood and gray matter off her face as best he could. He put a jacket on her to cover her naked torso and warm her body.

Brent opened the trunk. He lifted a thin carpeted panel and placed the murder weapon, along with the other guns, under the spare tire and out of plain sight. They would need to discard the murder weapon someplace very far away from the murder scene.

The police car had them blocked in. Brent peered around the alley before entering the vehicle. He expected a barrage of bullets to strike him from the dark.

Again, nothing came.

He sat in the driver's seat of the running vehicle. He noticed the center console, where the communication equipment was located, wasn't illuminated. A severed wire dangled just below the console.

After he moved the vehicle back ten feet, he managed to find the switch to stop the flashing lights. He then wiped his fingerprints from the steering wheel and door handle. Brent returned to the Mercedes and started the engine with a press of a button.

He eased the transmission into reverse to back out of the loading zone. He felt awkward using a turn signal to exit the gruesome crime scene. He turned down the road and let out a sigh.

He had a newfound respect for the woman in the back of the car. Brent watched Emily in the rearview mirror. She continued to stare ahead blankly. Her face and hair were wet and she appeared disheveled. Still, she was beautiful.

It was almost midnight. He planned to drive for a couple of hours. They needed to get as far away as they could. Annapolis would be crawling with police once the body in the alley was discovered.

He kept watch for a desolate hotel. A place where they could clean up and regroup. Everything had fallen apart, and they were in need of a new plan.

The Irishman used speed dial on his phone to place the call from the moving vehicle. The music playing in the background was interrupted by a dialing sound.

"Yes?" answered an ominous voice.

"The liability has been neutralized, per your request."

"Good."

"I will await further instructions." The Irishman expected the conversation to end. He could hear the man inhale smoke into his lungs.

When the man casually spoke, he exhaled. "Our needs have changed."

"Please advise," stated the Irishman.

"The liability needs to be eliminated, cleanly. No loose ends. No body."

"The liability has baggage, please advise."

"Including baggage." The call ended and techno music resumed to fill the cabin.

The Irishman pulled off Route 301 at the next exit with a vantage point of the westbound traffic. His prey would likely distance themselves from the city and head in his direction.

He pulled a tablet out of his bag to locate small hotels between Annapolis and DC. If they didn't pass him on the highway, they would likely seek refuge before the end of the night. *The game has begun again*, he thought with an almost imperceptible smile.

Chapter 38

Emily opened her eyes, but didn't recognize her surroundings. She blinked slowly as she tried to recall the previous night. A faint recollection of police lights reflecting off a brick wall came to mind. She couldn't remember anything else.

She sat up and looked around. She was in a hotel room. Alone. Without any idea of what hotel or how she came to be there, Emily wrapped the blanket around herself to appease some primal instinct.

Thoughts began to collect in her mind. A foul taste in her mouth broke her concentration. With her tongue, she managed to loosen an object wedged between her teeth and cheek toward the back of her mouth. She pushed a spongy material out of her mouth and onto her index finger. After a brief examination, last night's event began to flood her head.

Emily ran to the bathroom and lifted the toilet seat. She heaved and waited, but nothing came out. With the back of her hand, she wiped the saliva dangling from her lips. She opened the miniature soap wrapped in plastic and began to thoroughly wash her hands. Using her finger, she vigorously scrubbed her mouth and teeth.

She welcomed the awful taste of soap.

She visualized the young police officer, just before his head disappeared. Emily reluctantly looked in the mirror. Trace red smudges remained, but it was obvious someone attempted to wipe her face and clean her up. *Brent.*

The swelling on the right side of her face had subsided. A faint yellow-green bruise replaced it. It was sensitive to her touch when she gently pressed it with her finger.

A cursory glance of the hotel room didn't provide any helpful clues. She checked the desk. Directly underneath the hotel menu lay a glossy welcome guide for Fredericksburg, Virginia.

He drove us to a tourist trap, she thought. *Smart.* She was vaguely familiar with the small, historical town located about fifty miles south of DC. She had driven near it every time she visited her mother, but never stopped to visit.

Emily walked back to the bathroom, took off the men's T-shirt she wore, and entered the shower. She scrubbed her face and body in an attempt to erase the previous night, and maybe everything else that had happened to her. The blood circled the basin before flushing down the drain. The memories remained.

She got out of the shower and dried herself. With one towel around her torso and another on her head, she cleaned her undergarments in the sink and dried them with a hair dryer.

Emily nearly screamed when she came out of the bathroom. Brent was sitting at the desk. His lounging body swiveled in the chair as he faced her. "Don't do that again!" she said, pointing her finger at him. "You scared the hell out of me."

"You want me to leave?" he said. "Maybe give you a bit of privacy."

"No. Don't be silly."

"How are you feeling?" he asked with genuine concern.

Emily wasn't ready to talk about last night. She was mentally devastated, but decided to keep her emotions to herself. "I'm fine." Her pursed lips left no ambiguity.

"I got us some coffee," he said. He handed her one of the two coffees from the desk.

Emily inhaled the coffee aroma. A white paper bag, which appeared to be stained from a mixture of grease and condensation, sat next to Brent. She ignored the other that sat on the floor next to him. She lifted the lid off the coffee and took a sip.

"Mmm... I never thought the awful coffee from Starbucks could taste so good. Thank you." She took another sip. It helped alleviate the foul taste lingering in her mouth.

Emily opened the white paper bag and placed the Styrofoam container on the desk. She lifted the lid to find an omelet with roasted potatoes. After removing the fork from the plastic wrap, she began to dig in.

"In some ways, you haven't changed at all. You were never shy about eating."

"Why would I be?" she responded with a full mouth.

"It's called femininity. Lots of women have it." He smiled as he spoke.

"That's just fucking sexist," she replied with a laugh. "You obviously don't date the right women."

"Just leave some for me, please." He grabbed one of the coffees and took a sip.

"Here." She handed Brent a half piece of toast and took another generous bite of the omelet. She placed the container back on the desk. "What's in the other bag?" she asked.

"There was a second-hand store down the street. I thought you might want a change of clothes."

"I've never had a guy buy clothes for me," she said as she lifted them out of the bag.

"I guessed on size."

"Not bad," she said when she opened the shirt with outstretched hands. "And wow, the pants and shirt go quite well together. Is there something you're not telling me? What's his name? Bob?"

"What? Can't a guy know how to shop? And why Bob?"

"You can barely dress yourself. I'm just surprised, that's all."

"There's a difference, you know," he said defensively. "I know how to dress. I just don't typically care."

"Okay. Okay. Don't get your panties in a bunch."

"Hey, that's my line, lady," Brent said with an annoyed smile.

"I know. You used it on me a few times." After a pause, she spoke again. "Thanks."

"You're welcome. I hope they fit."

"No, *thank you*, Brent. For everything. I really don't completely understand what happened last night. It's all a blur."

"It's understandable. I really don't know where you get your strength. I certainly don't have it."

"Last night you did." Emily realized she was still in her towel. She started to put on the clothes from the shopping bag. She began with the underwear she had washed. They were mostly dry when she slipped them on underneath the towel wrapped around her body.

"Where do you get your strength? Seriously."

"Fear," she said without thinking. "I'm afraid. I'm afraid of what might happen if I fail. It's become patently obvious that these people will stop at nothing. I'm afraid of what might happen if we don't stop them."

While sitting on the edge of the bed, she lifted the pants up her legs. She faced away from Brent when she dropped the towel to the ground. After she slipped her arms through her bra and adjusted it with a quick tug to the thin wire frame, she turned to face him.

"I agree they need to be stopped. I'm just not sure we're the right people to do it," he replied. Brent continued to nonchalantly watch her as she dressed.

"Who else would stop them?"

"What do you mean?"

"Well, that's the thing," began Emily. "These people have power. They probably have contacts at the police, and maybe even the FBI. I know, I know. I'm being paranoid. But I have a pretty good reason to be that way. And that's why it's useless to go to them for help."

She slipped the shirt over her head, then grabbed the white Styrofoam box with the food. She sat barefoot on the bed with her legs bent underneath her.

"I see where you're going," he interjected. "We haven't been corrupted."

"Exactly. They're smart. If it were just our word against theirs, they would spin some one-sided, twisted, untruthful version that best fit their objective. We would be destroyed. Hell, my life will never be the same again."

"You're probably right," he said with a nod.

"Of course I am. We need proof. Something irrefutable," she said with her mouth full and the fork in the air.

"I can't believe I'm saying this, but I might have just looked the other way. Emily, you're a better person than I am. That's for certain."

"Don't be so sure. If I thought these people would leave me alone, I mean really let me go, like if they had never met me, I would consider walking away."

A fond memory of Scott at their favorite French restaurant entered her mind. Guilt immediately enveloped her.

"That'll never be the case now," she continued. "They've killed people. People like Mark. He was nothing to them. I'm becoming a threat. They won't hesitate to kill me."

"Then why did he let us go last night?" asked Brent. "The Irishman could have easily killed us." Brent shook his head slowly from side to side. "We were sitting ducks, literally. It doesn't make sense."

"I'm still trying to figure that out too," said Emily as she took another bite of potatoes. "Maybe they just want the police to hunt us. If we're the bad guys, we lose all credibility."

"Plus, we'll spend all our time trying to elude the authorities," Brent added.

"Giving them time to cover their tracks! Brent, that's it," she left the food on the bed and stood up.

Emily began pacing the room. "We can't lose our momentum," she continued. "We must be close. We have to strike while it still hurts."

"Okay..." Brent's expression did not convey confidence.

"Don't be such a *wuss*," she said with a playful punch to his shoulder. "We'll come out on top."

"I still don't understand where this certainty is coming from. Don't you see the odds stacked against us?"

"Positive thinking." She smiled before taking a sip of her coffee. "Besides, the alternative is that we'll be facedown in a ditch somewhere. And that's not a pleasant thought."

"I'm assuming you have a plan, right? We're not just driving aimlessly South?"

"We just needed a place to regroup. We need to review what you've done. You do have it accessible, right?"

"Of course." He pulled a flash drive out of his pocket and handed it to her.

"Let's have a look at what you've done." She booted her computer and inserted the device in the side.

She impatiently tapped on the keyboard while the files transferred to the hard drive. Brent cleared his throat to speak, but she cut him off. "Let me just review it first, okay?"

"You got it, Boss." Brent reached over to grab the Styrofoam container and began eating.

"Oh, stop the silly talk. It's just a habit I have. I prefer to review things from a fresh perspective." She quickly scanned the files.

"Wow," was the only word she managed to speak.

"I know," he said with a mouth full of food.

"We need access to the Internet."

"Let's just log-in here."

"Some hotels allow you to pay cash for the room, but the extras, including Internet access, require a credit card."

"Hmm. I didn't think of that."

"Wait," she said, grabbing the Fredericksburg visitor guide from the desk top. She flipped to the back page, which had a map. "I know where we can go. And it's less than two hours away."

"DC is less than two hours away. We're not heading back, are we?"

"I think it'll be good to stay away from there for a while. Charlottesville. That's where we're going."

"Why there?"

"We're going to seek the advice of one of the smartest guys I know. I'm not saying I don't trust my own judgment. I do. Or maybe I don't. It's all so confusing, you know? But the fact remains that people around us keep dying."

"Who is this guy?"

"Someone I've known a long time. I couldn't go to him before. I didn't have enough information. Now that we do, he'll be able to help us."

"I hope this guy knows his stuff."

"We're so close, Brent. He'll help get us over the goal line," she said. "Besides, we need a home base. We can't continue to be outlaws. Our funds can't get us very far. Unless we resort to robbing banks, any money we withdraw or credit cards we use will be tracked. Are you on board with this plan?"

"Okay. I trust you," said Brent as he looked at her as if he was trying to read her mannerisms. "I'll get the car," he said after a brief pause.

"Perfect," she exclaimed as he exited the hotel room.

Emily quickly gathered the few things they had with them. She threw out the trash from the morning's breakfast and looked around one last time before heading to the door.

She caught a glimpse of herself in the mirror. It was only for a fraction of a second. Emily saw the reflection of someone she no longer knew. The events from last night could not be undone. She had crossed a line she didn't know existed. She could never go back. The line was no longer there.

She examined the hands she used to take Jen's life. She rubbed them as if what she had done could be erased. It could not.

Chapter 39

Emily and Brent made the drive from Fredericksburg to Charlottesville in just under two hours to arrive mid-morning. The drizzle and clouds that covered much of the region the past few days were gone. They were replaced by a bright sun and blue sky.

The house they were to visit was on the outskirts of downtown and away from the commotion of the local university. They drove around the immediate vicinity before choosing a spot away from the property to park the car. Emily wanted to be sure they had an escape route if the Irishman somehow found them. It was an unfamiliar feeling that she was getting used to considering when making decisions.

"Is that the place?" Brent said, pointing to a house visible over the hill. It was located on a lake and surrounded by two and a half acres of wooded land.

"According to the map, yes." They walked on the perimeter of a neighboring property. Emily zipped up her coat after a breeze sent a chill through her body. The sun felt good on her face, but a seasonable chill remained.

"Are you sure we couldn't just park in the driveway?" complained Brent.

"Yes. And if he asks, we were dropped off with an expensive fare from DC. I'm just not sure how he'll react seeing a wanted murderer in his house."

"Now you're thinking about that? *Now*?" he asked.

"That's why we parked where we did. It won't be an issue. I've known him for many years. He's always been like a father to me."

"Do you even know if he's home?"

"I sure hope so. He's a homebody. Plus, like you, he's rather predictable. He's either working or drinking. Since it's not yet noon, he'll likely be working. Or drinking," she added. "It is almost noon, after all."

"I don't know how to take that comment," he said as they crossed onto the paved driveway.

"At face value," she quipped.

"I've always wanted a house like that," said Brent after the two-story English Tudor home was in sight.

"It certainly is something," she agreed as they made their way up the long driveway.

"It's like a castle on a hill," he continued. "I hope they don't raise the drawbridge before we get there," he jested.

"Please have some decorum when we get inside."

"I'm not an animal," he protested.

They arrived at the front door to a chorus of barks. Two dogs took turns barking as they paced back and forth in front of a second-story window.

Before Emily could knock on the door, a shadow appeared behind the leaded glass. She waited momentarily as someone unlocked the door and swung it open.

"My, my," said Terrance Sufferton. "Do my eyes deceive me?"

"No, it's really me," replied Emily. She dove into Terrance's open arms and subsequent embrace.

"You had me quite worried, child," he said in a fatherly voice. He wore neatly pressed slacks, a pinstriped button-down shirt, and loafers. His unkempt hair, white beard, and suspenders contrasted with his otherwise fashionable ensemble.

Terrance loosened his hold of Emily and put his hands on her shoulders. "You look horrible," he said with concerned eyes. He inched closer and adjusted his glasses. He gently turned her head with his hand as he inspected her bruised face. "It'll heal. You'll be fine," he added.

"Thanks," she responded, embarrassed and self-conscious of her injuries. She knew his kind words did not completely portray his thoughts.

"I can't imagine what you've been through. Come in." He glanced toward the street at the bottom of the driveway. He made a herding motion to Emily into his home.

Terrance stepped in front of Brent and looked him in the eyes as if he were assessing his character. After a pause, he offered him his hand. "I'm Terrance Sufferton. I usually know the names of people in my home."

"Brent. My name is Brent Gambel."

Terrance's handshake was firm, but short. He swung the door completely open and presented his home with a simple gesture of his open arm. "Please make yourself at home," he declared. "What's mine is yours."

"Thank you, Mr. Sufferton," Brent said. "Nice home," he added awkwardly.

Emily had never been to Terrance's second home, but he had mentioned it often. Everybody in the office knew about it. The closer he got to retirement age, the more time he spent working from it.

"Is Maggie home?" asked Emily.

"No, she's in DC. One of our daughters is visiting. I just needed some time to myself. I'll be meeting them tonight for dinner," he added after a slight pause. "Let's go to the kitchen." He led the way.

Marble tile lined the foyer, and premium wood floors were prevalent throughout the remainder of the first floor. They walked under the catwalk that anchored the east and west upper wings before arriving in the kitchen.

"I'd tell you to set your things down, except you didn't bring anything with you. Except that expensive-looking bag, I see. Well, you can set that anywhere, I suppose."

"We're traveling light. Our trip wasn't really pre-planned," stated Emily.

"That's understandable. I have to admit I was quite surprised to hear your name associated with Scott's murder. How are you holding up?"

"I haven't had time to grieve," she stated. "It's been hard. Very hard."

"The police interviewed me."

"I'm so sorry, Terrance. You should've never been involved in this mess."

"It's okay. They were fairly harmless. They just wanted to know when we spoke last and gathered general background information for profiling purposes."

"How's everyone at the office? I can only imagine what they must think of me."

"They all think you're completely innocent. As do I," he added as he placed his open hand on his chest. "None of this makes sense. They also mentioned something about some fellow named David. I don't recall his last name."

"They think I had something to do with David's death too?"

"They told me that his phone records indicated you were on the phone with him the morning of his death. They asked how close you were to him. You weren't in the office at the time of his death, and the park is only a short walking distance from the office. It's all circumstantial," he added. "No one thinks you were involved. Certainly not me."

"I can't dispute those facts," Emily admitted. She leaned against the kitchen cabinets for support.

"Emily, snap out of your self-pity," said Brent. "Terrance, I've been with her the past four days. We've had a murderous hound on our trail."

"Is that so?" asked Terrance as he looked at Emily.

"I'm afraid so," said Emily. "We've taken measures to ensure that we weren't followed here. We had a cab drop us off down the street. I really don't want to include you in this affair. If you want us to leave, please just say so."

"Of course not," Terrance responded. With a thoughtful expression, he added, "How can I be of assistance?"

"You're too kind. You've always been kind. Thank you."

"We'll get through this, child. You've always been like a daughter to me."

"And you've always been more than a mentor to me." She squeezed his hand to demonstrate her appreciation for all he had done. He gently patted her hand and returned her smile.

"This is great and all," started Brent, "but remember, we're dealing with some very disturbed people who want us dead."

"Of course. I understand," said Terrance. "What do you need from me?"

"Advice," stated Emily. "We want to present some information and talk through everything we've uncovered."

"Sounds like you've done some homework."

"Yes, we have. We're close. I think we have all of the pieces. We just need to put them together to tell a story. Your insight will definitely be appreciated."

"I'd be glad to provide any assistance I can." He removed his glasses and cleaned the lenses with the untucked portion of his shirt.

Before he put them back on, he paused. "Let's start with some swirly wine. I could use a drink."

Wine was one of Terrance's many eccentricities. He rarely made his purchases from retail stores. Instead, he bought wine through estate sales, where they were sold in cases of eleven. The twelfth bottle was sacrificed as a sample to potential buyers.

"I could use a good glass of wine," said Emily as she unconsciously stroked her brown hair.

"Me too," stated Brent with a shrug.

Emily saw Brent check his watch, then looked at her own.

It was twelve fifteen.

Part IV

Chapter 40

A large antique desk highlighted the exquisitely decorated office. Strategically placed at the back of the room, it granted a majestic view of the region's rolling hills. The desk occupied one end of an oversize ornate oriental rug that covered much of the wood floor.

Three full glasses of wine sat on the desk, next to the bottle that had held the deep purple liquid for nearly a quarter century. The wine, poured thirty minutes earlier, would remain untouched until Terrance deemed it ready.

Emily printed key documents housed on her flash drive with a seldom used printer and began to organize them. Terrance thoughtfully watched her from the chair he occupied behind the desk. Once the task was completed, she sat down on one of the two chairs stationed in front of the desk. Brent occupied the other one.

She began the conversation with an overview of the engagement with Owen and included highlights from their investigation. Terrance already knew the specifics, but this was the first time Brent had heard a complete description of the events.

When she detailed her encounter with Oscar at the train station and the subsequent meeting in Dupont

Circle, Brent's expression depicted amazement. She looked to Terrance. He seemed genuinely surprised by the encounter and adjusted his position in the chair, but didn't say a word. He never did when he reviewed an engagement with Emily. He always allowed her to finish before providing his thoughts.

Emily overlaid the deaths of Mark and David in the context of the investigation and what their roles were before they were murdered. She concluded the one-sided conversation after detailing her encounter with the Irishman at the restaurant and Scott's abduction.

"Is this all making sense?" she asked.

Terrance continued his thoughtful silence as he placed his thumb and index fingers on the stem of his glass. He rapidly swirled the wine. Once it settled, he proceeded to take his first sip.

"I have to admit," began Terrance. "This is much more elaborate than I would have thought. I had no idea that our client was so devious. And the man in the park? Can you provide any further detail on him?"

"Like what?" asked Emily.

"Who hired him or who he works for?"

"All I know is that he works with Owen. He has to. He's been following me. We've been lucky to evade him."

"I see that. You've been very lucky, indeed." He adjusted his glasses after he spoke.

"Have you ever seen someone matching his description with Owen?"

"No, but Owen isn't my client," Terrance stated plainly.

"What do you mean? Didn't he engage you as the firm partner?"

"No. This engagement was referred to me from Claudia. She didn't have time in her schedule, but I did."

"We need to tell her about Owen."

"I certainly think that would be wise," Terrance responded thoughtfully. "Before we do, let's see what you have." He gently banged his fist on the desk. "I want to understand everything you've uncovered."

The wall directly behind Emily was bare. The artwork that occupied the wall when they first entered the office had been neatly stacked by Brent in the corner of the room.

Emily switched her attention to a small stack of printer paper in front of her. She began writing the individual US account numbers on the paper. One account on each piece of paper. The pages were taped to the wall.

Once she finished, Emily picked up her wine glass and reviewed the matrix on the wall. "Our investigation really began when we learned about an investment in Uzbekistan."

"Okay," said Terrance as he tapped his chin in thought. "You mentioned that at our dinner last week. Enlighten me."

"Mark and I stumbled upon some investments Owen had in that country. At first glance, we didn't think much of it. But it led us to another account in Switzerland that housed a sizable amount of money. Over forty million," she added.

"I see," said Terrance. "That is a sizable sum."

"You see, there are eight subaccounts associated with the main account. The main account has twenty-one digits, which is typical for Swiss bank accounts. The eight subaccounts have nine digits, which indicates they are US bank routing numbers. We're the only country that uses nine digits."

Terrance nodded.

She placed a document from David's cloud drive on the wall. The Swiss bank insignia was visible. "I got this account summary from my friend David. He's the one who died in the park." Emily tapped the document on the wall for emphasis.

"This document..." Emily retrieved another document from the desk and handed it to Terrance. "This one is directly from one of the boxes given to us by our client. It has the same twenty-one-digit routing number as the Swiss bank account. The accounts match," she added.

Terrance examined the document. He glided his finger down the page to compare the account numbers to the ones posted on the wall. "So, they match. What does it mean?" He took off his glasses and began to clean them again with his shirt.

"It means a few things," Emily started. "First, there appears to be a consortium of eight people who share this account. Second, they own an interest in a Swiss bank account. Third, they own interests in public and private stocks, one of which is rather controversial." Emily reached over the desk and pulled out another document provided by David.

"One of the private stocks is an interest in a company in Uzbekistan. I've done some research regarding this investment. I think you'll like this."

Emily was feeling better. She had the complete attention of both Terrance and Brent. Everything was going as planned.

"I'm all ears," said Terrance with a smile.

"It appears that a hedge fund manager employed some unique investment strategies in the late 2000s. After the stock market crashed, investors began putting their money in precious metals."

"That's not surprising," stated Terrance. "That usually happens with a downturn in the economy. I think that specific trend was just exacerbated by the severity of the financial crisis."

"Exactly," said Emily. She continued her thought. "Now, this is where it gets more interesting. The fund manager is a guy by the name of Stan Murphy. After some research, it appears that his initial investments produced impressive returns."

"I've heard the name before," stated Terrance as he nodded.

"Me too," said Brent.

Emily continued, "Then you probably already know his strategy not only included precious metals, but also international mines. His investment strategy was highly speculative. I don't know if he just got lucky with his first investment, but his subsequent investments flopped."

"Oh, I know where this is going," interjected Brent. "I heard about him in the press. Didn't he have a Ponzi scheme?"

"Not exactly," said Terrance. "Highly speculative investments."

"Oh, that's right. It's coming back to me now. It was a few years back," Brent said, nodding his head. "He invested in mines that had been closed for some time. He made it seem as though they were still active, but they were actually..." Brent paused as he searched for the right word.

"Defunct," stated Emily.

"Exactly. Defunct. He was killed because of who he scammed, right? I read it was some sort of Russian group that did it."

"That's the way it was portrayed, but that's not the whole truth," replied Emily.

"What do you mean?" asked Brent.

"Apparently, he hid investments in Cyprus. A known tax haven."

"What? How did you figure that out?"

"I read it in one of Owen's emails."

"Is that so?" asked Terrance.

"Yes. During my reconnaissance of Owen's office, I copied his hard drive to this flash drive." She held up the small device like a trophy before placing it on the desk.

"You are certainly full of surprises," stated Terrance with a smile of disbelief. "I hope you made a back-up."

"Of course. I created a cloud storage account to house all of the data and documents I've uncovered. I can access it directly from my computer." She looked over to Brent, who was giving her a strange look. "What?"

"You went to his office undercover. You're fucking crazy."

Terrance shot him a disapproving glance.

"That's not all," Emily continued. "Owen met with Murphy in Cyprus just before his death. Murphy was in the process of withdrawing the funds before a significant tax levy was imposed by the Cyprus government."

"I know about the tax levy, but what does that have to do with the Swiss account?" asked Brent.

"Murphy got the funds out of Cyprus, but needed to put the funds somewhere. He was able to transfer them to a Swiss account. Good thing for us too."

"Why would you say that?" asked Terrance.

"If they hadn't been forced to switch banks, we wouldn't have found any evidence of Owen's involvement. Murphy just didn't have the time to mask who owned the investments before he died. It was the only real connection we found."

"Please elaborate," said Terrance.

"Okay. We identified a lot of small money transfers. They were in increments of less than $10,000 each. This allowed the money to be wired out of the country without alerting the banking authorities. The transfers were funneled to a Swiss account with direct ties to the US accounts. If he hadn't died, he likely would have been able to transfer the funds to other accounts without these ties."

"I see," stated Terrance. "Okay, let's circle back with what we know. Essentially, you have a Swiss account with ties to eight US bank accounts, a link to some shady investment in Uzbekistan, and funds transferred from a Cyprus bank account."

"That's right," stated Emily.

Terrance reviewed the information in front of him more closely. "At the end of the day, all we have is a list of bank routing numbers associated with some overseas investments. If we come forward now, we'll just have a wild accusation of wrongdoing without any concrete proof."

"I'm getting to that," stated Emily.

Terrance sat with his arms resting on his belly as he leaned back in his chair. Emily stood up and approached the wall with the account numbers.

She paced in front of Terrance and Brent as she spoke. "The people who own these accounts are smart people." She pointed to the account numbers for emphasis.

Brent interjected, "Wouldn't they just cover their tracks and divert the investments to hide any direct ownership?"

"I couldn't agree more. Why wouldn't they do that?" added Terrance.

"I've thought about that a lot. Something about Owen's visit to Cyprus bothered me. I did some investigating. After reading his emails, it was obvious there was friction between Murphy and his investors. I don't think he was trying to steal the money."

"Why would you say that?"

"It makes more sense considering that some of his clients, like the Russians, had mob ties. And look at the timing. He moved the funds to the Swiss account just a day before he died. He just didn't have time to move them out of that account."

"That's quite speculative."

"Yes, but I'm reading between the lines. That's what we do."

"Okay, say we accept this theory. What proof do you have?" asked Terrance. "For any of this?"

Emily pointed to the Swiss bank account and the investment in Uzbekistan. "We needed to create a link between these investments and the people who own them. Which is exactly why we researched the owners of the eight US bank accounts. Their interrelationships should shed some light on our investigation."

"I see," said Terrance again. The chair creaked when he sat forward.

"This is where Brent comes in," stated Emily as she pointed to him. "He has a banking background. He helped identify the individuals who owned the US bank accounts."

"Is that so?" said Terrance. He adjusted his glasses and swiveled his chair toward Brent. When he didn't immediately speak, Terrance gave him a reassuring nod.

"Of course. You want to hear what I've done. Okay." Brent stood up and walked over to the pages Emily had taped on the wall. He had a document in one hand, which he referenced, as he began writing on the pages with a pen. "I have identified these eight individuals as the owners of the Swiss bank account."

Chapter 41

Brent finished writing the names on printer paper and taped them on the wall. With an expression full of intrigue, Terrance got up from his chair and joined Emily next to the wall.

"Hmm," said Terrance as he gave his beard a thoughtful stroke.

"These are prominent people," said Emily to Terrance.

The eight names of the account holders were placed in a circular pattern on the wall: Owen Templeton, Lara Belinski, Margaret Welsh, Timothy Craft, Robert Nelson, Claudia Greene, Michael Thompson, and Katherine Hudson. To the right of the circle was the list of investments held in the Swiss bank account.

Terrance stood in silence as he reviewed the names.

"Lara Belinski is the Supreme Court Justice who was in the news two weeks ago," stated Brent.

"It makes you think about the car explosion a lot differently," added Emily.

"She was assassinated," said Brent.

"It certainly looks that way," agreed Terrance.

"A car bomb in the middle of DC?" asked Brent in a rhetorical tone. "Yeah, I think we could say she was assassinated."

"Fair enough," said Terrance.

"This name stands out," stated Emily as she pointed to Robert Nelson. "That's the US Attorney General."

Terrance adjusted his glasses. "He does share the same name."

"I don't recognize any of the other names, do you?" Emily asked both men as she pointed to the other names on the wall. All three of them concentrated on the printed names, as if staring at them would provide clarity.

"I can't say I do," stated Terrance. He lifted his wineglass to his lips. He swished the liquid in his mouth, then swallowed.

"No. Me, neither," added Brent.

"Well, we now have the names and the investments," stated Emily. "We need to determine the relationship between the people."

"What do you mean?" asked Brent. "Do you think these people are acting in concert?"

"What links everybody?" Emily asked in a rhetorical tone. "Before his murder, David indicated the people holding the investments were a prominent group. Looking at the names, I would have to agree. It's too much of a coincidence they just happen to share an international bank account in a tax haven. There's more to the story."

"I don't believe in coincidences," stated Terrance.

"Exactly. Neither do I. In consulting, I've learned there are no coincidences." Emily shook her head as she tried to look at the names from a different perspective. "Claudia Greene," she said to herself. There was something familiar about that name.

"What was that?" asked Terrance.

"That name." Emily pointed to the wall. "Claudia Greene. I've seen it somewhere. I just can't recall where."

Terrance looked at the name again. He shook his head. "It doesn't ring a bell."

Brent looked at Emily. "Do you think we have enough to go to the media?"

"Not yet."

"We have the accounts, we have the names. Why do we need to connect the dots? Can't someone else do that?"

"We have a listing of individuals associated with a Swiss bank account. We have a basic understanding of some of the investments held in that account. At the end of the day, I think all we have is a general accusation against some very influential people. We need specific accusations with evidence."

"We've done enough," said Brent.

"The puzzle is incomplete," said Emily. "I wouldn't place much credibility on these accusations if I were an outsider."

"Seriously?" asked Brent.

"Unfortunately, Emily is right," said Terrance with an air of authority.

"Shit, we've been through hell. We can't hold out forever. We just can't," Brent added. "We have a blood hound on our trail. Remember? He'll find us," he said, staring directly at Emily.

"I haven't forgotten. But we have to finish our work." She walked over to Brent and gave him a comforting squeeze on the hand.

Confused, Terrance looked at the two of them. "How do you two know each other again?"

"It's awkward," Emily responded. "We went on two dates a few years back. It didn't end well."

"That's an understatement," added Brent.

"I won't pry," said Terrance.

"If we're going to do this, let's get it done," said Brent to Emily.

She looked at Terrance. "Do you mind if we work in your office?"

"Of course not. Please use every resource I have." He smiled at her.

Emily heard the front door open. The sound was unmistakable. She glanced at Brent. Her heart sank. She immediately ran to Jen's purse, next to the desk, and pulled out her uncle's pistol.

"Hold on!" shouted Terrance when he saw the gun. He waved his hands back and forth as he approached Emily. "It's just my driver. I'm heading back to DC tonight. My daughter is in town. Remember? I'll be back in the morning."

Emily placed the gun behind her back right before his driver, Herb, entered the office.

"My bag's in the hall closet," he said to the man standing stoically in the doorway.

"Very well. I'll be waiting in the car. Please let me know if you need anything further from me." He turned around and exited the room as quietly as he came.

"Where did you get that?" asked Terrance.

"A lot has changed over the past week. I needed something with stopping power." Emily placed the gun back in Jen's purse.

"That would certainly do it."

"Why does he have a driver?" Brent asked Emily with a confused look.

"He doesn't drive," stated Emily. "He never has. It's a long story."

Terrance just gave a casual shrug as he dismissed the conversation. "Do you need anything further from me? I know you have some work to do, but I need to go." Before Emily could speak, he added, "Don't worry. I'll talk to Claudia."

"Good. Thanks, Terrance. Are you sure it's okay that we stay here to complete our investigation? We need to know more about the Consortium," she said as she glanced to the names posted on the wall.

"Of course. The Consortium? Sounds devious," he said with a playful smile. "I hope I've at least been somewhat helpful," he said as he approached her.

"You have," Emily replied. "Besides, we were not sure where else to go. We needed some time to figure everything out. Your hospitality is appreciated. Thank you."

Terrance embraced her. "Be careful," he said to her in a fatherly tone. "I mean it."

"I will," said Emily as she looked up. Their eyes met. She saw a sadness in him. "I'll be fine. Seriously."

"I don't have a car here for your convenience. Maggie took the car to DC."

"We're not planning on going anywhere," said Emily. "We have plenty of work here."

"Help yourself to the wine in the cellar. Start with a good Bordeaux. I have one that's very drinkable in the top drawer of my desk. Just make sure you give it adequate time to breathe."

"We will."

He turned his attention to Brent. "It was nice meeting you."

"You too, Terrance."

"Terrance, I need to use the ladies' room. At the sake of getting lost, could you direct me?"

"Of course. Down the hall and past the garage, you'll find it on the left." Before she could turn to leave, Terrance spoke again. "Emily, would you mind if I quickly check my email before leaving?" Terrance asked, pointing at her computer. "My phone is dead. That's why my driver came inside," he added. "He couldn't get a hold of me."

"Of course not. Help yourself." She unlocked the computer and waited for Terrance.

Terrance walked behind the desk and sat down. After just a minute, he spoke. "Oh, no."

"What is it?" asked Emily.

"Sorry, a client on another engagement is freaking out. I need to respond to him." He made eye contact with Emily. "I'll just need a minute."

"Sure." Emily headed toward the bathroom.

Terrance just spent a few more minutes at the computer, collected some personal items and exited the room.

By the time Emily returned, Terrance was gone. Brent sat at one of the seats in front of the desk, his attention focused on the wall where they had placed their evidence. She sat next to him and turned the computer around to face it in her direction.

"Okay, Boss," he said to her without taking his eyes away from the wall. "What's next?"

"Let's find out what we can about these people. They have to be connected somehow. I know where to start. One of the names really stands out to me. It really bothers me and I need to know why." She sat at the desk and began typing on her keyboard in search of an answer.

Chapter 42

"**W**hat exactly are you looking for?" asked Brent. He turned toward Emily, who stopped typing on the keyboard to address his question.

"The name *Claudia Greene* is familiar. I just don't know from where."

"That's a fairly common last name," stated Brent.

"It's more than that. Terrance knows something. He's just not telling us."

"His help seemed sincere to me. But what do I know, I just met the guy. What aren't *you* telling me?"

Emily stopped typing and looked up. She didn't look at Brent. She just stared in thought. "He was just different. He was purposefully being vague."

"Talk like a human," Brent said.

"He was hiding something. I just don't know what."

"I think you're crazy. He's obviously not involved. If he was, we would be dead."

Emily stopped listening. She didn't want to be distracted from her task. She refocused on the screen in front of her.

An initial Internet query of Claudia Greene didn't yield any significant results. Brent was right. The name was too common. Frustrated, she decided to research the other names.

"Okay, let's start from the top," she said to Brent as she voiced her thoughts. "We know about Owen Templeton, Lara Belinski, and Robert Nelson."

Brent got up from his chair. He walked to the names posted on the wall. "I'll fill in the background information on the *Consortium*. You talk and I write. Sound good?"

"Perfect," replied Emily. She began typing the names in her computer. She spoke every time she found something of interest.

"There are many Timothy Crafts, with the most prominent being a federal judge. I think we can go with this for now."

"I agree," replied Brent as he wrote it down.

After a few more minutes, Emily spoke again. "Katherine Hudson appears to be a judge. US District Court of New York," she added.

"Another lawyer, huh?" He scribbled her words on the wall.

"This is intriguing," said Emily. "It appears that Michael Thompson might be a law professor at Harvard."

"So far, they're all lawyers. Did Terrance go to law school?"

"No, he didn't."

"Well, wouldn't that discount him as part of the Consortium?"

"It might," she replied.

"The thought of him being part of the Consortium crossed your mind, right? I mean, before we got here and not just now."

"Of course I thought about it. I just can't see it. He's my friend."

"So was Jen."

"That was different. I've worked long hours with Terrance. You really get to know someone that way. It's just not in his character. Maybe I'm blind, but I just can't see it."

"All right, let's move on. There needs to be a connection between everyone," said Brent. "We haven't identified anyone in consulting. Have any of these people worked with Terrance or your firm?"

"I don't think so, but I know *someone* who is a lawyer. She just doesn't practice law." Emily looked around the room. Against the far wall of the office were family pictures organized on built-in shelves. Cabinets lined the bottom portion of the wall structure.

Emily got up and walked toward the pictures. In the center of the shelves were a collection of black-and-white photos from Terrance's wedding.

The centerpiece of the collection was a formal wedding picture. Wedged in the corner of the picture frame, against the glass, was a piece of paper. Her mouth dropped.

Emily pulled the piece of paper out of the frame. She stared at it in disbelief.

"What is it?" asked Brent. She didn't respond and continued to stare at it with her mouth agape. He approached her.

"I don't believe it." She handed the small piece of paper to Brent.

He glanced at it and immediately began to speak. "I don't get it, a wedding announcement?"

After a moment, he said exactly what Emily was thinking. "Oh, shit. This changes everything." He immediately made eye contact with her.

It was Terrance's wedding announcement. Written in ornate script, the document indicated that Terrance

Fitzgerald Sufferton was to marry *Margaret Anne Welsh* on May 13, 1978.

"So, Terrance's wife went to law school and is one of the Consortium members?" asked Brent with a blank stare.

"I can't believe this," stated Emily. "I feel like such a fool. I trusted him. He was instrumental in my career. How could I have been so blind?"

"How could you ever see this coming? It's not something a reasonable person would ever think about."

"But there must have been warning signs," she said as she mentally recalled past conversations. She needed answers.

"Don't focus on the past," stated Brent. "Let's figure out how this information can help us."

"Help us?" asked Emily as she looked at him. "He knows we'll figure this out."

"Maybe not," he replied.

"I think we're screwed." She began to pace and her mind raced.

Brent met her in the middle of the room. "The Emily I know doesn't think that way." He grabbed her shoulders and stared directly into her eyes. "We can do this if we work together."

"I don't know," she said with great uncertainty in her voice.

"That must be the reason he left so quickly."

"He's not going to meet his daughter in DC. I'm certain of that."

"How do you know?"

"He never meets them at his condo in DC. They always meet him here. I didn't think of that until just now."

"Then who is he going to meet?"

"The other members of the Consortium! That has to be it, right?"

"It sounds plausible. But how does that help us?"

"Just hear me out." Emily began to formulate her thoughts. "Ben said something to me the day they took Scott."

"What?"

"He said that I wouldn't be protected forever. Keyword, *protected*."

"I guess the old man has a soft spot for you."

"Exactly," she said as she pondered Terrance's actions.

"Whatever we do, we need to act quickly," said Brent. "Let's quickly finish our research while we have an Internet connection and then get out. We still haven't identified Ms. Greene."

The answer hit Emily. "That's it!" she said.

"What's it?" asked Brent with a confused expression.

"You're a genius," she said, looking at him.

"Explain."

"I'll explain in the car," she replied. "We need to get out of here. Besides, I'm the real genius anyway. Start collecting the documents. We need to take everything with us. There's something else here that I need to get before we go. I know it's here."

"Whatever gets us out of here faster."

Emily walked to the filing cabinets located below the built-in bookshelves. She tried opening one, then the others. All three were locked.

She began searching the room for the key. She didn't find it when she rifled through the desk and checked behind the picture frames. Frustrated, she left the room as Brent continued to collect documents.

Emily returned a few minutes later with a crowbar. She immediately began to pry open the middle cabinet. She struggled to get the proper leverage.

"Jesus Christ," said Brent when he looked up from the desk to see her actions. "I really hope you're right about Terrance. Otherwise, we'll have a lot of explaining to do."

"Help, please," she said as she continued to struggle.

Brent wedged the crowbar in the thin space between the drawer and the top of the cabinet. He began to push down on the handle to create leverage. It didn't budge. He worked at it for a few minutes, but couldn't open the drawer.

"Will this help?" asked Emily.

"Great. You found the key?" He looked over his shoulder, but she didn't have a key. She held a sledgehammer. "Jesus! Where do you keep finding these tools?"

"Apparently wealthy people have lots of tools in their garages."

"Lady, you have issues. Let me take that before you hurt yourself. Or me, for that matter," he added.

"Stand back," she said.

"Emily, *come on.*" He was about to take it from her, but was deterred by her stance. She held the weapon above her shoulder and behind her head. She looked like a baseball player preparing to strike a ball.

She hit the cabinet dead center. The impact of the sledgehammer crippled the structure with a resonating *thud.*

Brent inserted the crowbar in the space provided from Emily's blow to the cabinet. With a few hard thrusts, the drawer was free. He pulled it open to reveal a series of manila folders housed in green hanging folders.

Emily stepped forward and began to review the folders, which were meticulously organized. She glanced through the folders, moving through groups of them with a quick flick of her index finger until she got to the ones that started with the letter "*S*."

After removing a folder labeled "Sufferton & Waine" from the ruined cabinet, Emily knelt and placed the file folder on the ground. She looked behind her. Brent had resumed collecting their research and began placing everything in a banker box he found and emptied from Terrance's office.

"Are you finished?" she asked.

"Just about," he said as he looked toward her. "I'm taking this too." He held up a bottle of wine. "Can't let that go to waste," he added.

"Huh, not a bad idea."

"Find what you're looking for?"

"I still need a few minutes. Why don't you get the car? That should speed us up."

"Gotcha. I'll leave the box for you. Add whatever documents you find."

"Okay. Just hurry," she added. "I can't think of a more dangerous place for us to be right now."

After Brent rushed out of the room, Emily checked her watch. They were running short on time. The Irishman could already be on his way. Terrance had ample opportunity to contact the man while they were there. She just didn't know if he had. *He could still be protecting me.*

She resumed searching the contents of the folder. She thumbed through the documents, trying to find a specific one. *It has to be here.*

Emily finally found the document she sought toward the end of the manila folder. Her spirits rose as she lifted it out of the folder. "Here it is," she said to herself.

The document was labeled *Sufferton & Waine, LLC, Articles of Organization, August 1, 2002*. It contained all of the governing rules of the firm as agreed upon by its founding members.

Emily was not interested in the bylaws or any other substantive information contained in the document. She flipped directly to the last page. A nearly imperceptible smile flashed on her face. The name she stared at was amongst all the other signature lines of the firm's founding members.

She knew she recognized the name *Claudia Greene* from somewhere. She realized she must have seen Claudia's maiden name from an old engagement she reviewed when she first started at the firm. Emily didn't have time to gloat. There was much to be completed if she had any hope of staying alive.

Before taking her eyes off the document, something caught her eye that completely changed her perspective on the Consortium. She recognized almost all of the names on the document. They were the founding members' printed names and signatures. One name she did not recognize, *Dimitris Andreadis*. It wasn't his printed name that alerted her to his presence. It was what was stamped next to it.

Her finger reached toward the marking. The bird and olive branch insignia she had seen before. *What does this mean?*

She opened the lid to the banker box Brent used and placed the newly discovered document on top. She thought about the information it contained. It would be devastating if they lost it.

Emily decided to pull the key files out of the box. She began with the documents David provided. Next were the documents Brent provided as support for the account holders.

She also included the wedding announcement and the articles of organization. Finally, she picked a few key documents provided by Owen. There were a dozen documents in total.

She used her phone to photograph each one, and then sent them to the email account she had created last week. She placed the documents back in the box and put the lid on.

After copying the digital files to her computer, she looked for the flash drive she placed on the desk earlier. It wasn't there. She searched all around the desk, on the floor, in the drawers. Still nothing. Terrance had taken it. She remembered he had asked to use her computer before leaving.

Why would he take it? Her mind raced. He must have thought there was something incriminating that I failed to find. Emily accessed the back-up she had placed on the cloud drive.

Her heart sank when it opened. The cloud drive was empty with no way to get the data back.

"That bastard," she said. She opened the files on her computer. They too had been securely erased. "Shit!" she said as she slammed her hand on the table. She had been duped.

I have to get that flash drive back!

Emily turned off the computer and slid it into Jen's purse. She picked up the box and proceeded to the front door. Before exiting, she looked around the room.

It was in complete disarray, and documents were scattered over the floor. Against the far wall, the cabinets had been nearly destroyed by the sledgehammer. The center drawer hung at a forty-five-degree angle.

Emily had an unfamiliar feeling. Almost like the damage made her happy. *I'm not done yet.*

With one final thought, she walked to the corner of the room where Brent had placed the artwork taken down from the wall. She didn't need to look hard to find the piece she sought. She selected the most ornate frame. According to Terrance, it was hand-carved from a solid piece of wood.

Emily strode out of Terrance's front door. In one arm, she held just enough incriminating evidence to make Terrance and his cronies want to murder her and anyone who aided her effort. In her other arm, she held *Dante's Hell.*

Chapter 43

MONDAY. 5:27 PM.

The Mercedes' engine hummed in the driveway of Terrance's stately home. Brent sat in the passenger seat with the window rolled partly down. He stared at her when he spoke. "What the hell is that?"

"It's my new painting. I deserve it," she said with an oversize grin. "Besides, it's Terrance's favorite piece of artwork."

"It's ugly," cried Brent as he strained his head out the window to get a better view of it.

"Beauty is in the eye of the beholder. I think it's gorgeous." She placed the box of documents and the artwork in the trunk of the red two-door coupe.

She walked around the vehicle and sat in the driver's seat. "Couldn't handle the horsepower?" she asked.

"I just know you're crazy when it comes to cars. Besides, you really are a good driver."

"At least you know your place," quipped Emily.

"What are you planning on doing with that crazy painting?" he asked with his thumb pointed toward the trunk.

"If you are referring to the artwork I *stole*, we're going to make a quick stop at a post office. I'm going to mail it to Jen's condo."

"Why there?"

"She's not home, but they'll hold it in the office's storage room for some time."

"That makes sense, I guess."

"Besides," she continued, "If we make it out of this mess with our lives, I'm going to retrieve the painting and place it on my wall. It'll be a constant reminder not to trust anyone."

She placed the car in gear and sped down the long driveway. Soon, they were on the highway.

"I see we're heading north. I really don't have to ask where we are going, do I?" asked Brent.

"He stole my flash drive."

"Terrance?"

"Yep."

"Good thing we have a backup."

"He erased that too."

"He erased the cloud backup? Why did you leave him alone?"

"He asked to use my computer and made it seem like there was a client emergency. I fell for it. My cloud storage account doesn't require a password when you're logged-in."

"The wily old fuck."

"Yep."

"I can't tell if you're taking this well or not."

"I'm furious. He really screwed us."

"What information do we have?"

"We still have access to the documents from David's cloud storage, but nothing from Owen's computer. It's all gone."

"What was so important that Terrance had to risk stealing the flash drive and erase your backups?"

"I don't know."

"Then why are we trying to retrieve it?"

"Because Terrance believes there is something very important on it. Something I missed."

"How are we going to get it?"

"I don't know," she replied mostly to herself. "We'll do whatever it takes to get it back."

"So, it's safe to say, we're heading back into the fire."

"Yep. We had a good run," said Emily, smiling.

"Don't talk like that. It's not funny. So what's the plan?"

"I'm still formulating one." She kept her eyes fixed on the road.

"Do you know where we're heading, at least?"

"Yes."

"Care to share?"

Emily handed him her phone. The cellular signal was turned off, but the voicemail messages she previously heard were still there. "Listen to the last voicemail."

He looked at her phone. "The one from Terrance?"

"Yep."

He listened to it before he spoke. "He said he had a shareholder's meeting on Monday night, which is tonight."

"Exactly. He lied to us. He's not meeting his daughter. He's meeting the other shareholders. They always hold the meetings at Claudia's home."

"How do you know that?"

"He's mentioned them in the past."

"So, we're just going to crash the meeting and demand the flash drive?"

"No, first we're going to Old Town."

"Why would we head there?"

"There's a great oyster bar there. I'm starving, aren't you?" said Emily.

"I have to admit I'm not really thinking about food right now."

"We need to bide our time. We'll need the cover of darkness to complete our next task."

"I'm not sure I like the sound of that plan. Are we going to be wearing all black too, with *ski masks?*" he asked.

"Not a bad idea," said Emily.

"Actually, clam chowder sounds really good." His stomach growled from hunger.

"Now you're on board," she said, sounding pleased.

"How can you do this?"

"Do what?"

"Make me think about food given all we're going through," said Brent.

"We're just hungry, that's all," said Emily.

The seafood restaurant looked like every other seafood restaurant in the area, decorated with an abundance of light blue wainscoting. They sat in silence on the streetside patio.

The late afternoon sun made it feel almost warm. When the sun disappeared, the chill returned. A wait staff came by to light the gas heat lamps. The flames, covered by an ornate metal grate, provided a welcoming warmth.

"How are you holding up?" asked Brent after the clam chowder was served.

Emily casually opened a bag of salty oyster crackers. She tumbled the crackers into the hot soup.

"I'm actually okay." She poked the crackers to submerge them. Most popped back to the surface.

"You seem a little down, compared to earlier," said Brent. He blew on the chowder-covered spoon.

"I'm just a little worried about tonight."

"You are human, after all," he quipped.

"Ha-ha," replied Emily.

"So, I know where we're going, but am still a bit fuzzy on what we're going to achieve. How are we going to get the flash drive?"

"We're going to do some reconnaissance first," Emily stated plainly. Earlier, she'd identified their destination with a quick Internet query. She knew it was going to be dangerous, but their options were limited. "We know where Terrance will be tonight. We'll follow him and... get the flash drive somehow."

"That's not a plan. Do I really need to remind you that we're not qualified to do this?" said Brent.

"Who else will? There's something really fucked up going on here."

"Yes. I'm well aware of that by now. It's just dangerous, that's all."

"I know it is. People have lost their lives because of me."

"There it is," stated Brent. "You said *me*. You're making this too personal. It's blinding your judgment. These are our lives you're playing with here."

"You're right," replied Emily. "I'm completely aware of our situation. But I'm intent on seeing this out. To its completion. Are you reconsidering your role? I would understand if you don't want to be part of it anymore."

Brent was about to reply, but was interrupted by the waiter. He reached in front of Brent to remove his soup bowl and replaced it with a plate of fish and chips.

Emily smiled at the shrimp and chargrilled oysters on her plate. "Mmm, smells good."

"You're so annoying. Don't even try."

"Try what?" she innocently asked.

"Changing the subject, that's what. You know I'm in." His tone was resigned. "I just..." He sighed. "I just want to get through this alive."

"Me too," she said as she patted the thrift store shopping bag next to her chair. It was filled with clothes for their evening adventure. Black clothes.

Chapter 44

The unusually bright moon peered through a thin cloud covering. With her shadow seemingly staring back at her, Emily wished it were darker. Some things were simply out of her control. *Most things*, she thought with a sigh. The forecast called for rain, but she held hope the storm would miss them.

Her hope would be fruitless.

Emily had parked their red coupe out of sight from the street near the home they wanted to observe in the upscale and secluded suburb located just outside of DC. The nearest house was nearly one hundred yards away through densely populated trees and privacy shrubs. They walked toward the home along a forest preserve that separated the expansive homes from the Potomac River.

The coffee that once warmed their bellies was long gone. "I'm cold," stated Brent. "I can even see my breath," he said as he exhaled.

Emily ignored him as she concentrated on approaching the house undetected. She knew Terrance was there. They had passed his driver earlier, as he sat in a parked car some distance from the home.

The house had an attached garage. She assumed there had to be at least two other visitors given the two cars parked on the large circular driveway. Probably more.

"I can't see anyone, can you?" asked Emily.

"No. I don't think we should get any closer, either," he said. He looked to Emily, but she had already begun moving closer to the house.

As they approached, a twig beneath Emily's feet snapped. The sound seemed to echo in her head. She knew it wasn't as loud as she thought, but she stopped regardless. She watched the house intently, but didn't see any movement in the windows or around the perimeter.

Before she continued, a voice behind her spoke, "See anything?"

Emily flinched. "Jesus Christ!" she said in a loud whisper. "Don't do that again. You scared the bejesus out of me."

"Sorry," whispered Brent as he cringed and bared his teeth. "I'm trying to be quiet."

They slowly approached the house, using the vegetation as cover. Once they got to the home, they pressed their backs against the wall. Emily took a deep breath.

"Whew."

"This is crazy," said Brent.

"I know. But you don't have to keep saying that," said Emily. "We need to see who else is here."

"I suggest taking pictures of the license plates."

"That's not going to help us at this moment. We need to see faces."

"Yeah, but these faces have friends with guns."

"You keep stating the obvious," she said. "But so do we."

They had two pistols with them. The Beretta from her uncle's condo and the one the Irishman placed in Emily's hand after the young police officer was murdered.

They knew there was no use in disposing of the weapon to distance themselves from the murder. They needed two handguns and did not know how else to get one. She subconsciously put her hand against her back to ensure the weapon was still in her waistband.

The hard, metallic barrel was ice-cold and rubbed uncomfortably against her spine. She had checked to make sure the gun's safety was engaged three times before placing it there.

"I don't hear anything, do you?" she asked Brent.

"Nothing. I can't believe I'm saying this, but I think we need to move quietly around the perimeter."

"I agree," she replied.

The style and layout of the home reflected its age. The elongated design, consisting of many small rooms, made it difficult to effectively peer into the home.

As they made their way around the back, Emily watched for motion sensors or infrared cameras that would monitor the property. She didn't see any obvious devices as they passed the kitchen and living room.

A distinct odor entered Emily's nostrils. "Do you smell that?" she asked Brent.

"I used to love that smell," he replied. "Not anymore."

In a crouched stance, she moved ten feet away from the wall and looked back toward the house. She could see smoke emanating from one of the stone chimneys that rose from the slate roof.

"The smoke is coming from the east wing. It's around the house and down a way." She indicated the direction with a movement of her hands.

Brent took the lead as they carefully walked to the edge of the home. He peered around the corner. "I see some light..."

"What else do you see? Can we get closer?"

"Easy," said Brent as he put his open hand toward the ground in a pushing motion. He turned to her as he spoke. "There's a large wall of windows and, I think, glass French doors. At least that's what it looks like from the light pattern."

He looked around the corner again, before he continued his thought. "There's a patio off the room with a row of hedges. That would be our best vantage point."

She followed him as he led them toward the hedges. Observing the area, Emily noted the corner lot provided an abundance of privacy. Beyond the hedge, the property sloped steeply toward a canal.

Neither spoke a word as they moved carefully toward their destination. Their heads lifted slowly over the hedge as they peered into the home. A stately decorated office study came into view. At one end, there was an empty ornate wood desk. On the opposing end, there were four people positioned near an oversize fireplace.

"There's Terrance," she whispered. He sat on one of the two chairs closest to the roaring fire.

"And Owen too," said Brent, pointing to the other chair.

A stout woman paced back and forth in the study. She stopped numerous times in front of Terrance. She waved her finger at him as she spoke.

"I take it that's her?" asked Brent, even though it was obvious she was the only woman in the room. "She looks angry."

"Yes. That's Claudia Briggs. You'd recognize her name as Claudia Greene."

"No shit. So that's what you were looking for in the office."

"I got a document with her name and signature."

"I can't hear what's she saying, can you?" asked Brent.

"No, I can't. But she really likes the 'f' word," said Emily.

"I can see that. He's probably getting a lashing for letting you go."

"Probably," said Emily.

Emily almost felt pity for Terrance as she watched. He didn't defend himself as Claudia berated him. She was surprised by her reaction. He had lied to her. He put her in harm's way. But for some reason, Terrance was still her friend.

A fourth person stood on the perimeter of the room. Neither Emily nor Brent was able to make out a face, until he stepped out of a shadow.

"Oh, shit," stated Brent. "That's the guy I leveled with the vase."

It was Ben. She had hoped they wouldn't see him tonight. He wasn't one of the eight US account holders, but was Owen's right-hand man. She remembered their encounter at the office. *He will be armed*, she thought.

They waited in silence for what felt like an eternity. The tension appeared to rise in the room. Terrance yelled back as he began to stand his ground.

Owen never said a word. He seemed to be a bystander as Terrance and Claudia continued their heated debate.

"Emily, we're done," stated Brent. "We've confirmed the identity of Claudia Greene. No one else showed up. Were you expecting the president?" he asked in a condescending tone.

"We're not done. We need that flash drive. We'll wait until Terrance leaves and follow him. He either has it on him or it's at his DC condo. He hasn't had time to drop it anywhere else."

"Unless he hands it over to these people."

"Which is why we're here," said Emily as she kept her eyes fixed on the people in the room.

"What are we going to do, charge the room if he hands it over to them?"

"Of course not. I-I don't know what we'd do then."

Terrance got up from his chair to pour a drink. He walked over to Claudia. Before she could speak, he put his free hand up as if a final decision had been made.

A few additional words were spoken to Claudia before he abruptly turned around. Terrance downed his drink in one gulp. He placed it on the bar when he passed it on the way to the door.

"This might be it," stated Brent. "Thank God."

Claudia didn't say a word, but made eye contact with Ben. He had been standing quietly against the wall until he met Claudia's gaze.

Ben immediately reached inside his suit jacket. He pulled out a pistol and cocked the barrel with a swift movement of his hand.

"Oh no!" exclaimed Emily as an overwhelming sense of fear engulfed her.

Terrance turned around to see the gun trained on him. He didn't seem surprised. He didn't flinch.

Emily couldn't help but recall how the events unfolded when David was murdered in the park. She thought about how she froze and was unable to speak *before* the needle entered David's body.

She stood up.

"Get down," said Brent. He tugged her jacket from his crouched position.

Ben approached with the weapon aimed directly at Terrance's head. He stopped three feet in front of the man. His lips moved as his free hand stretched toward Terrance with an open palm. The pistoled hand remained steady.

"What's he doing?" asked Brent as his attention switched back to the action inside the room.

Emily knew the answer. Terrance produced a small device from the inside pocket of his blue blazer.

"Shit! That's the flash drive," he said as he rose to join his standing companion.

She found herself less concerned with the device as she pondered the fate of the man she had worked with for so many years. *He's a dead man.*

"What do we do now?" asked Brent.

She found her voice and spoke without any thought of the consequences. The single word screamed out of her mouth.

"Terrance!"

Ben turned toward the window. He then looked back to Claudia for instruction. She said three words that didn't need to be heard to be understood. *Go. Kill. Her.*

"What the fuck did you just do!" said Brent. It wasn't a question. It was a damning statement.

Chapter 45

Emily and Brent stood outside the study of Claudia Briggs's home. Emily's indiscretion had cost them their anonymity. They braced for what would come next.

Ben didn't immediately go toward them. Instead, he approached a wall. With a flick of his wrist, the room went dark. In that split second, they lost their only advantage.

It was now darker inside than it was outside. Emily couldn't see anyone in the room, but the moonlight left them exposed. She ducked behind the hedge. Brent joined her.

"Shit," spat Brent. "We're fucked. We need to get out of here." After a brief pause, he added, "Pronto." He began to run down the hill, toward the canal, in a crouched position. He looked at Emily after his fifth stride. She hadn't moved. "Are you deaf, or stupid?" he asked incredulously. "Let's go!"

He ran back for her. When he grabbed her arm, he saw the light in the study turn back on. Ben stood on the side of the window as his eyes scanned outside.

Terrance stood next to the light switch. He stared blankly out the windows.

Claudia appeared from behind the desk. She moved toward a second light switch. Before she could hit it, Terrance charged her. His belly twisted from side to side as he ran.

"Run, Emily!" he yelled. Ben turned and aimed his gun at Terrance. Before he could pull the trigger, the room went dark again.

Brent reiterated his plea to Emily. "Let's go, now!"

She began to turn, then stopped herself. There were two quick flashes in the room. The first flash revealed Owen had abandoned his position behind the chair next to the fireplace.

The second flash revealed Terrance had been shot. The bullet had flung him against the wall. Splattered blood covered the wall above him.

Emily pulled the gun from her waistband and aimed it at the wall of windows.

As she steadied the gun, a fleeting thought of her first hunting trip passed through her head. Her uncle had taught her the mechanics of using a weapon and how to respect the circle of life.

Aiming a weapon at a human being had nothing in common with that experience. It felt so terribly wrong.

She searched in herself to find the callousness necessary to see the people in the room not as human beings, but as dangerous objects.

She aimed at where Ben had stood before the lights went off and pulled the trigger once, twice, three times. The bullets obliterated the windows. Her accuracy was poor at first, but improved with every shot as she gained familiarity with the weapon's weight and recoil. She kept shooting and counted the shots in her head and stopped on the seventh.

Emily switched the focus of her aim and pulled the trigger five more times at Claudia. The flashes from her barrel did not provide the same illumination as Ben's gun inside the study. She could only witness silhouettes of chaos as glass shards and paper fragments from the desk littered the room.

The clip only held fifteen bullets. She fired the rest toward where Owen had been. With the gun clip empty, she dropped to the ground and rolled toward Brent. The terrified expression on his face indicated he wouldn't be of any help. She didn't have time to think about his well-being.

A barrage of bullets filled the air where she had just been moments ago. Emily pulled her face to the ground and covered the top of her head with her arms as fragments of wood and leaves fell around her.

She lifted her right elbow to peek at Brent. He had rolled partway down the hill, out of harm's way. They made eye contact. *That might have woken him up*, she thought.

Lying on her back to minimize her profile, she pulled the empty clip out and placed it in an outside coat pocket. She reached into her inner coat pocket to retrieve a second clip. The only one she had left. There were some loose bullets in her coat pocket, but she knew there wouldn't be time to fill a clip.

Emily shoved the clip into the pistol and cocked the weapon. Using the hedge as cover, she poked the gun barrel through. Another three blasts struck just to her right.

This time, Emily resisted the urge to recoil and held her position. She carefully aimed at the source of the flashes. She pulled the trigger eight times in quick succession. She varied her aim slightly to hit anything in the vicinity.

One of the bullet impacts made a distinctly different sound than the rest. Almost like bone cracking. She thought she saw a shape fall back and disappear, but couldn't be sure. *Did one of my bullets strike someone?* After the echoes from her blasts stopped, an eerie silence hung in the air.

Emily listened.

No other sounds came from the room. She looked around the yard to thwart any attempt to flank their position. There wasn't any movement.

"Brent," she said in a loud whisper.

"Yes," he replied. "I'm here."

"Provide a distraction."

"Why?"

"I'm going in."

"Are you crazy?"

"I have to get the flash drive," Emily stated.

"Don't go."

"Just cover me. I'm going." He crouched next to her. She took his gun and gave him hers. "There are seven shots left," she said to him.

"I think the one you have now only holds twelve," said Brent. "I think," he reiterated.

"It does." She checked the safety. It was still on. She gave him a condescending glance when she turned it off. "On three."

"You're crazy," he said again.

Emily held up one finger. They counted the remaining numbers in their heads. On three, Brent stood up and pulled the trigger three times. The first shot reflected off the wall above the French doors. The recoil caused the second and third shots to deviate even farther from the intended target.

The distraction provided Emily enough time to get to the house wall. She reached down and grabbed a handful of river rock from the landscaping near her feet. She then held up two fingers with the same hand, indicating to Brent that she was ready to go in.

He fired twice. This time she heard the bullets hit the room. She threw the rocks into the room. Her plan had been to jump through the broken window, but she didn't move. She looked to Brent, who gave her a confused expression. Nervous, she exhaled and prepared herself.

She held up two fingers as a signal to Brent that she wanted to try it again. She closed her eyes to summon courage. She was about to lower her hand when she heard a voice from inside the room.

"It's safe." The voice was undeniably Terrance's.

"I don't believe you," she said, concentrating to hear any sound emanating from the room. She couldn't hear anything other than Terrance's constricted breathing.

Terrance spoke again with short sentences and long pauses to draw oxygen into his lungs. "Ben is dead. The rest left. They're not fighters. Other people do their dirty work."

Emily peered into the room. Her eyes took a few moments to adjust to the low light. She saw one body on the floor and Terrance against the far wall. A significant amount of blood had pooled around him.

She cautiously entered the room and approached the far wall. She felt around for the light switch. The illuminated room confirmed there were only two other people in the room with Emily. Ben's skull had a large hole just near his left temple. He was indeed dead.

She approached Terrance. His eyes slit open briefly. Emily surprised herself with her next move. She raised the gun to his face. She expected to have compassion for him. Instead, all she felt was anger.

"Give me one reason why I shouldn't pull this trigger right now."

"You need me. Besides, you're not a murderer."

"I wasn't a murderer," Emily quickly replied. "I wasn't a lot things before you involved me in this hell. Jen is dead. My hands took her life." After a brief pause, she added, "You made me a murderer!"

Terrance opened his eyes again. This time he kept them open. The look on his face indicated genuine surprise.

"You're still not going to shoot me," he said again with a cough.

She kept the weapon aimed at Terrance. "You deserve to die, but I'm sure you know that. I trusted you. You returned my trust with betrayal."

"I know."

Emily could see a specific sadness in his eyes. "Why me?"

"It had to be you." He coughed twice, then wiped his mouth with a monogrammed handkerchief from his pocket. He examined the blood on it afterward.

"Explain."

"We needed our best consultant on the engagement. That's you."

"But Lisa was supposed to work on this one."

"They wanted you, I said no."

"So you put her brother in a coma?"

"I had nothing to do with that," said Terrance.

"You people are evil. And for what? Why did you need someone like me or Lisa?"

"We needed to know what you could uncover. It had to be someone in our firm for damage control."

"You used me? Was the plan to kill me like you did Mark?"

"No," he replied with another cough. "Everything got out of hand when Claudia took the reins from me. She's ruthless."

"That's a very convenient answer."

"It's true. I tried to protect you as best I could. I'm sorry I couldn't do more."

"I'll never forgive you," said Emily, uncertain if it was true.

"I'm a dead man. Even if you don't pull the trigger, they will."

"I'm not really focused on your well-being right now. Besides, I'm not sure you don't deserve it." She lowered the gun to her side. He was right, she wasn't a murderer.

Brent entered through the shattered glass door and clumsily aimed the weapon around as he surveyed the room. "Claudia and Owen aren't here," he said, stating the obvious.

"No, but they still might be in the house."

"I doubt it. I saw a pair of headlights reflect off some trees near the garage. They were leaving."

"Good."

"There's blood in that corner," Brent said, pointing. "Who else got hit?"

Emily looked to see a fair amount of blood in the corner closest to the fireplace. "Owen," she said.

"I hate always being the voice of reason, but we need to get out of here."

"Wait," said Emily. "We need some answers first." She looked to Terrance.

"Okay," replied Terrance in a defeated tone. "But, you already figured out who's involved." He paused while he coughed. "You uncovered more than we thought you would. We didn't think anyone would uncover the Cyprus connection. There's more to find. Keep digging," he added. "You'll be able to tie everyone with this." He handed Emily the flash drive he had clutched in his hand. "Look at Owen's calendar again. There's a pattern. We met quarterly."

"I know who's involved," said Emily to Terrance. "But, I'm still trying to understand the *why*?" She looked at the flash drive before placing it in her pants pocket.

"It's something *you* would never understand. Some people are wired differently. Power and greed. It's a symbiotic relationship. We all benefited handsomely."

"I think I understand some of it," stated Emily. "You needed a major incident to gain attention for Owen. The violent nature of the assassination was for his benefit. It allowed him to attack the policies of the president. Most importantly, it allowed him to enter the national stage with a resonant campaign message."

"Exactly," replied Terrance after another deep cough.

"But why Lara Belinski? She was part of the Consortium."

"She was planning on going to the FBI. She had to be eliminated. Claudia wanted someone in the White House who would further our reach. Owen's political career was beginning to bloom, and we used that to our advantage."

"And greed!" spat Emily.

"You're not wrong," replied Terrance with a tone of regret.

"But why the Cyprus account?" asked Emily.

"We had to pool funds to achieve our goals. It was also necessary to distance ourselves from the money to ensure no trails led directly to any of us."

"The financial crisis in Cyprus created a weak link, didn't it?"

"Yes. The money needed to be moved quickly. The crisis made it nearly impossible to move the funds out of Cyprus. As you figured out, Stan Murphy moved everything in small denominations. To facilitate the transfer, he used an account already created. The Swiss account. He just didn't get a chance to mask the individual accounts associated with the main account."

"Then why did you kill him? It was the Consortium, wasn't it?"

"We had no choice. The Russians learned about the transfer out of Cyprus and beat us to Stan. We eliminated him as a defensive move. Better dead than have the Russians get access to the funds."

"But the money is still there."

"If they had gotten him, the money would most certainly be gone. Eliminating him gave us a chance to get the funds back."

"Does the Consortium have any Russian ties?" she asked.

"No. The Russians had no direct link to us. Stan managed some of their investments, but he couldn't get their money out of Cyprus. Accounts with Russian ties faced more scrutiny." Terrance shook his head. "Bad luck, I guess."

"It shouldn't surprise me that all of this is about power and greed, but it does."

"Like I said, some people are wired differently. Once you get a taste of it, it's addictive."

"Terrance, I've known you for many years. You're certainly not a politician. You never even attended any political events."

"You're right. I've never had any political ambitions. They fed me clients in return. I was financially rewarded for my involvement. And so were you," he added. "Your salary was paid with these relationships."

"My life has been taken from me. I don't have anything left," said Emily. "All because you wanted *more money.*"

"Don't be so naive. Besides, you're still alive," stated Terrance. "You've been much more resilient than anyone gave you credit for. I certainly didn't expect you to show up tonight." His eyes drifted away from her when he spoke next. "But you need to listen to Brent. Get out of here."

"What haven't you told me?" asked Emily.

"Claudia is very vindictive. She certainly made a call once she left the home."

The implications were clear. Brent spoke. "Great, the Irishman. Now are you going to listen, Emily?"

"Fine. Let's go." She looked at Terrance with equal pity and anger.

"Finally," said Brent. "We need to leave now."

"There's a garage full of cars," said Terrance. "Take one. They keep the keys in the vehicles."

"This isn't over between us," she said to Terrance.

"I wouldn't expect it to be," he replied. His eyes remained closed when he spoke.

"We're just going to leave him?" asked Brent.

Emily reached into Terrance's pocket to pull out a cell phone. She placed it on his hand. "Call your driver."

With a grimace, he nodded his appreciation. His eyes closed as his head found a comfortable resting position against the wall.

Emily and Brent walked through the house with their weapons ready. They still didn't know where Claudia and Owen had gone.

They opened the door that led to the garage. One of the three bays was empty, and the large garage door remained open.

"Looks like she left," said Brent.

"Let's still be careful," replied Emily. "I heard those eyes roll," she added after a brief pause.

"I'm glad it was that obvious," he quipped.

Emily approached the vintage BMW coupe. She loved the control a manual transmission provided.

"I'm not even going to pretend I know how to drive that thing," stated Brent as he shook his head.

"Just get in," stated Emily. "We need a quick getaway."

Brent looked at the other car in the garage, a recent model Mercedes sedan. "Wouldn't that be better?" he said, pointing to it.

"Newer cars all have tracking devices. An older one won't. Besides, we need speed and agility. This one is perfect."

They entered the car. After a quick turn of the key, the engine came to life. Brent made the sign of the cross on his body. Emily put the transmission in first gear and expertly engaged the clutch. She launched the expensive vehicle out of the garage and down the private drive.

Chapter 46

MONDAY. 9:02 PM.

Emily and Brent raced down the street in the showroom-quality BMW. Claudia's home quickly vanished in the rearview mirror. Emily was glad to leave, but was acutely aware of who *hunted* them. The Irishman.

She had been lucky so far. But luck doesn't last. The Irishman was a trained assassin. She wasn't sure what she was anymore. A consultant? Certainly not. Those days were over.

She resisted the urge to swerve the speeding vehicle into a large tree to end the nightmare. Instead, she downshifted through a sharp turn before launching the vehicle down a straightaway. Brent gripped the door handle with white knuckles.

"Slow down," he said. "Please," he pleaded.

She eased the vehicle toward the posted limit. Brent let go of the door handle to pull out his phone. "The forecast calls for rain," he said. "Whoa, there's a pretty big storm on the radar."

Emily looked over. "Is that your personal phone?"

"Yes, why?"

"Turn that off, you idiot! What if they can track your cell phone somehow?"

"Can they really do that?"

"I honestly don't know, but why risk it?"

With a nod, Brent obliged her request.

Emily saw a pair of headlights a mile behind them. Police cruisers in the area were typically only one of three car models. She found them fairly easy to recognize by their lights. *It's not the police.*

"Are you okay, Emily?" asked Brent. "The last few days have been crazy. I feel like I'm going crazy. I can only imagine how you feel."

"I'm just trying to keep my head above water. To be honest, I've had to disassociate myself from everything, mentally, to prevent being overwhelmed."

"I didn't know that was possible," he replied.

"Neither did I."

"Where are we going now?" He stared at her, waiting for a response. Her long hair draped down the side of her face and over her left shoulder.

"The Washington Post."

"Finally. What changed your mind?"

"The last twenty-four hours have gotten completely out of control. I thought I could handle it, but it's just too much. Our work isn't done, but I think we have enough for someone to at least listen to the evidence we've uncovered. Don't you?"

"I think so."

"Considering the time, it'll have to be tomorrow."

"Then where do we go tonight?"

"I'm still trying to figure that out," she said without taking her eyes off the road. "Some shady hotel, I suppose."

"And a six-pack of beer," added Brent.

"Agreed. I'm buying."

Going public with the information wouldn't be easy. Even with all the information she possessed, it would likely be met with great skepticism.

Plus, she was a fugitive. Her life would never be the same again. Maybe Brent's world could return to normal. She wanted to help him get his life back, if at all possible.

They crossed a road connecting Maryland with Virginia. Emily turned onto a regional parkway.

"Why west?" asked Brent.

"We need to get away from the heavily populated areas."

"And away from the police," stated Brent.

"Exactly."

Emily used the rearview mirror to scan the road behind them. Satisfied they weren't being followed, she focused on the road ahead.

Brent exhaled, then moved around in his seat before he found a comfortable position. He looked at her again. "We're doing the right thing. You should be proud that you stood up to these villains."

"It sounds so cool when you put it that way," said Emily. "Battling villains. Huh. So we're like superheroes, then?"

"Fuck, that makes me Robin, doesn't it? Man, I don't want to be the weenie one."

They laughed. It lessened the tension and allowed them to refocus. She looked at Brent. It was never like this a few years back. "We've both changed, haven't we?"

"I guess we have."

She wanted to keep the conversation lighthearted, but gratitude welled up and spilled over instead. "Thank you for all you've sacrificed." She removed her hand from the stick shift and patted his leg. "I really didn't expect the events to transpire as they have."

"That's an understatement," he said with a half-laugh. "It's been a real cluster fuck. Do you think Terrance is okay?"

"I suspect he'll be fine. I'm sure his driver is taking him to some private hospital, where he doesn't need to explain his injuries."

"What about Claudia's house? The police, or worse, the FBI, will canvass the home for clues. I really don't want the FBI on my ass."

She didn't want to tell him she was going to the authorities alone. *He'll figure it out when I'm gone in the morning.* She planned on leaving him a burner phone and most of the money she had left. *That should be enough to get him home.*

"I wouldn't make that assumption," she said, continuing their conversation. "I don't think the FBI will get involved."

"Why not? It seems logical to me."

"These people have too much to lose. Think about it. Would it be advantageous to any of them if what happened tonight was made public?"

"Of course not," replied Brent. "It would put their entire operation in jeopardy."

"Exactly. Now you're thinking like them."

"How do you think like this?" asked Brent.

"Training. I have always had to consider how the other side would react."

"I never really understood consultants. A lot of the work seemed rather abstract. And don't get me started on the interview process. I don't really care how many manhole covers there are in Manhattan."

"It's not the answer they're looking for," Emily explained with a chuckle. "It's the logic you provide to support a reasonable conclusion. That's why we've put so much effort trying to determine all of the puzzle pieces. We needed to put together as many as possible to tell a complete story. One based on facts and not inferences."

"This is not a game, Emily."

"I know." She was preparing to elaborate on her position, but something caught her attention. A dark sedan was racing up the on-ramp. *A dark blue Cadillac*, she noted.

"Do you see that car?" she asked.

"Yes." He turned his head to track the car behind them. "It doesn't seem to be making any ground on us. Probably nothing."

After a few tense moments, Emily spoke. "Let's test the theory." She accelerated the vehicle. The Cadillac held its course, and the distance between them increased.

"See? You're just being paranoid," stated Brent.

"You're probably right. I just don't want to take any chances." Without a turn signal, Emily veered toward the exit. They drove down the off-ramp and immediately took a quick right. Emily maintained a view of the exit ramp with the rearview mirror.

Brent turned his head around. No car appeared. "Looks like we're clear," he said. "Let's stay off the highway, just in case."

"Agreed. We're less likely to encounter someone on the side roads." They proceeded through the rolling hills of northern Virginia. Dots of moisture began to appear on the windshield.

"Here comes the storm."

Emily almost laughed at the words. *The storm has already been raging for days*, she thought.

The rain built steadily over the next fifteen minutes until it was a complete downpour. Their vehicle idled at a red light as the wipers aggressively worked to hold the rain at bay. Their vision through the side windows was limited. The light turned green, but their car didn't move.

"It's green," said Brent, pointing at the light.

"I know. That car isn't slowing down. I don't think they saw the light turn red."

"The Volvo across from us?" asked Brent. "It hasn't moved."

"Not that one. To our left," said Emily. Brent looked to see a car approaching from the cross street. It didn't indicate any signs of slowing. Just before the car entered the intersection, it swerved to the right to head directly toward them.

"It's the Cadillac!" yelled Brent. "Punch it!"

Emily popped the clutch. The back wheels spun momentarily before gaining traction. The car shot forward, but it was too late.

The Cadillac clipped the back quarter panel of the vintage car, causing it to spin out into the intersection.

The Cadillac also spun into the intersection before it stopped. The two cars now faced each other. Only twenty feet of road separated them.

Brent uttered the only word spoken in the car: "*Shit.*"

Emily glanced at her companion. His nervous mannerisms indicated that he didn't want to be here. She could certainly relate. It seemed their journey was about to come to an abrupt end.

Chapter 47

Emily watched as the bystander from the Volvo station wagon exited his car and began approaching the Cadillac. The folded newspaper he placed over his head provided limited relief from the pouring rain.

A lightning flash provided a glimpse of the other car's occupant. It was *him*. Emily pursed her lips, and she gripped the steering wheel tight with her left hand. The clutch remained disengaged with her foot. With a quick movement of her right hand, she shifted out of first gear. She didn't need that gear right now.

This was her one chance to escape. Emily wanted to take advantage of the bystander's altruistic action. He was now blocking the Cadillac's path. The damage to their vehicle was likely superficial. Emily popped the clutch and the vehicle surged backward.

Brent wasn't braced for the backward motion. The seat belt caught him at an awkward angle. He reached out to the dashboard.

Using the rearview mirror to guide the vehicle, Emily pushed herself against the back of the seat with the force she applied to the gas pedal. The lack of rear wipers greatly limited her field of vision through the rain. There was no choice but to accept the risk.

Her eyes darted to the front window. The Cadillac launched forward. The bystander attempted to get out of the way, but lost his footing on the wet cement. By the time he gained his balance, it was too late.

The four-thousand-pound machine slammed into the man, catapulting his body into the air. He flew over the hood and glanced off the windshield before crashing awkwardly onto the pavement.

"Do you know what you're doing?" asked Brent.

"Not really," answered Emily.

"We can't outrun him in reverse."

Emily kept the accelerator to the floor. Their three-second head start quickly shrank. Their vehicle's single reverse gear could not match the Cadillac's eight.

"I know we can't outrun him. I have another plan."

"You better not do what I think you're going to do," stated Brent. He watched as the Irishman raced toward them and braced himself for a violent collision.

When the impact seemed imminent, Emily spun the wheel. She gave it a quarter turn to the right, before reversing direction a full turn and a quarter with the palm of her hand.

The maneuver didn't work as she had planned. Instead of causing the vehicle to turn one hundred eighty degrees with speed, the car began to spin out. The Cadillac maintained a straight line toward them as Emily fought a losing battle to regain control. She slammed on the brakes to avoid a direct impact with the front of the charging car.

The sides of the cars collided, damaging the entire passenger side of the coupe and forcing it onto the shoulder. The Irishman jammed on the brakes after his car shot past them. It came to a complete stop thirty feet behind them.

The maneuver didn't work, but their car now faced away from the Irishman and toward the intersection they had just left. She engaged the clutch after jamming the transmission into first gear and stomped on the accelerator.

"Are you okay?" she asked Brent.

"I think I'm going to throw up."

"Do whatever you need to do, but get out your gun. We need him off our tail."

They approached the intersection with the stationary Volvo, where the man sat directly under the stoplight. He was drenched by the rain and appeared unable to move his legs. He attempted to gain their attention by gingerly waving one of his injured arms toward them. Their car raced around the man as they ran through the red light overhead.

"I can't believe he's still alive," said Brent. "That lucky son of a bitch."

"Maybe he'll be okay," said Emily as she glanced at him in the rearview mirror. "If someone calls the police," she added.

"It's not going to be us, though."

"No, it's not," she said. "I'm sure he has a cell phone in his car."

Brent pulled out Emily's gun and checked it. "There are only two bullets left."

"I have more." She released her hand from the gearshift to reach into her coat pocket. She dropped a handful of bullets into the cup holder and glanced in the rearview mirror again.

The Irishman sped through the intersection, clipping the bystander and sending him sprawling. She closed her eyes in disgust.

"What?" asked Brent after she cringed. "He didn't, did he? That bastard."

She tried to focus on their own predicament. The vehicle sped down the hill. She felt her stomach drop when the car reached the bottom of one hill and began to climb the next. Gravity pulled their bodies when they drove over the next crest.

"Have I told you lately that you're crazy?" said Brent. Unable to steady his hands during the erratic driving, he dropped a few bullets on the floor. He retrieved some, but the others rolled under his seat.

"Just pay attention to what you're doing," replied Emily.

The rolling hills and curved streets tested her driving skills. She performed well, but knew they needed more speed if they were to lose the man in pursuit.

After Brent finished loading the clip, he peered behind them. "I see him," he said when a pair of headlights appeared over a hill.

Emily took her eyes off the road to view the pursuing car in the mirror. The rain impaired her vision, and it took her a few moments to locate the car rounding a bend. When she refocused on the road ahead there was another sharp turn. She downshifted and applied the brakes at the same time, but it was too late.

The car careened back and forth across both sides of the two-lane road. She couldn't regain complete control and was forced onto the shoulder, where she crashed into the only mailbox visible in the area, adjacent to a hidden driveway.

The four-by-four wood post snapped in two. The mailbox smashed onto the hood, causing a large dent before deflecting into the passenger side of the front window. It finally landed in the middle of the road behind them.

The right wheel glanced the wooden post in the ground, forcing the tire high into the wheel well of the car, causing a loud thud in the cabin. Both passengers were jarred by the impact.

The car came to a complete stop after another thirty feet of sliding over the loose, wet rubble on the shoulder. Rain continued to pound the windshield. Water began to enter the cabin from a golf ball-sized hole in the windshield in front of Brent.

"Shit," exclaimed Emily. "I lost control."

"Just go!" yelled Brent.

She accelerated down the narrow road. When they got to the top of the next hill, Emily grew frustrated. The tussle with the mailbox had cost them most of their lead.

"I can't believe I'm saying this," said Brent, "but you need to go faster."

"I can't."

"What? Why not?"

"The alignment is out of whack," said Emily.

"I'll try to slow him down. You just concentrate on driving."

"What are you going to do?"

Brent didn't answer. He unbuckled his seat belt and turned around. He knelt on the car seat and readied his pistol. "When he gets close, I'll start firing."

"Be careful," she said.

"It's too late for that."

Emily kept the car on the road as best she could. Speeds greater than eighty shook the wheels and caused a significant loss in traction on the slick pavement. A quick check of the rearview mirror indicated the Irishman had nearly caught up to them.

When less than ten feet separated the vehicles, Brent aimed the pistol and pulled the trigger twice. The bullets shattered the back window. A deafening blast echoed in the car. "Sorry," he yelled.

Emily cringed from the blast. "Some advance notice would have been nice," she yelled back.

"That's the only shot I had."

"Did you hit the car?"

"I don't think so."

"Try again!"

A steady growl from the Cadillac's V8 engine resonated through the rain and into the cabin. Brent aimed at the engine. He pulled the trigger four times. The first three shots connected with the target, but the car kept gaining.

The fourth bullet completely missed its target when their car hit a bump in the road. Brent lost his balance, and his face smashed into the headrest. After adjusting his position in the seat, he strained to steady the weapon for a clean shot. The car behind had crept closer. Through the high-intensity light beams, he could see an ominous outline of the occupant. Brent aimed directly toward it.

Desperate to put distance between them, Emily pressed the gas pedal harder. The vehicle began to shake as they approached another hill crest.

Brent pulled the trigger twice. The first bullet penetrated the windshield, but the motion of the car affected his accuracy. The bullet tore a hole in the windshield to the left of the driver's position. The second pull of the trigger ended with a distinct click of an empty chamber.

One last surge from the car in pursuit was all that it took to cement everyone's fortune. Neither Emily nor Brent saw the sign located just before the hilltop. It advocated caution and indicated a sharp turn was imminent.

The blue sedan inched past the rear bumper of the coupe on the driver's side. Emily took one hand off of the wheel to shield her eyes from its blinding high beams. With an expert side-to-side motion of the pursuing vehicle's steering wheel, the front end hit the rear wheel well of the BMW.

The impact sent the coupe into an uncontrollable spin. The road underneath the vehicle disappeared as it dipped down the hill and veered to the right. Their vehicle was now airborne.

Both Emily and Brent froze as the scene continued to change around them. The spinning vehicle grazed the top of some small trees as they continued down an embankment. Emily crossed her arms in front of her face. Brent was unable to brace for the impact. His unrestrained body lifted off the seat as the car descended.

With no airbags or safety devices to deploy, the vintage car made a metallic crunching sound as it deflected off the trunk of a large tree. It flipped over once before coming to an abrupt stop. The wheels continued to spin for a moment, then stopped.

The Irishman's car came to a screeching halt on the bend's shoulder. The headlights lit the wooded area as the rain continued to drench it.

After two long minutes, Emily's eyes opened. Disoriented, she tried to regain her faculties. She felt an enormous pressure from her shoulder to her waist. She tried to look around, but couldn't see anything. Her long, dark hair flowed downward to obstruct her field of view.

Water streamed through the roof underneath her in the upside-down vehicle. Mud seeped through the window frames and shattered glass to mix with her dripping blood as it pooled below.

She tried to move, but couldn't. The seat belt held her firmly in place. She reached for the seat belt release with her left hand, but her arm didn't move. The pain made it obvious that it was broken.

She found the release with her right hand. After four attempts, the lock disengaged. Her body fell awkwardly into the bloody mixture below. "Ahh!" Her scream was silenced when her face sank into the mud.

She laid on her right side, unable to push herself over with her broken left arm. Emily managed to flip over using her body momentum. The excruciating pain made the reality of her situation clear. She would not be able to escape *him*.

With a bloodied hand, she gingerly pushed the hair and mud away from her eyes. She saw Brent staring at her. He didn't say a word. He didn't have to say anything.

She immediately understood his plight.

Chapter 48

MONDAY. 10:03 PM.

Emily couldn't help staring at her friend. Brent's disfigured body attempted to move, but he couldn't dislodge himself from the wreck. Sharp, mangled metal fragments had pierced his body in multiple places.

Brent had suffered the brunt of the vehicle's impact with the tree. With the hair and mud out of her face, she could finally see what remained of the car around her. It was completely destroyed. Brent and the vehicle had become one.

"I fucked up," stated Emily. "I'm so sorry. I shouldn't have involved you in this mess. I really didn't mean to. I didn't."

"We both fucked up. I couldn't leave you on your own. Sorry I didn't do more."

"Thank you," said Emily sincerely. A mother-like desire to soothe him overcame her. She reached out to touch his face. She did her best to remain composed, but tears began to stream down her cheeks when she couldn't reach him.

Her left leg remained entangled with the seat belt dangling above her. She tried to move closer, but an agonizing pain stopped her. She continued to stare at her friend.

He returned her gaze with a placid numbness. "Don't cry. You're too beautiful to cry." Blood trickled down his face. He wouldn't leave the cabin alive. They both knew it. A tear from his eye mixed with the blood on his face before reaching his chin.

They heard rocks slide down the embankment about ten yards away. Neither needed to look to know who was coming.

"Get out of here," said Brent. He didn't understand the extent of her injuries.

"I can't."

"Yes, you can. You have to go on." He grimaced before continuing. "You have to stop these people."

"I'm not getting out of here alive. Neither of us are." She wasn't sure she cared anymore. If her life ended at that moment, she would have been strangely content. She had tried to stand up for what she thought was right. *Sometimes, good does not prevail over evil*, she thought.

Her body became tired. Emily closed her eyes. It was almost a relief not to care anymore.

"Stop that. Wake up." Only a coarse whisper left his lips when he spoke.

"I can hear you," said Emily with her eyes still closed.

"I've always liked that smell," Brent randomly stated as gasoline fumes permeated the cabin.

"You've always liked strange smells," she said with a diffused laugh. She grimaced from the pain the laugh caused.

Footsteps approached. Emily resigned her life.

"Holy smokes," said a voice from outside. The strong Irish accent was unmistakable. "Do you mind if I smoke?" He laughed. "Of course you don't."

Emily heard a match strike. She expected the car to explode. It didn't. She opened her eyes to see *him*.

"Hello," said the Irishman. He had bent over as he examined the extent of the damage inside the car. "I can't stay long," he continued. "You never know who might stop and help. I can't believe that good Samaritan at the red light. The bloke seemed so eager to lend a helpful hand. Not anymore."

"Go to hell," Emily said with no emotion.

"Now, now, missy. Don't be rude." He took a long drag on the cigarette and continued to survey the people trapped inside.

"Just shoot me," she exclaimed. "You'll get your due."

"I just wanted to introduce myself. I don't typically do that, but then again, I've never been presented such a unique opportunity. We've known each other for some time. Well, I've been acquainted longer with you than you have with me," he added.

"Fuck off. I hope your *fag* gives you throat cancer."

"Ha," he laughed at the cigarette slang reference. "And one hell of a driver. You had a bit of bad luck with the mailbox. And don't even get me started on that last bend. Bad luck, indeed. I didn't see it coming, either."

"Please stop talking and get this over with."

"Oh, you think I'm just going to *off* you, huh?" He shook his head slowly back and forth. The rain flowed off his English cap and down his black trench coat. He looked dry and perfectly content as he continued his gaze.

The Irishman glanced at Brent. "He's dead. Well, not yet. Who are we kidding, he's as good as dead." He laughed again. This time he flashed his white teeth before exhaling smoke through the gaps.

"I'm not going anywhere with you," she said.

"You've pissed off the wrong people, missy." He crouched closer to the vehicle. Reaching through the broken window, he untangled her injured leg from the dangling seat belt. It dropped to the ground, providing her a momentary relief from pain.

He grabbed her ankles and dragged her out of the car. His disregard for her injuries was evident from his recklessness.

She couldn't help but scream from the pain as she passed over the broken glass and through the metal door frame.

"Stop," whispered Brent.

"My job is to bring you back alive, if possible. I didn't think you were when your car flew off the road. A damn miracle, if you ask me. They have some questions for you. They want to know exactly what you know, and more importantly, who else you have spoken to. Miss Claudia was very specific about a certain electronic device you might possess."

The Irishman patted her down and searched her pockets until another smile crossed his face. "Here it is." He examined the small device he found. "All of this fuss over this little thing." He shook his head in disappointment. He propped her against a neighboring tree. "I know you're not going anywhere," he added.

She had cuts on her neck and cheek, her clothes were torn, and she was covered in blood. Besides a broken arm, her leg had been seriously injured.

"Your actions have caused a lot of people to get hurt. You've been very careless." He reached into his pocket and pulled out a matchbook. He opened it and placed the flash drive behind the paper matches. He closed the cover underneath the paper lip to secure it before putting the book back in his pocket. "I'm not careless," he added with a pat to his pocket.

The Irishman walked back to the car and switched his attention to Brent. "Now, you, my friend. I'm sorry to say, but there's no stay of execution for you."

He opened his coat to retrieve a weapon from the holster under his arm. He calmly pulled the pistol slide.

The Irishman puffed on his cigarette before pulling it out of his mouth. He inspected it. A rain drop had extinguished it. Annoyed, he put the unlit cigarette back into his mouth. With his left hand, he retrieved the matches from his left pocket.

A clicking sound emanated from the vehicle, causing the Irishman to laugh. "I know you're antsy, boy. Don't worry, I'm coming."

As only a seasoned smoker could, the Irishman expertly opened the match cover and lit it using only one hand. He lifted the dancing flame to the end of his cigarette. The lip of his hat shielded it from the rain. The tobacco flashed red as he puffed.

"Any last words?" said the Irishman as he bent down. With the cigarette hanging from his mouth, he inhaled the smoke into his lungs. When he exhaled, he took one last look at the man in the car.

Emily closed her eyes tight as the tears that streamed down her face mixed with the rain. The sound of the single blast was drowned in the downpour. A subsequent sound of loose rocks surprised her. Her eyes shot open.

The Irishman was no longer standing next to the car. Only a book of matches lay where he had just stood.

"Brent!" she exclaimed with a grimace. A tempered hope lifted her spirits. The Irishman must have toppled down the hill.

Emily stood on her second attempt. Her injuries were great, but she could stand. She shuffled and stumbled to the car, dragging her left foot. She grimaced after dropping to one knee. Emily peered into the wrecked car. "Brent, are you okay?" His dire situation remained unchanged.

"I hated that guy," stated Brent. His speech was slow and slurred.

"I got him, Emily. Fucker."

Emily didn't ask where he got the bullet. She knew. If he hadn't dropped some earlier, everything would have turned out much differently.

"Let me help you out."

"You can't, Emily." He looked down to acknowledge the metal shard protruding from the side of his abdomen. "He stood two feet in front of me. That's the only reason I got him." Brent gave her a weak half-laugh.

Even in death, he had a sense of humor. "I'm not going to leave you."

"You can't linger. Get out of here. Just do me one favor," he said with a fading voice.

"Anything," said Emily.

"Finish the job. Do it right," he added.

"I will. I promise," she said, wiping tears and rain from her face.

"You know that means eliminating all evidence in this car."

"What do you mean?"

"There can be no fingerprints or evidence of you being here. The police will link you to this crime scene. It will ruin everything."

"Now you sound like me," she said.

"I've learned from the best." He tossed the gun as far as he could throw it. It only went ten inches. Emily reached into the car to pick it up.

"I love you," he said as he looked at her. "Even though you're crazy as shit." He tried to smile. "I always have."

"I know." She wasn't sure if her own calloused heart could love anymore.

"I'll finish it," she promised again. It was the best she could offer. She wished she could hug him or provide him some sort of comfort.

Emily offered him one last smile. She tried to memorize his face. Not what it looked like at that moment, but what it looked like without the gruesome injuries. The image of him at the bar three nights ago came to mind. His skeptical expression while she asked for his help was etched into her memory.

Brent closed his eyes. With each exhale, his breath became more shallow. A content smile appeared upon his bloodied face.

Emily turned around to pick up the book of matches the Irishman had dropped on the ground. She stood up using the side of the car as support. She paused for a moment as she fought back tears. A sharp pain shot up her leg. It brought her back to the moment and reminded her of what she needed to do next.

After a few hobbled steps, she turned to face the car. The breached gas tank on top of the overturned vehicle continued to leak high octane fuel down the sides. The translucent liquid had pooled around the car.

Emily opened the book of matches. She ripped out a paper match adjacent to the flash drive and struck it against the graphite strip on the back of the matchbook. She hesitated.

She concentrated on the burning match. It burnt halfway down the matchstick before she could summon the courage to finish the job.

Emily closed her eyes before tossing the lit match. Orange flames immediately engulfed both the interior and exterior of the wreckage. She could feel the heat on her eyelids. Popping noises and hissing sounds filled her ears as raindrops met the high-intensity fire.

She turned around before opening her eyes again. She didn't want to witness what she knew was happening to Brent. She limped away, wondering if the muffled screams were real or if her guilt had gotten the best of her. She pretended it didn't matter either way.

The bright headlights of the blue Cadillac on top of the embankment guided her way. The slow trek of her battered body allowed her an unfortunate amount of time to reflect.

Am I a murderer, now? rang repeatedly through her head.

She hated what they had put her through. She hated what she had done. Most of all, she hated herself. She tried to refocus her anger on the people responsible for her anguish. Her head hurt.

Chapter 49

Emily had spent the next two days recuperating. Her injuries weren't insignificant, but she knew they could have been much worse. A trip to the hospital would have raised too many questions. This forced her to tend to her own injuries.

She had painfully straightened her broken arm using a metal rod and a tightly wrapped fabric bandage. Whiskey dulled the pain. Open wounds were closed with adhesive bandage strips found in a well-equipped medical kit in the Irishman's car. Her bandaged body was reminiscent of a mummy when she finished dressing the wounds. The injuries would eventually heal, but the scars would be a constant reminder of her recklessness.

More whiskey dulled the emotional pain.

Her head swirled with emotions as she stared at the ceiling of a decrepit hotel room. She forced herself out of the squeaky bed. So many had people died, but she was still alive. Their deaths needed purpose.

There hadn't been any mention of the shootout or car wreck in the news. Her speculation of a cover-up was correct. She didn't have the luxury of time. People were actively hunting her. If she wanted to live, she needed to act decisively.

Two days prior, she had scheduled two appointments for that day. Before attending the first appointment, she visited her uncle's condo to set the dominos in motion. Surfaces were wiped, all garbage collected, and everything was placed as it had been before she arrived. Her injuries made even the simplest task arduous.

Jen's body was positioned on the floor in the kitchen. She had removed it from the tub, where it had been thawed after a quick visit the night before.

A bucket of siphoned gasoline stood strategically on the kitchen floor. The flammable liquid had been used to douse the carpets and floors. To ensure all evidence of her presence was erased, Emily had also breached the main gas line.

Emily selected a match from the Irishman's matchbook. She lit it and threw it toward the gasoline filled bucket. The fumes immediately burst into flames.

She kicked the bucket over, sending a wave of orange flames through the kitchen and around Jen's body. A chain reaction began as the trail of flames raced throughout the condo.

It would be destroyed, leaving only a charred body for the police to identify. The death would be greeted with suspicion, but her plan was to use it to her advantage. Emily opened the door to the garage. Disposing of the Cadillac was next.

After driving back to Claudia's neighborhood, she parked the Cadillac behind Jen's Mercedes. She pulled a gasoline container out of the trunk. With a drenched rag, she wiped the flammable substance over the steering wheel and any other surface she had touched. She saturated the blood-stained driver's seat.

She stuffed the rag in the mouth of the container and placed it on the floor in front of the driver's seat. After lighting it, she drove away in Jen's car. Emily lingered just long enough at the end of the block to ensure the flames engulfed the car.

As a kid, she remembered seeing the destruction of a fire. A neighboring home had been completely incinerated. The fear she once held had now become a welcoming rebirth.

Emily checked her watch. The first appointment was a fifteen-minute drive away. She needed to hurry to keep on schedule. Timing was key.

An odor emanated from her hands clutching the steering wheel. She had tried many times, but the gasoline smell couldn't be removed with the wipes found in Jen's purse. The smell became oddly soothing. It reminded Emily of her late friend.

Emily didn't want to draw attention to herself and tried to mask her injuries as best she could. A cane limited her limp when she approached the main counter. For her appointment, she wore a Niagara Falls turtleneck and sweatpants she had found in the condo. Makeup had never been a large part of her morning routine. The heavily applied foundation to mask her bruises made her feel like a hooker.

"My name is Stella Fisher. I'm here to see Doctor Bohgan," said Emily from behind a pair of oversize sunglasses. A decorative scarf covered the bandages on her neck. If it weren't for the injuries and the awful clothing, she would have felt like Jackie Kennedy.

This was the second of Emily's scheduled appointments. Her first one had gone exactly as planned. She employed the same strategy for this appointment.

"I see you're scheduled at eleven, Miss Fisher. Let's get you checked in. I understand it's your first time getting your teeth cleaned with us." She offered Emily a large smile as if trying to demonstrate the effectiveness of their services. "Let me print the forms you need to fill out."

"Great. Thank you." Emily placed an extra-large coffee on the counter, just in front of the chubby receptionist. When she looked away, Emily's knuckle gave the cup a slight nudge. The black liquid, which boiled in a convenience store microwave only ten minutes earlier, covered the woman's forearms and desk while she typed.

"Goodness!" the woman screamed as she shot up from the desk, now covered in coffee. She gave Emily a spiteful look through her bespectacled eyes.

Just like the woman at the first office, thought Emily. "Oh my God, I'm so sorry."

The woman acted quickly to wipe the hot coffee from her arms with some nearby tissues. She grimaced from the discomfort and inspected the resulting redness.

Emily knew the hot liquid would only cause temporary discomfort. It was important to make the woman think it might be worse.

"Wait. I just happen to have something that might help." Emily handed her a tube of ointment. "You should use it to prevent any blistering. I'm so sorry," she reiterated. The woman gave Emily a confused expression. She must have thought it was odd that someone would carry ointment, but accepted it anyway. Emily wasn't surprised.

After the woman excused herself, Emily had her opportunity. With a grimace, she walked as fast as her injured leg would allow to the filing cabinets behind the desk. Using the patient's last lame, Hendricks, she quickly found the folder she sought.

A quick examination of the folder's contents indicated her plan had a good chance of success. She knew the exchange wouldn't be perfect, but it didn't need to be. She pulled specific documents out of the folder. As best she could, Emily replaced the contents using the file from her first appointment. She focused on key documents and film. What she couldn't adequately replace, she removed without substitution.

The office would get a request from a government agency to view the folder for Emily Hendricks. From her call yesterday, she knew the office used physical film for their documentation and didn't house any digital version of the X-rays. Likely, only a cursory glance to ensure her file contained major documents would be performed before handing the file to the requesting authority.

Once satisfied, Emily put the document file back in the cabinet. She left the office before the woman came back from the bathroom. The whole exchange took less than ninety seconds.

Emily opened the door to her newly rented apartment. Jen's identity would be extremely useful. It wasn't a permanent solution, but for now, it allowed her mobility.

The Consortium believed Jen was dead. Terrance surely would have told them about their conversation and her confession to him. They would have no reason to search Jen out. She was just a pawn.

The government now had proof Emily was dead. An autopsy would be performed on the body from the Annapolis condo. Jen's dental records were now located in Emily's dental file. No one would be looking for Emily anymore. She tried not to think about her family. That life no longer existed.

Her first official action as Jen Myers would be to quit her job so that no one would be looking for her. *I might just be able to pull this off*, she thought. She ordered blue contact lenses to match Jen's eye color and made an appointment at a salon to match her hair style.

Chapter 50

The Thai food she had ordered sat mostly untouched. The contents of the banker box were spread across the table. Emily sat, deep in thought, with her legs bent underneath her at the coffee table in the living room. She thoroughly reviewed the report in front of her one last time.

Emily had started the investigation from the beginning with a fresh perspective. Determined to leave no stone unturned, she had pored over all of the documents in her possession numerous times.

Terrance had said the Consortium had quarterly meetings. She found references in Owen's calendar and email communications to support his statement. She didn't have calendar schedules to tie each person to every quarterly meeting, but she was able to piece information from public appearances near the meeting dates for some of the prominent members.

It wasn't necessary to tie every single person and event together. She just needed to make the claims public. The Consortium members would have to defend their innocence. In the court of public opinion, the defendant was often guilty until proven innocent.

During her investigation, she paid special attention to the additional signature on the document taken from Terrance's home. *Dimitris Andreadis* was not a founding member of the firm. He was listed as a witness. The name listed by itself would not have drawn her immediate attention, but the insignia did.

She uncovered much about Dimitris. She found his law firm in Cyprus, *Kyrkos & Andreadis*. The letters at the top of the insignia took on new meaning. They were not a lower case "*k a*," but rather, Greek letters representing the law firm.

She contacted the law firm under the pretense she was a wealthy widow intent on hiding family assets from a much younger future husband. After discussing a healthy fee structure, Dimitris was more than willing to discuss tax haven strategies and ensured her that no government agency had ever investigated his law firm. She recorded the conversations and received a contract letter from the firm to provide financial services. The firm insignia was stamped on the front page of the contract.

Over the past weeks, she had documented everything she had uncovered in a report she labeled, *The Cyprus Papers*. She included specific references and account numbers for the international bank accounts in Cyprus and Switzerland. She also included the names and US bank account numbers for the eight Consortium members.

Emily detailed every assertion, including direct references to the Supreme Court Justice assassination, the murders of Scott, David, Brent, and Mark, and an Internet link to Owen's campaign. Given Owen's prominence, Emily was confident that a substantiated claim of his involvement would be investigated by either the media or a government agency.

The report wouldn't be complete without acknowledging the individual personally responsible for the heinous acts. She admitted to herself she didn't know a lot about the Irishman. Not his name. She only knew his nickname. Even his accent might have been a ruse.

She did, however, possess one piece of incriminating evidence. She picked up a clear Ziploc bag to examine it one last time. A single, seemingly innocuous, matchbook. She visited a private detective under the pretense that a cheating husband's girlfriend left it in her car, and that she needed the fingerprint identified for an upcoming divorce proceeding. She provided her own to ensure he captured the correct one.

The digitalized fingerprint would be provided as a supporting source when she turned over her report. Surely he would have gotten caught committing a crime somewhere, probably in his youth. Someone had to know his name. Hopefully, the fingerprint would help unlock his identity.

Emily made copies of the report and placed the electronic information on numerous flash drives. She included the contents of Owen's computer from the flash drive in the matchbook and the supporting files initially provided by Owen. Lastly, she included the Irishman's single fingerprint.

Ten boxes on the counter contained complete sets of the report and supporting evidence. She used gloves when she assembled the boxes to conceal her fingerprints and identity. She addressed them to prominent news agencies, both domestic and abroad. Someone would care. Someone would investigate.

The truth needed to be told. She owed it to the people who lost their lives because of not only their actions, but also her own. Emily hoped that doing so could in some way alleviate her tremendous sense of loss and accompanied guilt.

She glanced at the full glass of the fine wine poured from the bottle taken from Terrance's house. She took his advice and allowed it the proper time to breathe before pouring it into an ornate crystal wineglass. She swirled the wine before her first sip.

"Mmm," she said to herself. *Terrance did have good taste in wine.* Emily raised her glass toward the fireplace as a ceremonious *thank you.* The unwavering gaze of *Dante's Hell,* strategically perched above the mantle, almost seemed to smile back.

It was time.

Chapter 51

DECEMBER.
ITHACA, NEW YORK.

Emily sat in the first row. The event wasn't scheduled to begin for another forty-five minutes. She had marked it on her calendar the day it was announced and arrived early to ensure she got a prime seat.

As the time grew nearer, a crowd of over four hundred people slowly formed around the main square of the small town in upstate New York. The sun was out and kept the air unseasonably warm. It was a perfect day.

The crowd in back began to cheer when a black limousine stopped at the square. Everyone around Emily stood up. She remained seated with a clear view of the raised stage fifteen feet in front of her.

A man slowly approached the stage from the left side as the cheering crowd opened before him. He religiously shook the hands of everyone in his path before climbing the five-stepped staircase to the platform. Once at the top, he stopped and faced the crowd. His arms shot triumphantly toward the sky. His right shoulder did not have the same range of motion as his left. One of the bullets from Emily's pistol had struck him during their encounter in Maryland.

The crowd responded with a synchronized chant. "O-wen. O-wen. O-wen." He smiled as he pumped his fists in encouragement.

Owen confidently strode to the podium. The smile never left his face as the chant continued. The crowd showed no letdown when he began to speak.

"Thank you all. Thank you all for joining me today." The crowd cheered louder.

"I couldn't be happier to be here with *you* today. *We* are going to change a lot of lives *together*." The roars continued.

He teased the crowd with playful political banter as he eloquently attacked his opponent's stances on various issues. They cheered every statement he made. He then resumed his speech with a more serious tone.

"There's no secret that a lot has changed in my life. I wanted to let you know that nothing can stop us from reaching our goals." He paused for dramatic effect as the ruckus increased.

In the days following the event, various news reports had indicated he was shot during an attempted robbery. The reports had also stated the assailant fled and was never found. *The lies never stop,* she remembered thinking when she heard the news.

The media made Owen a hero for standing up to crime. His picture covered nearly every magazine. He made the headlines on CNN. Her account of the incident was much different.

Owen managed to quiet the crowd. When there was a brief pause in his speech, he flashed a politician's smile. He spoke each word deliberately when he resumed his speech.

"I'm here today to announce my candidacy for President of the United States of America!" He didn't have to pause this time. Nobody could hear him over the rambunctious noise. The people around Emily jumped in excitement.

The red, white, and blue balloons, released after his last statement, raced high in the sky. Confetti shot from behind the stage. Emily remained patiently seated.

A large billboard occupied the stage behind Owen. Emily had watched them place it there the evening before. A gold braided cord and tassel was attached to a decorative blue sheet that covered the billboard.

"Thank you again, everyone," continued Owen. "I wouldn't be here without the support of my friends and family." He flashed a smile to his family standing silently to his left. They requited his smile and then waved to the audience.

"But I would like to thank *you* most of all." He redirected his attention and focus to the crowd. They reciprocated with another large cheer. He put his hands up to calm them.

"Since we are officially kicking off my presidential bid—I like the sound of that, don't you? *President.*" The crowd erupted once again.

"I'd like to unveil my official campaign slogan." With the crowd's support, he dramatically inched toward the billboard just a few feet behind him. He reached for the gold cord, but paused before pulling it. He adjusted his angle as a slew of cameramen approached the stage to get the *money shot* that would be replayed throughout the country on the evening news.

With the crowd's abundant support, Owen gently tugged the cord. The presidential blue sheet dropped elegantly to the ground. Owen focused his attention on the cameras and the crowd as he offered his best presidential smile.

The crowd's tone changed. The exuberance that filled the air immediately dissipated. Owen's smile faded once he looked at the billboard.

The slogan had been defaced. What originally read, "America First! America Forever!" now had a large X in red paint over it. In the same red paint, a new slogan prevailed.

"Our Greed is Murderous. TheCyprusPapers.com."

Emily had aroused the attention of a decentralized hacking community via a private chat room. They were more than eager to lend their services once she was able to support her seemingly outlandish claims. Her only request was to delay the website launch until today.

In addition to the ten boxes she had sent to the media outlets, all of the evidence was available for immediate download on the website. The Consortium would have no chance to quell the storm.

The demeanor of the crowd had irreversibly changed. Some cheering continued, but only from the most loyal supporters. Appearing frustrated, Owen examined the audience for the first time. Everyone in the front row stood, with the exception of one person. In the middle of that row, sat Emily.

With a stoic demeanor, she stared at the man on the stage. She knew from his subtle reaction that he recognized her. His eyes turned to his campaign team. All he saw from his team was genuine confusion.

He put his hands in the air again as he confidently stepped back to the podium. He was about to continue his speech, but looked once more to the first row. She was gone. He stumbled over his first few words before regaining his focus.

Emily walked out of the back of the crowd. Owen's speech continued in the background, but she didn't have any interest in listening to his lies any longer. A genuine smile found her face for the first time since the car crash.

It was foolish to show herself at the event. She just knew it was unlikely she'd get an opportunity like this again. Once he became a viable candidate, the Secret Service would be watching over him.

Emily looked in the visor mirror as she sat in the red Mercedes coupe. She missed her old self. She removed her wig and set it on the floor. She put her head next to the mirror as she carefully placed a blue contact lens in each eye. She blinked until they fit comfortably in place.

Epilogue

Emily finished her shopping at the bodega. She purchased only items she intended to cook that night. Her life had been greatly simplified since starting over in a new city. New York was an ideal place to blend in and the perfect city to stay anonymous.

It was a relief to distance herself from the chaos that transpired in DC. Owen was no longer involved in politics. He maintained his innocence, but had his lawyer's number on speed dial. Donors wouldn't touch his campaign.

The Attorney General had been forced to resign. The other members of the Consortium were still in the news and had been forced into hiding. Their greedy ambitions had been effectively ended. All affiliates, both political and non-political, had ended any relationship with them in the interest of self-preservation.

Since the news broke, the law office of Kyrkos & Andreadis had been raided. Three of its partners had been caught trying to illegally enter Bulgaria, including Dimitris. Rumors of celebrities and wealthy people involved with the firm swirled wildly.

After putting her groceries in a backpack, she wrapped a hand-knit scarf snugly around her face and neck. Four inches of accumulating snow and swirling wind greeted her outside. Emily began the three-block walk to her apartment on the upper west side.

A figure in the distance caught her eye through the narrow slit in her scarf. A man in a black fedora stood motionless on the street corner. Snow filled the dimple on his hat, and his foot tracks had been partially covered.

Visions of the nightmare she thought she had eluded flooded her mind. She changed course and ducked into an alley. *There was a good chance he didn't see me.* She had intentionally selected an apartment that had everything she needed nearby and featured multiple access points. She had no idea she'd be using one so quickly.

After traveling through a few more alleys and a back entrance, she brushed the snow off her clothes and ran up the three flights of stairs to her apartment while clutching her key. She quickly opened and closed the door. With her back against it, she audibly exhaled.

Two men approached from inside the apartment. Her attempt to open the door was forcibly thwarted as one of the men slammed it shut. They didn't say a word as they removed her backpack and outer garments before placing her on a chair in the living room of her small apartment.

One man sat across from her on a couch. The other man stood in front of the door with his arms crossed. She knew how this was going to end. As if on cue, a bare knuckle rapped twice on the aged wood door. The man in front of the door moved to the side as he opened it to present his boss.

The man with the black fedora brushed the snow off his shoulders and tipped the snow from his fedora. After a quick stomp of his feet, he walked casually through the doorway and gently hung his coat on a wall hook. He had obviously been to the apartment before.

"Well, well, Miss Myers. We finally meet."

Emily was confused. He greeted her using Jen's name and not her own. *He must think I'm really Jen. Maybe they had never met or known each other was involved with the Consortium.* She quickly thought how she could use this knowledge to her advantage.

"I'm listening," she replied stoically. *Keep your replies short. Let him speak.*

"You're a hard person to find. I've had to search high and low for you. Much more of an ordeal than I would have originally thought when I first found you smoking in the park."

"I've changed." *Wait, the park?* she asked herself. Jen was confused about who he thought was her real identity. *He met Emily in the park, not Jen.*

"Indeed, you have. A lot of people have been hurt because of your actions."

"Some of them deserved it." She thought about the members of the Consortium when she stated it, but knew he would think she referred to Scott, David, Brent, and Mark.

"You don't know who I am, do you?"

"I think I have a clear understanding," replied Emily.

"I don't think you do."

"Please. Enlighten me." *Keep him talking.*

She watched him intently as he reached into his pocket and pulled out a small silver case. He opened the case and offered her a business card pinched between his thumb and index finger.

"Just call me Ted."

Emily read it. "What?" was the only response she could muster.

"It's true."

"What about the park?" she asked.

"I never actually stated my affiliation. I just omitted certain highly relevant facts."

"Why?"

"I had to maintain a cover. If I had said who I worked for, you would have told someone. I didn't know the extent of their network. My cover would have been blown."

"What do you want from me?"

"We would like to thank you."

"For what?"

He continued to speak as if she hadn't spoken. "As you know, a major investigation of Kyrkos & Andreadis has been launched. You helped launch it. The law firm wasn't on anyone's radar screen. The document you provided gave probable cause to raid the office. What we found goes way deeper and wider than anyone could have imagined. Politicians, billionaires, famous actors, people from all over the world. The law firm was quite good too."

"They had dozens of people like Stan Murphy who funneled money to them. Their office was an absolute treasure trove. We acted swiftly enough to catch them with their pants around their ankles." He let out a boisterous laugh. "We're going to get them, and we wanted to thank you."

"We?" she asked as she examined the business card once more. *Special Agent Theodore William. Federal Bureau of Investigations.*

"And that's it? You just wanted to thank me?"

"Not exactly."

His reply didn't surprise her. Part of her was glad it was finally over. She could stop running and resume her identity as Emily Hendricks. *Albeit in prison.*

"We would like to speak with you about a career change," declared Ted in a calm voice.

Her head spun. "Why in the world would you want someone like me?" She couldn't help blurting out the question.

"You have strong investigative skills. You're particularly good with numbers. A skill my profession desires given all of the white-collar crime. Also, your adaptation skills are impressively strong. It's beneficial to know how to assume an identity. It's less a skill you are taught and more a skill you innately possess. You certainly have it. I honestly would have never found you if I hadn't been watching that woman you met for lunch."

"You were there?"

"Yes, and it was the best fried chicken I'd ever eaten."

"What about Old Ebbitt? I saw you there."

"I was watching Terrance that day. I saw you and thought you were someone else. It wasn't until that lunch with the other woman that I began to take an interest in you."

"How could you possibly consider me given everything I've done?" Emily almost professed her real identity, but stopped herself.

"We know who you are, *Jen*. We are also innately aware of Emily's charred body found in an Annapolis condominium. It was a shame too. Such a nice young woman."

"It's a good thing that you, *Jen*, do not have any close surviving relatives. Given your nomadic lifestyle,"—he paused to glance disapprovingly around the sparsely decorated rooms, where only a few picture frames covered the otherwise bare walls—"a career with the FBI might be just what you're looking for to get your life back on track."

Emily had trouble processing his words, as if he had just spoken a foreign language. After a few moments, it sank in. It would be impossible to say no. They could arrest her on the spot if she did. Before she could reply, Ted spoke again.

"If you need any convincing, this may help."

Emily expected a threat, but none came.

Instead, Ted casually walked to the wall and removed a picture frame. He handed it to her with a smile.

"We still haven't had any leads. It's my number one priority. It comes straight from the top. I think the new Attorney General is a fan of yours, as well," he added with a hardy laugh.

Emily didn't need to look at the object to know what he had handed her. She kept just two mementos from her ordeal. One was a hand-carved picture frame that housed *Dante's Hell.* But that was locked away in a safety deposit box.

The other was a book of matches she had recently framed.

Made in the USA
Middletown, DE
05 December 2017